D1065013

Darkest Heart

By the Same Author:

Sunglasses After Dark (10th Anniversary Edition)

Midnight Blue: The Sonja Blue Collection

A Dozen Black Roses

Angels on Fire

For all these titles and more, visit **www.white-wolf.com/fiction**

Darkest Heart

Nancy A. Collins

A Sonja Blue Novel

Cover Art by Thom Ang.

ISBN: 0-7394-3216-8
First Edition: September 2002
Printed in Canada

White Wolf Publishing
1554 Litton Drive
Stone Mountain, GA 30083

For LuAlice

Author's Note

Part One of **Darkest Heart** first appeared as an original chapbook published by Cross Roads Press in 1992 under the title *Cold Turkey*. It would later appear in 1995, in a slightly rewritten format, as Chapter Three of **Paint It Black**. Because **Darkest Heart** concerns characters and events from *Cold Turkey*, and since more than five years have passed since the publication of **Paint It Black**, I have chosen to reprint it here.

Part One

New Orleans: Ten Years Ago

Oh I'll be a good boy,
Please make me well,
I'll promise you anything,
Get me out of this hell.

Cold Turkey, John Lennon

She had to give the dead boy credit; he had the trick of appearing human nailed down tight. He'd learned just what gestures and inflections to use in his conversation to hide the fact that his surface gloss and glitz wasn't there merely to disguise basic shallowness, but an utter lack of humanity.

She'd seen enough of the kind of humans he imitated: pallid, self-important intellectuals who prided themselves on their sophistication and knowledge of "hip" art, sharpening their wit at the expense of others. Like the vampiric mimic in their midst, they produced nothing while draining the vitality from those around them. The only difference was that the vampire was more honest about it.

Sonja worked her way to the bar, careful to keep herself shielded from the dead boy's view, both physically and psychically. It wouldn't do for her quarry to catch scent of her just yet. She could hear the vampire's nasal intonations as it held forth on the demerits of various artists.

"Frankly, I consider his use of photo-montage to be inexcusably *banal*. If I wanted to look at photographs, I'd go to Olan Mills!"

She wondered where the vampire had overheard—or stolen—that particular drollery. A dead boy of his wattage didn't come up with witty remarks spontaneously. When you have to spend conscious energy remembering to breathe and blink, there is no such thing as top-of-your-head snappy patter. It was all protective coloration, right down to the last double entendre and Monty Python impersonation.

It would be another decade or two before this vampire with the stainless steel ankh dangling from one earlobe and the crystal embedded in his left nostril, could divert his energies to something besides the full-time task of insuring his continuance. Not that the dead boy had much of a future in the predator business.

She waved down the bartender and ordered a beer. As she awaited its arrival, she caught a glimpse of herself in the mirror backing the bar. To the casual observer she looked to be no more than twenty-five. Tricked out in a battered leather jacket, with a stained Circle Jerks T-shirt, patched jeans, mirrored sunglasses, and dark hair twisted into a tortured cockatoo's crest, she looked like just another college-age gothic chick checking out the scene. No one would ever guess she was actually forty years old.

She sucked the cold suds down, participating in her own form of protective coloration. She could drink a case or three of the stuff with the only effect being she'd piss like a fire hose. Beer didn't do it for her anymore. Neither did hard liquor. Or cocaine. Or heroin. Or crack. She had tried them all, in dosages that would have put the entire US Olympic Team in the morgue, but no luck. There was only one drug that plunked her magic twanger. Only one thing that could get her off.

And that drug was blood.

Yeah, the dead boy was good enough he could have fooled another vampire. Could have. But didn't.

She eyed her prey. She doubted she'd have any trouble taking the sucker down. She rarely did, these days. Least not the lesser undead that lacked major psionic muscle. Sure, they had enough mesmeric ability to gull the humans in their vicinity, but little else. Compared to her own psychic abilities, the art-fag vampire was packing a peashooter. Still, it wasn't smart to get too cocky. Lord Morgan had dismissed her in just such a high-handed manner, and now he was missing half his face.

She shifted her vision from the human to the Pretender spectrum, studying the vampire's true appearance. She wondered if the black-garbed art aficionados clustered about their mandarin, their heads bobbing like puppets, would still consider his pronouncements worthy if they knew his skin was the color and texture of rotten sailcloth, or that his lips were black and shriveled, revealing oversized fangs set in a perpetual death's-head grimace. No doubt they'd drop their little plastic cups of cheap Chablis and back away in horror, their surface glaze of urbanite sophistication and studied ennui replaced by honest, good, old-fashioned monkey-brain terror.

Humans need masks in order to live their day-to-day lives, even amongst their own kind. Little did they know that their dependence on artifice and pretense provided the perfect hiding place for a raft of predators, such as the vampire pretending to be an art-fag. Predators like her.

Sonja tightened her grip on the switchblade in the pocket of her leather jacket.

"Uh, excuse me?"

She jerked around a little too fast, startling the young man at her elbow. She was so focused on her prey she had been unaware of his approaching her. Sloppy. Really sloppy.

"Yeah, what is it?"

The young man blinked, taken aback by the brusqueness of her tone. "I, uh, was wondering if I might, uh, buy you a drink?"

She automatically scanned him for signs of Pretender taint, but he came up clean. One hundred percent USDA Human. He was taller than her by a couple of inches, his blonde hair pulled into a ponytail. There were three rings in his right ear and one in his left nostril. Despite the metalwork festooning his nose, he was quite handsome.

Sonja found herself at a loss for words. She was not used to being approached by normals. She tended to generate a low-level psychic energy that most humans found unnerving, if not actively antagonistic. In layman's terms, she tended to either scare people away or piss them off.

"I— I—" She shot her prey a glance out of the corner of her eye. *Shit!* The bastard was starting to make his move, hustling an entranced human in the direction of the back door.

"I realize this is going to sound like a really dumb, cheap come-on," the young man with the nose ring said, giving her an embarrassed smile. "But I saw you from across the room—and I just had to meet you. Please let me buy you a drink."

"I, uh, I—"

The vampire had his prey almost out the door, smiling widely as he continued to discourse on modern art.

"There's something I have to take care of—I'll be right back! I promise! Don't go away!" she blurted, and dashed off in pursuit of her target for the night.

***

She scanned the parking lot, checking for signs of the vampire's passage. She prayed she wasn't too late. Once vamps isolated and seduced humans from the herd, they tended to move quickly. She knew that much from her own experience at the hands of Lord Morgan, the undead bastard responsible for her own transformation.

The vampire and his prey were sitting in the backseat of a silver BMW with heavily tinted windows; their blurred silhouettes moved like shadows reflected in an aquarium. There was no time to waste. She would have to risk being spotted.

The imitation art-fag looked genuinely surprised when her fist punched through the back window, sending tinted safety glass flying into the car. He hissed a challenge, exposing his fangs, as he whipped about to face her. His victim sat beside him, motionless as a mannequin, his eyes unfocused. The human's erect penis jutted from his open fly, vibrating like a recently struck tuning fork.

Sonja grabbed the vampire by the collar of his black silk shirt and pulled him, kicking and screaming, through the busted back windshield. The human didn't even blink.

"Let's get this over with, dead boy!" Sonja snapped as she hurled the snarling vampire onto the parking lot gravel. "I got a hot date waiting on me!"

The vampire launched himself at her, talons hooked and fangs extended. Sonja moved to meet the attack, flicking open the switchblade with a snap of her wrist. The silver blade sank into the vampire's exposed thorax, causing him to shriek in pain. The vampire collapsed around her fist like a punctured balloon, his body spasming as his system reacted to the silver's toxin.

Sonja knelt and swiftly removed the vampire's head from his shoulders. The body was already starting to putrefy by the time she located the BMW's keys. She unlocked the trunk and tossed the vampire's rapidly decomposing remains inside, making sure the keys were returned to his pants pocket.

She looked around, but there were no witnesses to be seen in the darkened lot. She moved around to the passenger side and opened the door, tugging the human out of the car.

He stood slumped against the rear bumper like a drunkard, his eyes swimming and his face slack. His penis dangled from his pants like a tattered party streamer.. Sonja took his chin between her thumb and forefinger and turned his head so that his eyes met hers.

"This never happened. You do not remember leaving the bar with anyone. Is that clear?"

"N-nothing h-happened," he stammered.

"Excellent! Now go back in the bar and have a good time. Oh, and put that thing away. You don't want to get busted for indecent exposure, do you?"

***

She was buzzing by the time she reentered the bar. She liked to think of it as her *après*-combat high. The adrenaline from the battle was still sluicing around inside her; juicing her perceptions and making her feel as if she was made of lightning and spun glass. It wasn't as intense as the boost she got from blood, but it was still good. She scanned the bar for the young man with the nose ring.

Give it up, he's forgotten you and found another bimbo for the evening.

Sonja fought to keep from cringing at the sound of the Other's voice inside her head. She had managed to go almost all night without having to endure its commentary. A second later she was rewarded by the sight of him at the bar. After a quick spot-check for any telltale signs of blood or ichor that might still be clinging to her, she moved forward.

"You still interested in buying me that drink?"

The young man's smile was genuinely relieved. "You came back!"

"I said I'd be back, didn't I?"

"Yeah. You did." He smiled again and offered her his hand. "I guess I ought to introduce myself. I'm Judd."

Sonja took his hand and smiled without parting her lips. "Pleased to meet you, Judd. I'm Sonja."

"What the hell's going on here?"

Judd's smile faltered as his gaze fixed itself on something just over Sonja's right shoulder. She turned and found herself almost nose-to-nose with a young woman dressed in a skin-tight black sheath, fishnet stockings, and way too much make-up. The woman's psychosis covered her face like a caul, with pulsing indentations marking her eyes, nose and mouth.

Judd closed his eyes and sighed. "Kitty, look, it's over! Get a life of your own and let go of mine, alright?"

"Oh, is *that* how you see it? Funny, I remember you saying something different! Like how you'd *always* love me! Guess I was stupid to believe that, huh?"

Kitty's rage turned the caul covering her face an interesting shade of magenta. The way it swirled and pulsed reminded Sonja of a lava lamp.

"You're not getting away *that* easy, asshole! And who's this slut?" Kitty slapped the flat of her hand against Sonja's leather-clad shoulder in an attempt to push her away from Judd.

Sonja grabbed Kitty's wrist with the speed of a cobra strike. "Don't touch me."

"Let go of me, bitch!" Kitty snarled as she tried to pull herself free of Sonja's grasp. "I'll fucking touch you anytime I want! Just you stay away from my boyfriend, bitch!"

C'mon, snap the crazy bitch's arm off, purred the Other. *She deserves it!* Sonja closed her eyes, fighting the urge to break Kitty's wrist in front of Judd.

"I said let go!" Kitty shrieked as she tried to rake Sonja's face with her free hand. When Sonja snared that wrist as well, Kitty was forced to look directly into her face. Suddenly the other woman stopped struggling and the blood-red rage that suffused the caul was replaced by a sunburst of yellow fear.

Sonja knew the other woman was seeing her—*truly* seeing her—for what she was. Only three kinds of human could perceive the Real World: psychics, poets and lunatics. And Kitty definitely qualified for the last category.

Sonja released the girl, but kept her gaze fixed on her. Kitty massaged her wrists, opened her mouth as if to say something, then turned and hurried away, nearly tripping over her high heels as she fled.

Judd's cheeks were red with embarrassment. "Man, I'm so sorry you had to deal with that. But it's not what you think. . Kitty and I lived together for a few months over a year ago, but she was incredibly jealous. It got to the point where I couldn't take any more, so I moved out. She's been dogging my tracks ever since. She scared off the last two women I was interested in."

Sonja shrugged. "I don't scare easy."

***

He wasn't afraid of her. Nor did she detect the self-destructive tendencies that usually attracted human men to her kind. Judd was not a tranced moth drawn to her dark flame, nor was he a closet renfield in search of a master. He was simply a good-natured young man who found her physically attractive. The novelty of his normalcy intrigued her.

He bought her several drinks, all of which she downed without effect. But she *did* feel giddy, almost lightheaded, while in his company. To be mistaken for a human woman was actually quite flattering. Especially since she'd stop thinking of herself as human some time back.

They ended up dancing, adding their bodies to the surging crowd that filled the mosh pit. At one point, Sonja was amazed to find herself laughing, genuinely *laughing*, one arm wrapped about Judd's waist. And then Judd leaned in and kissed her.

She barely had time to retract her fangs before his tongue found hers. She slid her other arm around his waist and pulled him close, grinding herself against him. He responded eagerly, his erection rubbing against her hip like a friendly tomcat. And she found herself wondering how his blood would taste.

She pushed him away so hard he staggered backward, nearly falling on his ass. Sonja shook her head as if trying to dislodge something in her ear, a guttural moan rising from her chest.

"Sonja?" There was a confused, hurt look on his face.

She could *see* his blood beckoning her from just beneath the surface of his skin: the veins traced in blue, the arteries pulsing purple. She turned her back on him and ran from the temptation, her head lowered. She shouldered her way through a knot of dancers, sending them flying like duckpins. Some of the bar's patrons hurled insults in her direction, a couple even spat at her, but she was deaf to their anger.

She put a couple of blocks between her and the bar before slumping into a darkened doorway, staring at her shaking hands as if they belonged to someone else.

"I liked him. I honestly *liked* him and I was going to… going to…"

Like. Hate. What's the difference? Blood is the life, wherever it comes from.

"Not like that. I never feed off anyone who doesn't deserve it. *Never.*"

Aren't we special?

"Shut up, bitch."

"Sonja?"

She had him pinned to the wall, one forearm clamped against his windpipe in a chokehold before she recognized his face. Judd clawed at her arm, his eyes bugging from their sockets.

"I'm…sorry…" he gasped out.

She let him go. "No, I'm the one who should be sorry. More than you realize."

Judd regarded her apprehensively as he massaged his throat, but there was still no fear in his eyes. "Look, I don't know what it is I said or did back there that put you off…"

"The problem isn't with you, Judd. Believe me. Look, I gotta go." She turned and began walking away, but he hurried after her.

"I know an all-night coffeehouse near here. Maybe we could talk ..?" "Judd, just leave me alone, okay? You'd be a lot better off if you just forgot you ever met me."

"How could I forget someone like you?"

"Easier than you realize."

He was keeping pace alongside her, desperately trying to make eye contact. "C'mon Sonja! Give it a chance! I—damn it, would you just take your shades off and *look* at me?"

Sonja stopped in mid-step to face him, her expression unreadable behind her mirrored sunglasses. "That's the *last* thing you want me to do."

Judd sighed and fished a pen and piece of paper out of his pocket. "You're one weird chick, that's for sure! But I *like* you, don't ask me why." He scribbled something on the scrap of paper and shoved it into her hand. "Look, here's my phone number. *Call* me, okay?"

Sonja closed her fist around the paper. "Judd—"

He held his hands out, palms facing up. "No strings attached, I promise. Just call me."

Sonja was surprised to find herself smiling. "Okay. I'll call you. Now will you leave me alone?"

***

When she revived the next evening, she found Judd's phone number tucked away in one of the pockets of her jacket. She sat cross-legged on the canvas futon that served as her bed and stared at it for a long time.

She'd been careful to make sure Judd hadn't followed her the night before. Her current nest was a drafty loft apartment in the attic of an old warehouse in the neighborhood just beyond the French Quarter. Save for her sleeping pallet, an antique cedar wardrobe, a Salvation Army-issue chair, a mini-fridge , a cordless telephone, and the scattered packing crates containing the esoteric curios she used as barter, the huge space was otherwise empty. Except for those occasions when the Dead came to visit. Such as tonight.

At first she didn't recognize the ghost, as he had lost his sense of self in the years since his death, which blurred his spectral image somewhat. He swirled up through the floorboards like a gust of blue smoke, gradually taking shape before her eyes. It was only when the phantom produced a smoldering cigarette from his own ectoplasm that she recognized him for who he once had been.

"Hello, Chaz."

The ghost of her former renfield made a noise that sounded like a cat being drowned. The Dead cannot speak clearly—even to Pretenders—except on three days of the year: Fat Tuesday, Halloween, and Candlemas. The ghost-light radiating from him was the only illumination in the room. "Come to see how your murderer is getting on, I take it?"

Chaz made a sound like a church bell played at half-speed.

"Sorry, I don't have a Ouija board, or we could have a proper conversation. Is there a special occasion for tonight's haunting, or are things just boring over on your side?"

Chaz frowned and pointed at the scrap of paper Sonja held in her hand. "What? You don't want me to call this number?"

Chaz nodded his head, nearly sending it floating from his shoulders.

"You tried warning Palmer away from me last Mardi Gras. Didn't work, but I suppose you know that already. He's living in Central America right now. We're very happy."

The ghost's laughter sounded like fingers raking a chalkboard. Sonja grimaced. "Yeah, big laugh, dead head. And I'll tell you one thing, Chaz; Palmer's a damn sight better in bed than you ever were!"

Chaz made an obscene gesture that was rendered pointless since he no longer had a body from the waist down. Sonja laughed and clapped her hands, rocking back and forth on her haunches.

"I *knew* that'd burn your ass, dead or not! Now piss off! I've got better things to do than play charades with a ghostly hustler!"

Chaz yowled like a baby dropped in a vat of boiling oil and disappeared in a swirl of dust and ectoplasm, leaving Sonja alone with Judd's phone number still clenched in one fist.

Hell, she thought as she reached for the cordless phone beside the futon. *If Chaz doesn't want me to call the guy, then it must be the right thing to do....*

***

The place where they rendezvoused was a twenty-four hour establishment in the French Quarter that had once been a bank, then a show-bar, then a porno shop, before finally deciding on being a coffee house. Judd's hair was freshly washed and he smelled of aftershave, but those were the only concessions made to the mating ritual. He still wore his nose– and earrings, as well as a Bongwater T-shirt that had been laundered so often the silk-screened image was starting to flake off.

Judd poked at the iced coffee with a straw. "If I'm not getting too personal—what was last night all about?"

Sonja studied her hands as she spoke. "Look, Judd. There's a lot about me you don't know—and I'd like to keep it that way. If you insist on asking about my past, I'm afraid I'll have to leave. It's not that I don't like you—I *do*—but I'm a very private person. And it's for a good reason."

"Is there someone else?"

"Yes. Yes, there is."

"A husband?"

She had to think about that one for a few seconds before answering. "In some ways. But, no; I'm not married."

Judd nodded as if this explained something. It was obvious that some of what she said was bothering him, but he was trying to play it cool. Sonja wondered what it was like, living a life where the worst things you had to deal with were jealous lovers and hurt feelings. It seemed almost paradisiacal from where she stood.

After they finished their iced coffees they hit the Quarter. It was after midnight, and the lower section of Decatur Street was starting to wake up. The streets outside the bars were decorated with clots of young people dressed in black leather, sequins, and recycled Seventies rags. The scenesters milled about, flashing their tattoos and bumming cigarettes off one another, as they waited for something to happen.

Someone called Judd's name and he swerved across the street toward a knot of youths lounging outside the Crystal Blue Persuasion Dance Club. Sonja hesitated before following him.

A young man dressed in a black duster, his shoulder-length hair braided into three pig tails and held in place by Tibetan mala beads carved into the shapes of skulls, moved forward to greet Judd.

Out of habit, Sonja scanned his face for Pretender taint, but it came up human. While the two spoke, she casually examined the rest of the group loitering outside the club. Human. Human. Human. Hu—

She froze.

The smell of *vargr* was strong, like the stink of a wet dog. The only reason she had not noticed it before was the reek of fish and freshly slaughtered poultry from the nearby French Market. The odor was radiating from a young man with a shaved forehead, whose hair at the back of his head was extremely long and held in a loose ponytail, making him look like a punk mandarin. He wore a leather jacket whose sleeves might well have been chewed off at the shoulder, trailing streamers of mangled leather and lining like gristle. He had one arm draped around a little punkette, her face made deathly pale by powder and grease paint.

The *vargr* met Sonja's gaze and held it, grinning his contempt. Her hand closed instinctively around her switchblade.

"I'd like you to meet a friend of mine—"

Judd's hand was on her elbow, drawing her attention away from the teenaged werewolf. Sonja struggled to conceal the disorientation from having her focus broken.

"Huh?"

"Sonja, I'd like you to meet Arlo, he's an old buddy of mine…"

Arlo frowned at Sonja as if she'd just emerged from under a rock, but offered his hand in deference to his friend. "Pleased to meet you," he mumbled.

Sonja shot a sideways glance at the *vargr* twelve feet away. He was murmuring something into the punkette's ear. She giggled and nodded her head and the two broke away from the rest of the group, sauntering down the street in the direction of the river. The *vargr* paused to give Sonja one last look over his shoulder, his grin too wide and his teeth too big, before disappearing into the shadows with his victim.

That's right. Pretend you didn't see it. Pretend you don't know what that grinning hellhound's going to do with that girl. You can't offend lover boy here by running off to do hand-to-hand combat with a werewolf, can you?

"Shut the fuck up, damn you," she muttered under her breath.

"What did you just say?" Arlo snapped, jerking his hand free from her grip.

"I'm sorry," she said hastily. "I was thinking about something else." Arlo grunted and nodded his head, but cast a hard look over his shoulder in Sonja's direction as she and Judd continued on their way. She could feel suspicion and hostility tingeing his thoughts.

Jesus, Judd's got himself another head case.

As they passed one of the seedy bars that catered to the late-night hardcore alcoholic trade, someone's mind called out Sonja's name, and a black man, his hair plaited into dreadlocks, stepped from the doorway of the Monastery. He wore a black turtleneck sweater and immaculate designer jeans, a gold peace sign the size of a hood ornament slung around his neck. "Long time no see, Blue."

"Hello, Mal," Sonja said with a weary sigh.

The demon Malfeis smiled, exposing teeth that belonged in the mouth of a shark. "No hard feelings, I hope? I didn't want to sell you out like that, girlchick, but I was under orders from Below Stairs."

"We'll talk about it later, Mal...."

The demon nodded in the direction of Judd. "Got yourself a new renfield, I see."

"Shut up!" Sonja hissed. Mal lifted his hands, palms outward. "Whoa! Didn't mean to hit a sore spot there, girly-girl."

"Sonja? Is this guy bothering you?" Judd was hovering at her elbow. He gave Mal a suspicious glare, blind to the demon's true appearance.

"No. Everything's cool." Sonja turned her back on the grinning demon and tried to block the sound of his laughter echoing in her mind.

"Who was that guy?"

"Judd—"

"I know! I promised I wouldn't pry into your past."

Sonja shrugged. "Mal is a—business associate of mine. That's all you need to know about him, except, no matter what, *never* ask him a question. *Ever.*"

They walked on in silence for a few more minutes, and then Judd took her into his arms. His kiss was warm and probing and she felt herself begin to relax. Then he reached for her sunglasses.

She batted his hand away, fighting the urge to snarl. "Don't do that."

"I just want to see your eyes."

"*No.*" She pulled away from him, her body rigid as a board.

"I'm sorry—"

"I better leave. I had a nice time, Judd. I really did. But I have to go."

"You'll call me, won't you?"

"I'm afraid so."

***

Why don't you fuck him? He wants it bad. So do you. You can't hide that from me.

The Other's voice was a nettle wedged into the folds of her brain, impossible to dislodge or ignore. Sonja opened the mini-fridge and took out a bottle of whole blood, cracking its seal open like she would a beer.

Not that bottled crap again! I hate this shit! You might as well go back to drinking cats! Wouldn't you rather have something nice and fresh? Say a good B negative mugger or an O positive rapist? There's still plenty of time to go trawling before the sun comes up... or you could always pay a visit to lover-boy.

"Shut up! I've had a bellyful of you tonight already!"

My-my! Aren't we being a touchy one? Tell me, how long do you think you can keep up the pretense of being normal? You've almost forgotten what it's like to be human yourself. Why torture yourself by pretending you're something you're not simply to win the favor of a piece of beefsteak?

"He likes me, damn it. He actually likes me."

And what exactly are you?

"I'm not in the mood for your fuckin' mind games!"

Welcome to the fold, my dear. You're finally one of us. You're a Pretender.

Sonja hurled the half-finished bottle of blood into the sink. She picked up the card table and smashed it to the floor, jumping up and down on the scattered pieces. It was a stupid, pointless gesture, but it made her feel better.

***

She knew it was stupid, even dangerous, to socialize with humans, but she couldn't help herself. There was something about Judd that kept drawing her back, against her better judgment. The only other time she'd known such compulsion was when the thirst was on her. Was this love? Or was it simply another form of hunger?

Their relationship, while charged with an undercurrent of eroticism, was essentially sexless. She wanted him so badly she did not dare do more than kiss or hold hands. If she should lose control, there was no telling what might happen.

Judd, unlike Palmer, wasn't a Sensitive. He was a basic, garden variety human, blind and dumb to the miracles and terrors of the Real World, just like poor, doomed Claude Hagerty had been. Rapid exposure to the universe in which she lived could do immense and irreparable damage to those unequipped to handle it.

To his credit, Judd hadn't pressed the sex issue over much. He wasn't happy with the arrangement, but honored her request that they "take it slow."

This, however, did not sit well with the Other. It constantly taunted her, goading her with obscene fantasies and suggestions concerning Judd. Or, failing to elicit a response using those tactics, it would chastise her for being untrue to Palmer. Sonja tried to ignore its gibes as best she could, but she knew that something, sometime was bound to snap.

***

Kitty wiped at the tears oozing from the corner of her eye, smearing mascara over her cheek and the back of her hand. It made the words on the paper swim and crawl like insects, but she didn't care.

She loved Judd. She really, truly loved him. And maybe after she did what she had to do to save him, he'd finally believe her. He needed proof of her love. And what better proof than to rescue him from the clutches of a monster?

Dearest Judd,

I tried to warn you about That Woman. But you are blind to what she Really Is. She is Evil Itself, a demon sent from Hell to claim your Soul! I knew her for what she truly was the moment I first saw her, and she knew I knew, too! Her hands and mouth drip blood! Her eyes burn with the fires of Hell! She is surrounded by a cloud of energy as red as blood. She means to drag you to Hell, Judd. But I won't let her! I love you too much to let that happen. I'll take care of this horrible monster, don't you worry. I've been talking to God a lot lately, and He told me how to deal with demons like her. I Love you so very, very much. I want you to Love me too. I'm doing this all for you. Please Love Me.

Kitty

***

Judd woke up at two in the afternoon, as was usual for him. He worked six-to-midnight four days out of the week and had long since shifted over to a nocturnal lifestyle. After he got off work he normally headed down to the Quarter to chill with his buddies or, more recently, hang with Sonja until four or five in the morning before heading home.

He yawned as he dumped a heaping tablespoons of Guatemalan into the hopper of his Mr. Coffee.

Sonja. Now there was a weird chick. Weird, but not in a schizzy, death-obsessed art-school freshman way like Kitty. Her strangeness issued from something far deeper than bourgeois neurosis. Sonja was genuinely *out there*, wherever that might be. There was something about the way she moved, the way she handled herself, which suggested she was plugged into something Real. And a frustrating as her fits of mood might be, he could not bring himself to turn his back on her.

Still, it bothered him that none of his friends liked her—not even Arlo, who he'd known since junior high school. Some of them even seemed to be *scared* of her. Funny. How could anyone be *frightened* of Sonja? Sure, she could be intense... but scary?

As he shuffled in the direction of the bathroom, he noticed an envelope shoved under his front door. He stooped to retrieve it, scowling at the all-too-familiar handwriting.

Kitty.

Probably another one of her damn fool love letters, alternately threatening him with castration and begging him to take her back. Lately she'd taken to leaving rambling, wigged-out messages on his answering machine, ranting about Sonja being some kind of hell-beast out to steal his soul. Crazy bitch. Sonja was crazy, too, but not in such a predictable, boring way.

Judd tossed the envelope, unopened, into the trashcan and staggered off to the bathroom to take a shower.

***

Sonja Blue greeted the night from atop the roof of the warehouse where she made her nest. She stretched her arms wide as if to embrace the rising moon, listening with half an ear to the baying of the hounds along the riverbanks. Some, she knew, were not dogs. But the *vargr* was not her concern tonight. She'd tangled with a few of their breed over the years, but she found hunting her own kind vastly more satisfying. Since warehouse's exterior fire escape was badly rusted and groaned noisily with the slightest movement, Sonja avoided it altogether. She crawled, headfirst, down the side of the building, moving like a lizard on a garden wall. Once she reached the bottom, she routinely pat-checked her jacket pockets to make sure nothing had fallen out during her descent.

There was a hissing sound in her head, as if someone had abruptly pumped up the volume on a radio tuned to a dead channel, and something heavy caught her between the shoulder blades, lifting her off her feet and knocking her into a row of garbage cans.

She barely had time to roll out of the way before something big and silvery smashed down where her head had been a second before. She coughed and black blood flew from her lips; a rib had broken off and pierced one of her lungs.

Kitty stood over her, clutching a three-foot long, solid silver crucifix like a baseball bat. While her madness gave her strength, it was still obvious the damn thing was *heavy*. Sonja wondered which church she'd stolen it from.

The dead channel crackling in Sonja's head grew louder. She recognized it as the sound of homicidal rage. Shrieking incoherently, Kitty swung at her rival a third time. While crosses and crucifixes had no effect on her—on any vampire, for that matter—if Kitty succeeded in landing a lucky blow and snapped her spine or cracked open her skull, she was dead no matter what.

Sonja rolled clear and got to her feet in one swift, fluid motion. Kitty swung at her again, but this time Sonja stepped inside her reach and grabbed the crucifix, wresting it from the other woman's hands.

Kitty staggered back, staring in disbelief, waiting for Sonja's hand to burst into flames as she hefted the heavy silver cross. It was at least three inches thick, the beams as wide as a man's hand, and at its center hung a miniature Christ fashioned of gold and platinum. "What the hell did you think you were going to solve, clobbering me with this piece of junk?" Sonja snarled.

Kitty's eyes were huge, the pupils swimming in madness. "You can't have him! I won't let you take his soul!"

"Who said anything about me stealing—"

"Monster!" Kitty launched herself at Sonja, her fingers clawing at her face. "Monster!"

Sonja instinctively defended herself, swatting Kitty with the crucifix. The mad woman dropped to the alley floor. The only thing still holding her head onto her body were the muscles of her neck. *Way to go, kiddo! You just killed lover-boy's bug-shit ex-girlfriend! You're batting a thousand!*

"Shit." She tossed the crucifix aside and squatted next to the body. No need to check for vital signs. The girl was d-e-a-d.

What to do? She couldn't toss the corpse in the dumpster. Someone was bound to find it, and once the body was identified New Orleans Homicide would take Judd in for questioning. Which meant they'd be looking for *her*, sooner or later. And she couldn't have that.

I've got an idea, crooned the Other. *Just let me handle it.*

***

Stealing the car was easy. It was a '76 Ford LTD with a muffler held in place with baling wire and a *Duke for Governor* sticker on the sagging rear bumper. Just the thing to unobtrusively dispose of a murder victim in the swamps surrounding New Orleans during the dead of night.

Out in New Orleans East, there was what was to have been yet another cookie-cutter housing development built on the very fringes of the marshlands of Lake Pontchartain. The contractors got as far as pouring the concrete slab foundations before the oil slump hit, then the money dried up. The condos were never built, but the access road from the interstate still remained, although there was nothing at its end but an overgrown tangle of briars and vines that had become a breeding ground for snakes and alligators.

She drove the last mile without lights. Not that she needed them. She could see just fine in the dark. Having reached her destination, she cut the engine and rolled to a stop. Except for the chirring of frogs and the grunting of gators, everything was quiet.

Sonja climbed out of the car and opened the trunk with a length of bent coat hanger. She stood for a second, silently inventorying the collection of plastic trash bags. There were six, total: one for the head, one for the torso, and one apiece for each limb. She'd already burned Kitty's clothing in the warehouse's furnace and disposed of her jewelry and teeth by tossing them into the river.

She gathered up the bags and left the access road, heading in the direction of the swamp. She could hear things splashing in the water, some of them quite large.

She paused for a second on the bank of the bayou. Something nearby hissed at her, then slithered out of the way. She tossed the bag containing Kitty's head into the murky water.

The assembled gators splashed and wrestled amongst themselves for the tender morsels like ducks fighting for scraps of stale bread.

Sonja was tired. Very tired. After this was over she still had to drive the stolen car to a suitably disreputable urban area and set it on fire. She looked down at her hands. They were streaked with blood. She absently licked them clean.

When she was finished the Other looked through her eyes and smiled.

The Other wasn't tired. Not in the least.

***

It hadn't been a very good night, as far as Judd was concerned. He'd gotten chewed out concerning his attitude at work, Arlo and the others had treated him like he had a championship case of halitosis, and, to cap the evening, Sonja pulled a no-show. Time to pack it in. It was four o'clock when he got home. He was in such a piss-poor mood he didn't even bother to turn on the lights.

His answering machine, for once, didn't have one of Kitty's bizarro messages on it. Nothing from Sonja, either. He grunted as he removed his shirt. Was she mad at him? Had he said or done something the last time they were together that ticked her off?

It was hard to figure out her moods, since she refused to take off those damn mirrored sunglasses. Judd wondered how she could navigate in the dark so well while wearing those fuckers.

Something moved at the corner of his eye. It was the curtain covering the window that faced the alley. Funny, he didn't remember leaving that open…

Someone stepped out of the shadows, greeting him with a smile that displayed teeth that were too sharp. Judd felt his heart jerk into overdrive as the adrenaline surged into his system. Just as he was ready to yell for help, he recognized her.

"S-Sonja?"

"Did I scare you?" Her voice sounded like something out of *The Exorcist*. She sniffed the air and her smile grew even sharper. "Yes. Yes, I *did* scare you, didn't I?" She moved toward him, her hands making slow, hypnotic passes as she spoke. "I *love* the smell of fear in the morning."

"Sonja, what's wrong with your voice?"

"Wrong?" The Other chuckled as she unzipped her leather jacket. "I *always* sound like this!"

She was on him so fast he didn't even see her move, lifting him by his belt buckle and flinging him onto the bed so hard he bounced. She grabbed his jaw in one hand, angling it back so the jugular was exposed. Judd heard the *snikt!* of a switchblade and felt a cold, sharp pressure against his throat.

"Sonja, what are you doing?"

"Do not struggle. Do not cry out," she whispered, her voice as harsh and as cold as a metal rasp pressed to his ear. "Do as I command, and maybe I'll let you live. Maybe."

"What do you want?"

"Why, my dear, I just want to get to know you better." The Other removed the sunglasses protecting her eyes with her free hand. "And vice versa."

Judd had often wondered what Sonja's eyes looked like. Were they almond-shaped or round? Blue, brown, or green? However, he had never once pictured them as blood red with pupils so hugely dilated they resembled shoe buttons.

The Other smirked, savoring the look of disgust on Judd's face. She pressed her lips against his, thrusting his teeth apart with her tongue, and penetrated his will with one quick shove of her mind.

Judd's limbs twitched convulsively then went still as she took control of his nervous system. The Other disengaged, physically, and stared down at him. He couldn't move, his body locked into partial paralysis. Satisfied her control was secure, she moved the switchblade from Judd's throat.

"I can see why she finds you attractive. You're a pretty thing… *very* pretty." The Other reached out and pinched one of his nipples until it began to purple. Judd didn't flinch. "But she's much too old fashioned when it comes to sex, don't you agree? She's afraid to let herself go and walk the wild side. She's so *repressed.*" The Other shrugged out of her leather jacket, allowing it to fall to the floor. "I will explain this to you once, and once only. I *own* you. If you do as I tell you, and you please me, then you shall be rewarded. Like *this.*" She reached into his cortex and tweaked its pleasure center. Judd shuddered as the wave of ecstasy swept over him, his hips involuntarily humping empty air.

"But if you fight me, or displease me in *any* way—then I will punish you. Like *so.*"

Judd emitted a strangled cry as he was speared through the pain receptor in his brain. It felt as if the top of his skull had been removed and someone had dumped the contents of an ant farm on his exposed brain. His back arched until he thought his spine would snap. Then the pain stopped as it it'd never been there at all.

"Hold me."

Judd did as he was told, dragging himself upright and wrapping his arms around her waist. The Other knotted her fingers in his hair, pulling his head back so she could look into his eyes.

"Am I hurting you? Say yes."

"Yes."

"Good."

She smiled, exposing her fangs, and with a cold shudder he realized that the worst had not even begun.

***

They fucked for three hours straight, the Other skillfully manipulating his pleasure centers so that he remained perpetually erect, despite his physical exhaustion. She randomly induced orgasms, until they numbered in the dozens. After the seventh or eighth climax, he was shooting air. She seemed to enjoy his wails each time he spasmed.

As dawn began to make its way into the room, she severed her control of Judd's body. He fell away from her in mid-thrust, his eyes rolled back behind flickering lids. The Other dressed quickly, her attention fixed on the rising sun. Judd lay curled in a fetal position amongst the soiled and tangled bedclothes, his naked body shuddering and jerking as his nervous system reasserted its control.

"Parting is such sweet sorrow," purred the Other, caressing his shivering flank. Judd gasped at her touch but did not pull away. "You pleased me. *This* time. So I will let you live. *This* time."

She lowered her head to his neck, brushing his jugular lightly with her lips. Judd squeezed his eyes shut in anticipation of the bite. But all she did was whisper: "Get used to it, lover boy."

When he opened his eyes again, she was gone.

***

The Other took a great deal of pleasure in telling Sonja what it had done to Judd, making sure not to leave out a single, tasty detail as it reran that morning's exploits inside her skull.

Sonja's response to the news was to scream and run headfirst into the nearest wall, then to continue pounding her skull against the floorboards until her glasses shattered and blood streamed down her face and matted her hair. She succeeded in breaking her nose and fracturing both cheekbones before collapsing.

***

"Girly-girl! Long time no see! What brings you into my little den of iniquity this time?"

The demon Malfeis sported the exterior of a flabby white male in late middle age, dressed in a loud plaid polyester leisure suit with white buck loafers. A collection of gold medallions dangled under his chins and he held a racing form in one hand.

Sonja slid into the booth opposite the demon. "I need magic, Mal."

"Don't we all? Say, what's that with the face? You can reconstruct better than that...."

She shrugged, one hand absently straying to her swollen left cheek. The bone squelched under her fingertips and slid slightly askew. Heavy-duty facial reconstruction required feeding in order for it to be done right, and she'd deliberately skipped her waking meal.

"You tangle with an ogre? One of those *vargr* punks?"

"Leave it be, Mal."

Malfeis shrugged. "Just trying to be friendly, that's all. Now, what kind of magic are you in the market for?"

"Binding and containment."

The demon grunted and fished out a pocket calculator, his exterior flickering for a moment to reveal a hulking creature that resembled an orangutan with a boar's snout. "What kind of demon are you looking to lock down?"

"I wish to have myself bound and contained."

Malfeis glanced up from the calculator, a sour look on his face. "Are you shitting me or what, girlchick?"

"Name your price, damn you."

"Don't be redundant, girlchick."

Sonja sighed and hefted a knapsack onto the tabletop. "I brought some of my finest acquisitions. I've got hair shaved from Ted Bundy's head just before he was to go to the chair, dried blood scraped from the walls of the LaBianco home, a spent rifle casing from the grassy knoll, and a cedar cigar box with what's left of Rasputin's penis in it. Quality shit. I swear by its authenticity. And it's all yours, if you do this one thing for me."

Malfeis fidgeted, drumming his talons against the table. Such close proximity to so much human suffering and evil was bringing on a jones. "Okay, I'll do it. But I'm not going to take responsibility for anything that happens to you."

"Did I ask you to?"

***

"Are you *sure* about this, Sonja?"

"Your concern touches me, Mal. It really does."

The demon shook his head in disbelief. "You really mean to go through with this, don't you? Sonja, once you're in there, there's no way you'll be able to escape, unless someone on the outside breaks the seal."

"Maybe."

"There's no *maybe* to it!" he retorted.

"The spell you're using is for the binding and containment of vampire energies, right?"

"Of course. You're a vampire."

She shrugged. "Part of me is. And I'm not letting it out to hurt anyone ever again. I'm going to kill it or die trying."

"You're going to *starve* in there!"

"That's the whole point. If I'm lucky, maybe I'll starve that side of myself to death, so that I can walk away clean and human."

"Whatever you say, girly-girl. But if you ask me, you're out of your fucking mind."

Sonja hugged herself as she stared into the open doorway of the meat locker. It was cold and dark inside, just like the Other's heart. "I'm not paying for your opinions, just your hoodoo. Let's get this show on the road."

Malfeis nodded and produced a number of candles, bottles of oil, pieces of black chalk, and bags of white powder from the Gladstone bag he carried. Sonja swallowed and stepped inside the meat locker, drawing the heavy door closed behind her with a muffled thump.

Malfeis lit the candles and began to chant in a deep, sonorous voice, scrawling elaborate designs on the outer walls of the locker with the black chalk. As the chanting grew faster and more impassioned, he smeared oil on the hinges and handle of the door. There was an electric crackle and the door glowed with blue fire.

Malfeis' incantation lost all semblance of human speech as it reached its climax. He carefully poured a line of white powder across the threshold, made from equal parts salt, sand and the crushed bones of human babies.. Then he stepped back to assess his handiwork.

To human eyes it looked like someone had scrawled graffiti all over the face of the stainless steel locker, nothing more. But to Pretender eyes, eyes adjusted to the Real World, the door to the locker was barred by a tangle of darkly pulsing *vévé*, the semi-sentient protective symbols of the *voudou* powers. As long as the tableau remained undisturbed, the entity known as Sonja Blue would remain trapped within the chill darkness of the meat locker.

Malfeis replaced the tools of his trade in the Gladstone bag. He paused as he left the warehouse, glancing over his shoulder.

"Goodbye, girly-girl. It was nice knowing you."

***

"I'm looking for Mal."

The bartender looked up from his racing form and frowned at Judd. After taking in his unwashed hair and four days' growth of beard, he nodded in the direction of the back booth.

Judd had never been inside the Monastery before. It had a reputation as being one of the sleazier—and most uninviting—French Quarter dives, and he could see why. The booths lining the wall had once been church pews. Plaster saints in various stages of decay were scattered about on display. A Madonna with skin blackened and made leprous by age regarded him from above the bar with flat, faded blue eyes, an equally scabrous Baby Jesus, cradled in her rotting arms.

Judd walked to the back of the bar and looked into the last booth. All he saw was a paunchy middle-aged man dressed in a bad suit smoking a cigar and reading a dog-eared porno novel.

"Excuse me...?"

The man in the bad suit looked up at him, arching a bushy, upswept eyebrow, but said nothing.

"Uh, excuse me—but I'm looking for Mal."

"You found him."

Judd blinked, confused. "No, I'm afraid there's been some kind of mistake. The guy I'm looking for is black, with dreadlocks..."

The man in the bad suit smiled. It was not a pleasant sight. "Sit down, kid. He'll be with you in just a moment."

Still uncertain of what he was getting himself into, Judd slid into the opposite pew.

The older man lowered his head, exposing an advanced case of male pattern baldness, and hunched his shoulders. His fingers and arms began vibrating, the skin growing darker as if his entire body had suddenly become bruised. There was a sound of dry grass rustling under a high wind and thick, black dreadlocks emerged from his scalp, whipping about like a nest of snakes. Judd was too shocked by the transformation to do anything but stare.

Mal lifted his head and grinned at Judd, tugging at the collar of his turtleneck. "Ah, yes. I remember you now. Sonja's renfield."

"My name's not Renfield."

Mal shrugged indifferently . "So, what brings you here, boychick?"

"I'm looking for Sonja. I can't find her."

"That's because she doesn't want to be found."

"But I *have* to find her! Before she does something stupid, like kill herself, maybe."

Mal regarded the young human with a look of mild amusement in his dark eyes. "Tell me more."

"She sent me this letter a few days ago." Judd fished a much-folded envelope out of his back pocket and held it out to Mal. "Here, you read it."

The demon took the letter out of its envelope like a gourmet removing an escargot from its shell. He unfolded the paper, carefully noting the lack of signature and the smears of blood in the margins.

Judd,

I can never be forgiven for what was done to you, even though I was not the one who did those thing. Please believe that. It was her. She is the one that makes me kill and hurt people. She is the one who hurt you.

I promise I'll never let her hurt anyone, ever again. Especially you. I'm going to try something I should have done years ago, before she became so strong. She is sated now, at least for the moment. Which means she is asleep. By the time she becomes aware of what I'm planning, it will be too late. I'm going to kill her. I may very well end up killing myself in the bargain, but that's a chance I'm willing to take. I won't let her hurt anyone ever again, damn her. I love you, Judd. Don't try to find me. Escape while you can.

"She doesn't understand." Judd was close to tears as he spoke. "I *do* forgive her. I *love* her, damn it! I can't let her *die*!"

"You know what she is," Mal said flatly. It wasn't a question.

Judd nodded. "I know. And I don't *care*."

"So why have you come to me?"

"You know where she is, don't you?"

Malfeis shifted in his seat, his eyes developing reptilian slits. "Are you asking me a question?"

Judd hesitated, recalling Sonja's warning that he should *never*, under *any* circumstance, ask Mal a question. He took a deep breath and nodded his head, his lips pressed into a tight line.

Mal smiled, displaying shark's teeth. "Before I respond to any questions put to me, you must pay the price of the answer. Is that understood, boychick?"

Judd swallowed and nodded.

"Very well. Tell me your name. All of it."

"That's all you want?" Judd frowned, baffled. "My name is Michael Judd Rieser." "To know a thing's name gives one power over that thing, my sweet. Didn't they teach you that in school? Come to think of it, I guess they don't."

"What about my question? Do you know where Sonja is?"

"Yes, I do." The demon scrawled an address on the back of the letter Judd had given him. "You'll find her here. She's inside the meat locker on the ground floor."

"Meat locker?"

"I wouldn't open it if I were you."

Judd snatched up the address and slid out of the pew. "But I'm *not* you!"

Malfeis watched Judd hurry out of the bar with an amused grin. "That's what *you* think, boychick." He leaned back and closed his eyes. When he re-opened them, he was white with shoulder-length hair pulled in a ponytail, a ring in his nose, and a four days' growth of beard.

***

It was cold. So very, very cold.

Sonja sat huddled in the far corner of the meat locker, her knees drawn up to her chest. Her breath drifted from her mouth and nostrils in wispy flumes before condensing and turning to frost on her face.

How long? How many days had she been here? Three? Four? Twenty? A hundred? There was no way of telling. She no longer slept. The Other's incessant screams and curses made sure of that.

Let me out! Let me out of this hellhole! I've got to feed! I'm starving!

"Good."

You stupid cunt! If I starve to death, you go with me! I'm not a damned tapeworm!

"Couldn't prove it to me."

I'm getting out of here! I don't care what you say!

The Other forced her stiffened limbs to bend, levering her onto her feet. Her joints cracked like rotten timber as she moved. She staggered in the direction of the door. In her weakened condition she had difficulty seeing in the pitch black of the meat locker, forcing her to abandon her sunglasses.

Her groping hands closed on the door's interior handle. There was a sharp crackle and a flash of blue light as she was thrown halfway across the locker. She screamed and writhed like a cat hit by a car, holding her blistered, smoking hands away from her body. This was the twentieth time the Other had tried to open the door, and several of her fingers were on the verge of gangrene.

"You're not going anywhere. Not now. Not *ever!*"

Fuck you! Fuck you! I'll get you for this, you human-loving cow!

"What? Are you going to *kill* me?"

Sonja crawled back to her place in the corner. The effort started her coughing again, bringing up black, clotted blood. She wiped at her mouth with the sleeve of her jacket, nearly dislocating her lower jaw in the process.

You're falling apart. You're too weak to regenerate properly....

"You're the one who pounded your head against the fuckin' wall trying to get out."

You're the one that got us locked up in here! Don't blame me!

"I *am* blaming you. But not for that."

It's that fucking stupid human again! You think you can punish me for that? I didn't do anything that you hadn't already fantasized about!

"You *raped* him, damn you! You could have killed him!"

I didn't, though. I could have. But I didn't.

"I *loved* him!" Sonja's voice cracked, became a sob.

You don't love him. You love being mistaken for human. That's what you're really mad at me about. You're upset that I ruined your little game of Let's Pretend!

"Shut up."

Make me.

***

Judd checked the street number of the warehouse against the address that Mal had given him. This was the place. It was one of the few remaining warehouses in the district that had not been turned into an overpriced yuppie ghetto. There was a small, hand-lettered sign posted on the front door that read Indigo Imports, and a heavy chain and double padlock wrapped about the handle. A quick check of the ground floor confirmed that all the windows were secured with burglar bars.

He rounded the side of the building and spotted the loading dock. After a few minutes of determined tugging, he succeeded in wrenching the sliding metal door open wide enough for him to slide under. The inside of the warehouse was lit only by the mid-afternoon sunlight slanting through the barred windows and the place smelled of dust and rat piss. The meat locker was on the ground floor, just where Mal said it would be. Its metal walls and door were covered in swirls of spray-painted graffiti. What looked like a huge line of cocaine marked the locker's threshold. Judd grabbed the door's handle and yanked it open. There was a faint crackling sound and a rush of cold, foul air. He squinted into the darkness, covering his nose and breathing through his mouth.

"Sonja?"

Something moved in the deepest shadows of the freezer. He stepped in the direction of the movement. "Sonja, it's me, baby. "

"Go away." It sounded like she was talking through a mouth full of mud. "You don't know what you're doing."

Judd took another step into the locker, his eyes finally adjusting to the gloom. He could see her now, crouching in the far corner with her knees drawn against her chest, her face turned to the wall.

"No, you're wrong, Sonja. I know *exactly* what I'm doing."

"I let her hurt you, Judd. I could have stopped her, but I didn't. I let her—let her—" Her voice trailed off as her shoulders began to shake. "Go away before I hurt you again."

Judd kneeled beside her. She smelled like a side of beef gone bad. Her hands were covered with blisters and oozing sores, and some of her fingers jutted at odd angles, as if they had been broken without being properly set. She pulled away at his touch, pressing herself against the wall as if she could somehow squeeze between the cracks.

"Don't look at me."

"Sonja, you don't understand. I *love* you. I know what you are, what you're capable of—and I love you *anyway*."

"Even if I hurt you?"

"*Especially* when you hurt me."

She turned her head in his direction. Her face looked like it had been smashed, then reassembled by a well-meaning, but inept, plastic surgeon with only a blurry photograph to go by. Her eyes glowed like those of an animal pinned in the headlights of an oncoming car.

"What?"

Judd leaned closer, his eyes reflecting a hunger she knew all too well. "At first when it happened, I was scared. Then, I realized I wasn't frightened anymore. I've never known anything like it before! It was *incredible!* I love you, Sonja! *All* of you! I want to be your slave forever."

She reached out and caressed his face with one of her charred hands. She had feared this would happen since the moment she first met him. The Other had transformed Judd into a vampire junkie, and turned her into his fix. "I love you too, Judd. Kiss me."

***

She sat behind the wheel of the car for a long time, staring out into the dark on the other side of the windshield. Nothing had changed since the last time she'd been out here, disposing of Kitty.

She pressed her fingertips against her right cheek, and this time it held. Her fingers were healed and straight again as well. She readjusted her shades, opened the car door, and slid out from behind the wheel of the Caddy she'd bought off the lot, cash-in-hand.

Judd was in the trunk, divvied up into six garbage bags, just like Kitty. At least it'd been fast. Her hunger was so intense she drained him dry within seconds. He hadn't tried to fight when she buried her fangs in his throat, even though she hadn't the strength to trance him. Maybe part of him knew she was doing him a favor.

She dragged the bags out of the trunk and headed in the direction of the alligator calls. She'd have to leave New Orleans, maybe for good this time. Kitty might not have been missed, but Judd was another story. Arlo was sure to mention his suspicions concerning his missing friend's weirdo new girlfriend to the authorities.

It was time to blow town and head for Merida, maybe pay Palmer a visit and check on how he and the baby were making out. Funny how she'd forgotten about him. Of all her human companions, he was the only one she'd come closest to truly loving. Before Judd, that is.

She hurled the sacks containing her lover's remains into the water and returned to the car. She tried not to hear the noise the gators made as they fought amongst themselves.

She climbed back into the car and slammed a cassette into the Caddy's tape deck. Lard's *The Last Temptation of Reid* thundered through the speakers, causing the steering wheel to vibrate under her hands. She wondered when the emptiness would go away, or at least be replaced by pain. Anything would be preferable to the nothing inside her.

I don't see why you had to go and kill him like that. We could have used a renfield. They do come in handy, now and then. Besides, he was kind of cute....

"Shut up and drive."

Part Two

One is the loneliest number that you'll ever do.

Two can be as bad as one,

It's the loneliest number since the number one.

One, Harry Nilsson

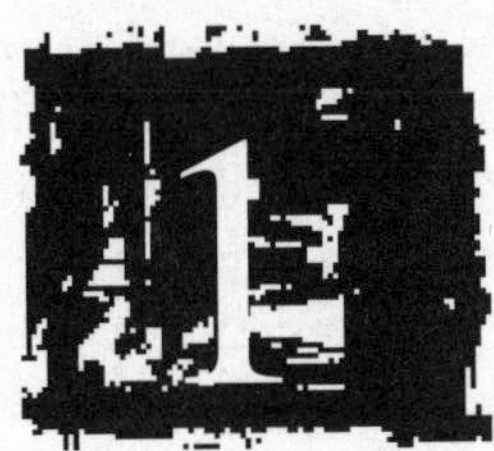

The important thing he had to remember was, no matter what his eyes might see, he dared not trust it. He had learned that whatever he hunted might look like, it was nothing but falsehood, wrapped in illusion. It didn't matter if the mask they showed him was one of drab normalcy or that of youth and beauty, underneath its surface was nothing but horror and rot.

But most of all, he had learned to be wary of those who always smiled. They did so not because they were happy to see him, but because they were thinking about ripping out his throat. Of course, he had learned this truth the only way he could... the hard way.

The sweet little old lady tending her knitting in front of the fireplace; that saucer-eyed school child skipping down the sidewalk on her way to the playground; or the gray-flannel yuppie with his attaché case in one hand and cell phone in the other: they all could be fiends from pits far darker than any charted by Dante.

That is why he kept trophies. They reminded him that no matter how mundane such creatures might appear on the outside, on the inside they were monsters. In the end, not matter how innocuous their outward visages, when the moment of truth finally arrived they all dropped their masks and showed him their real faces.

In the years since he first dedicated himself to the eradication of the secret plague upon mankind, he had not allowed his hand to waver once, no matter how pitiful their pleas. Some of them cried; others tried to convince him he'd made a horrible mistake, whimpering and wailing for their miserable lives until it made him sick. He would have thought they would have more self-respect than that, but what could he expect from such creatures?

Their kind had robbed him of his parents, his innocence and his childhood. They had tainted him by making him a part of their nightmare world. So he made them pay for it, one by one. Yet, for all of this, he was no closer to finding the bastard who made him what he was than on the day he first left the hospital.

***

Their mouths are the only things that seem alive. The lips are full and red and eager, wet and trembling with anticipation, waiting for the moment when the hard and waiting fangs may be shown, like a samurai who can only sheath his sword after it has been anointed with blood. When set in pale, otherwise unremarkable faces, such raw vitality seems more appropriate of genitals. Which isn't too far from the truth, since for them to feeding is breeding. The drive to continue the species and sustain the self has been fused in an obscene parody of replication, where Thanatos is inextricably wed to Eros.

In the living world, species that destroy what they mate with are doomed to extinction, but amongst the undead such creatures are profligate. Indeed, it is only the vampire's innate selfishness that keeps their population in check. There is a certain safety in numbers—provided their fellows share the same Maker, otherwise they will battle one another to their final deaths.

These pathetic creatures pretend to be human the way alligators pretend to be logs—in order to ambush unwary prey and consume them at their leisure. They mimic human society and its foibles without fully understanding why they do so, like chimps smoking cigars or bears riding bicycles. Even the centuries-long grudge matches and guerrilla wars amongst the Ruling Class are the result of dead flesh parodying the darker passions of the living.

In truth, they all were once living beings who had known love, warmth, kindness, and all those other things that make humans what they are. But with death comes darkness, erasing all the higher emotions, and leaving only base appetite and self-interest behind. In this manner the undead are little more than sentient beasts, concerned with one thing and one thing only: continuing their existence.

***

On the outside, the loathsome creature was the very picture of normalcy. It dressed like any other human on the street—not too current, not too dated. It seemed no different from any of the other well-groomed, well-fed young urbanites hanging out at the bar, the only noticeable eccentricity being a four-foot-long braid of blood-red hair. But since he knew what to look for, he could see it for what it truly was.

There was something about their body language that gave them away. The manner in which they moved their hands and positioned their bodies was very deliberate, almost stylized. It was hard to explain, but once he saw it, there was no mistaking it.

While recovering in the hospital, he read one of Dr. Morrissey's books on non-verbal communication between humans. It described various body postures and how they subliminally represent various emotional states: passivity, dominance, aggression, fear. It was the author's contention that even the most paranoid patient could be manipulated into trusting an utter stranger, provided the proper non-verbal signals were used.

He had been of two minds about that, until he saw these creatures at work. They moved with a studied nonchalance, a deliberate ease… no motion unintended, no gesture accidental. Yet it all seemed strangely alien to them, like martial artists whose fighting stances imitate the movements of tigers, cranes or snakes.

Another means of detecting them was for him to get close enough to look into their eyes. That was dangerous, but surefire. The real trick was not letting them know he was looking, for their features restructured themselves the moment they were no longer being observed. Most humans who gained this knowledge learned it far too late to do them any good, but he had been lucky so far. If you could call what he had undergone "luck."

When they smiled, he noticed it never reached their eyes. The corners of the mouth pulled up, but it was more a nervous tic. The eyes possessed a hunger that was completely out of context with human emotion; as if something much more ancient and dangerous were looking out at the world.

His eyes had been like that; fixing him with a gaze no child should ever see, except from something locked safely behind the bars of a zoo.

***

The dead girl's not half bad at pretending she's alive. Then again, the level of artifice at dance clubs makes it easier for her kind to pass. That's why I make a point of checking raves for infestations.

This one's got the look and the moves that attract human males down pretty well: the skin-tight designer jeans, the pastel spaghetti-strap baby-doll T-shirt and the clunky platform shoes. She's even got the navel ring and the Hello Kitty lunchbox that doubles as a purse. She's broadcasting vulnerability and availability. The one jarring note to her ensemble is the three-foot-long braid, thick as man's wrist. Most observers would simply assume she's wearing a hair extension of some sort. Judging from the length of the braid, I'd peg her somewhere between eighty and a hundred years old. Probably was Made before bobbed hair was all the rage. Vampires wear the goofiest shit. The females tend to favor hairstyles that were popular during their original lifetime, while the males lean more towards outdated clothes, especially shoes. I can't tell you how many dead boys I've snuffed over the years who went to their final grave wearing spats and wing tips. Which leads me to question that resurgence of swing music a couple of years back, but that's another story.

When I'm on patrol, I sometimes feel like the sole watchman on the ramparts, keeping lonely vigil while the city parties itself into a coma. It used to not be this way. In ancient days, strangers who looked and behaved differently were automatically suspect. Then came the rise of the city, the upshot being humans so alienated and under-socialized that no one thinks twice about someone who smells a little off or is dressed twenty years out of fashion. So now its up to me to keep an eye out for the lions amongst the lambs or even worse, the Judas goats sent to lead the sheep to the slaughter.

***

The creature chose her victim for the night; a young male dressed in jeans with pants legs that flared out like the ears of a charging African elephant and a leather billfold fastened to his belt-loop by a length of chrome chain. The combination of grossly oversized clothing, reversed baseball cap and Day-Glo pacifier dangling from a cord around his neck made him look more like a preschooler than a college student.

She hung onto his arm, her tongue tickling his ear. A swell of lust washed over the victim, as a wave overtakes a novice swimmer. At first his eyes burned bright and wet with excitement, then suddenly grew dull, like windows obscured by frost. By the time she led him towards the door, numb hand in hers, her intended victim was little more than a sleepwalker.

He waited a beat before following, making sure they remained in his line of sight. He couldn't afford to lose them in the crowd.

***

I cut across the dance floor, oblivious to the multicolored laser light and the pulsing, molar-rattling beat from the speaker towers; my attention is fixed on the dead girl and her prey. Suddenly a laughing youth dressed in a towering multi-colored stovepipe hat and a Dr. Seuss T-shirt jumps out of the crowd, spraying Day-Glo silly string in my face.

My response is as immediate as it is instinctual: I slap the can out of the boy's hand and grab him by the throat. The raver's pupils, already dilated by meth, expand even further once he realizes his feet are no longer touching the floor. I wipe the silly string from my sunglasses with my free hand as the music continues to pound away in the background. The raver's face is turning blue. The other partygoers are still dancing, oblivious to what's going down in their midst. The only ones who seem to have noticed are those nearby, who I assume to be his friends. They're staring at me open-mouthed. I give a dismissive snarl and toss him aside, like a lioness batting aside a bothersome cub. The boy staggers backward, spittle flying from his lips as he gasps for air. He has no idea how lucky he is. I can only hope that his ill-timed playfulness hasn't cost his fellow partygoer his life.

The rave is being held in an old warehouse in a questionable landscape of overgrown lots, rusted-out cars, abandoned gravel pits and stagnant ponds. The moon shines like a huge luminous skull, pouring its light upon the bleak cityscape below, but there is no sign of the dead girl or her party boy. I toss my head back and take a deep breath. I catch a whiff of putrescence and depravity, mixed with the reek of snake house. It is the stink of the undead. I smile without humor and trot off in the direction of my prey. As I head down the darkened alley, I catch a second, all-to-familiar odor: sweat, blood and fear combined with the unadulterated stench of mortal combat. I round the corner and see a figure kneeling over a prone body in the shadows of the alley.

I curse the idiot in the stovepipe hat, but then I realize the raver is lying unconscious on the ground a few feet away from me. His skin is gray from shock and his eyes are rolled back in his head, but seems to be otherwise unharmed.

The shadowy figure straightens from its task and turns to face me, a Bowie knife in one hand and the dead girl's head in the other. The stranger is a man dressed in a long black duster, black jeans, a long-sleeved black shirt, and black cowboy boots with silver tips. His head is bare, his long, prematurely white hair pulled back from his face in a simple ponytail. His gray eyes have all the warmth of the yawning doors of a walk-in freezer.

He slides the big knife into a sheath fastened to his belt, next to the leather gun holster tied to his right leg. I can tell he's trying to decide whether or not he should kill me. Although I never laid eyes on him before in my life, a thrill of recognition still ignites my nerve-endings.

"Back the fuck up," he snarls.

"You got it, ace," I reply, holding my hands palms out, so he can see I'm not carrying a weapon.

I take a step backward, using the opportunity to drop my vision into the occult spectrum. I scan the stranger for signs of Pretender taint, but his aura comes up clean. Whatever else he might be, at least he's human.

"What are you doing here?" he asks tersely.

"Funny, I was about to ask the same of you."

The dark-clad stranger tilts his head to one side, his brows knitted tightly together, as if he's trying to read a newspaper through me. Suddenly there's a gun in his hand. I have to admire his reflexes. The boy's quick, I'll give him that. The silenced muzzle makes a slow, methodical searching movement up and down my torso, like a police dog sniffing out contraband.

"Look, man, there's no need to get hostile...."

The gun in his hand bucks and there's a muffled sound, like the pop of an old-fashioned flashcube. He stands snapshot-still as the gun smoke blows back into his face. I instinctively grab my wounded shoulder, momentarily turning my attention away from the stranger. When I look back, seconds later, it is to see him running down the alley, the dead girl's braid flapping behind him like the tail of a fox.

I should—and could—give chase, but I'm not keen on risking a second bullet between the eyes. The slug in my shoulder is no misfire. He could have put me down, if he'd had a mind to do so. I use the switchblade to dig the bullet out. It hurts, but I've endured far worse.

I hold the blood-smeared .38 caliber bullet in the palm of my hand, rolling it back in forth so that its silver jacket reflects the moonlight. I shake my head in disbelief, a rueful smile on my face. After all these years, it seems I've finally stumbled across a fellow vampire slayer.

***

At first it seemed like it would go down like the other kills. The vampiress was too preoccupied with keeping her most recent victim under her spell to notice that she herself was being stalked. He watched from a safe distance as she led the boy into a secluded alley and behind a dumpster. Thinking she was alone, the vampiress began giggling in a hideous little-girl voice. That's when he knew it was time to call her out.

"Undead."

He said it loud and distinctly, so she would know he wasn't crying out in fear, but naming her, as a doctor would diagnose a disease. She stepped away from her prey and turned to face him with a nimble, feral movement, her eyes cisterns leading down to sunless depths. A long strand of saliva dripped from her exposed canines.

"This does not concern you, human."

He fired twice before she could move against him, splashing the wall behind her with blood and vertebrae. The vampiress hit the ground and stayed there, but she wasn't completely dead yet. The bullets had severed her spinal cord, but such injuries were not instantly fatal to her kind. The killing blow would come from the silver, which, as he had learned, inflicted a painful, agonizing death. The vampiress' upper torso squirmed like a worm on a hot sidewalk as her flesh turned a pale, bluish purple, sloughing off her bones like the meat of a stewed chicken. She looked up at him, scarlet sparks of loathing spitting from her fading eyes, her lips smeared with the black ichor that served as her blood. She clicked her fangs together rapidly; making a sound like the buzz of rattler's tail, then went still.

Satisfied she was truly dead, he knelt to take his trophy. He had been thinking for most of the night about where he would put it. The braid would definitely have to be part of the display.

As he decapitated the creature, he became aware of being watched, like a hunter who has come to the stream to fill his canteen, only to find himself opposite a cougar that has wandered down from the hills to slake its thirst.

She was standing less than thirty feet away, dressed in a well-worn leather motorcycle jacket, faded black jeans, scuffed harness boots, and a ragged Skinny Puppy T-shirt. She was tall and built like an acrobat, with dark, unruly hair that hung about her face like an abbreviated lion's mane, her eyes hidden behind mirrored sunglasses.

At first he thought she was one of the revelers from the rave who had wandered into the alley to either relieve herself or do drugs. But there was something in the way she held herself that told him she wasn't a mere party girl. Despite her pretense at casualness, he was reminded of a panther pretending to doze before springing on its zookeeper.

Something in the way she dipped her head slightly, looking over the top of her sunglasses at him for a brief second without managing to show her eyes, was genuinely disquieting. She studied him for a long moment; the way cats will break away from grooming themselves to stare intently at nothing at all. Whatever it was she saw, or didn't see, made her relax her stance slightly—but not completely.

Since he wasn't sure she was one of them, he fired at a part of her body that would not be normally fatal. If she were undead, the silver alone would do its job. If she were human, she would escape with a broken collarbone. Granted, it wasn't the fairest of calls, but it was better than either of them being dead.

It wasn't until he was in the van, tearing ass back to base, that it occurred to him who the stranger had been. He swore out loud and hammered his forehead with a doubled fist, cursing his stupidity.

After years of hunting the most dangerous game known to mortal man, he had finally come face-to-face with the only other vampire hunter on the face of the earth. And what did he do?

He shot the Blue Woman.

The sun is rising in the east, chasing away the night and all the things that dwell within it. Including myself.

I sigh and let the heavy blackout curtains fall back in place. I have yet to develop a fatal allergy to sunlight, but it does not feel pleasant upon my skin, and the minutest exposure hurts my eyes, even when I wear the darkest of my sunglasses. I pace back and forth uneasily. I am weary, and the wound in my shoulder throbs. I know I should allow myself to regenerate, but there is too much on my mind to surrender to the *petite mort*.

The events of the night's hunt have done much to disturb and, yes, excite me. I can't shake the image of the white-haired hunter from my mind. I must know more—who is he? What's his name? Where does he come from? Why is he here? Is he a friend? An enemy? Something in between?

If I have learned one thing from my existence, it's that knowledge is power. This is why I forced myself to learn how to use a computer. Pretenders have a problem with electronics. Perhaps it's because machines are things of human making, or perhaps it's simply too difficult for them to break centuries-old habits, but most of them refuse to keep abreast with the latest advances in the sciences. That's why they surround themselves with human servants; it guarantees that they can exploit technology without ever having to interface with it directly.

I unplug my laptop from its recharger and place it on the card table that serves as my desk, jacking the modem into the phone line. The LCD flickers into life as I turn on the juice, typing in my password as I go. I take out the hands-free headset and plug it into a port on the side of the laptop. I type in an address and hit the ENTER key. The screech of the computer modem fills my skull. I grimace and spin down the volume on the earpiece.

A computer-generated image fills the laptop's LCD. It's a three-dimensional picture of a man's head, perpetually rotating in cyberspace through three hundred and sixty degrees. The head is transparent and where the brain should be there is a mass of cobwebs. As the head spins and tilts, the strands of the spider web shimmer with electric blue foxfire and purple heat lightning.

I turn the volume up on the earpiece and hear a short buzzing sound, kind of like a cross between the rings of a doorbell and a telephone. Suddenly a smaller rectangle opens up within the upper right hand corner of the screen, revealing a man in his late twenties with a shaved head, the folds and creases of a human brain tattooed directly onto his bald pate. As if this was not adornment enough, there's a third eye etched upon his brow. Upon magnification, the center of the tattooed eye turns out to be a perfectly circular hole in his skull.

"Who is it?" The voice speaks before the lips move, like that of an astronaut circling the moon. Although I can see the tattooed man thanks to the digicam mounted on his computer monitor, he can't see me.

"It's Sonja," I reply, identifying myself.

The bald man's broad lips pull into a wide smile. "Sonja! Long time no see—so to speak."

"Back at ya. How's the virtual world treating you, Webhead?"

He shrugs bare shoulders covered in spider-web tattoos. "I was scheduled for a second trepanation, but the dude who was going to drill me got cold feet."

"Bummer."

"Yeah, but you didn't log on for small talk. What do you need?" He reaches off-screen to retrieve what appears to be a defused mortar shell.

"What do I always need you for?"

"Besides the hot monkey sex?" he leers, firing up the bong.

I snort good-naturedly. It's part of our ritual banter. "In your nightmares, kiddo! I need a search done—newspaper archives, police databases, the discussion groups that cater to true crime and serial killer buffs, that kind of thing. I'm looking for unsolved homicides involving decapitations. Oh, and filter out those with known sexual assault."

Webhead lifts an eyebrow, his interest piqued. "Time frame?"

"The last five years."

"You want me to charge it to the Swiss account?"

"Sure."

"You got it. I'll beep you when it's ready."

The PIP disappears, signaling our business transaction is at its end. I log off and stare at the blank face of the laptop's display for a long moment. There is no guarantee that Webhead will turn up anything of any real use to me, but it would be a start. Whoever the mystery man I ran into in the alley might be, it's clear he has his moves down. And you don't get that smooth without practice in the field.

I yawn and strip off my leather jacket, draping it over the back of the chair, one of the few pieces of furniture in the loft I've made my base of operations. Its getting harder for me to locate suitable space to crash out in during the day—most of the old warehouses are in the process of being renovated into yuppie condos.

I kick off my boots and drop onto the old mattress that serves as my bed. The ticking is stained and torn, and there are no bedclothes. Not that it matters. I never feel cold.

The ache in my shoulder pulls at my consciousness, urging me to surrender to the *petite mort*. I can already feel my blood pressure dropping, plummeting like a stone hurled down an empty well. My heart slows its beating. My lungs fold in on themselves like paper lanterns. I close my eyes, only to be swallowed by the dreamless void, and I am still as death and…

The sun is down.

I know this because my eyes are open again. I lay there, flat on my back, my hands folded in repose atop my breastbone, and wait for my heart to resume its pumping. I emerge from death, as easily as another woman would climb from a bath, feeling rejuvenated and restored. The pain in my shoulder is gone, the bone completely mended, the flesh bearing only the slightest trace of a scar.

I reopen my laptop and find an email with an attachment awaiting me. The file Webhead has compiled keeps the printer busy for over an hour. Most of it consists of archived newspaper accounts of badly decomposed bodies found in ditches, but that's not all.

There's a series of articles from the Portland and Seattle papers detailing "ritualistic" murders committed in 1995 by a killer dubbed the "Headhunter" because of his (or her, as the reporters were Politically Correct enough to point out) removal of the victims' craniums.

An unusual aspect of the Headhunter's killing spree was that all but two of the victims remained unidentified, and those two had each been listed with Missing Persons for several years. The killings, which transpired over a four-month period between several major metropolitan areas in both Oregon and Washington, ended abruptly in April of 1995. To date, the seven murders remain unsolved, the cases still open.

In May of that same year, three murders occurred in Chicago, the modus operandi bearing an eerie similarity to those in the Pacific Northwest. These slayings were attributed to the so-called "Head-Man."

In the spring of 1996, Toronto was terrorized by a faceless killer known only as the "Skid Row Butcher," who took the heads of four victims in the span of six weeks. During 1998 and most of 1999, several headless bodies were found at rest areas along major Eastern Seaboard turnpikes, although the various investigative agencies involved didn't connect the murders.

Of far greater interest to me are the FBI files Webhead hacked into. While local law enforcement never saw a pattern amongst the various slayings, the same did not hold true for the Feds. Although J. Edgar's boys never announced to state and metropolitan law enforcement agencies that a serial killer with over twenty notches on his belt was on the loose, that has not kept them from compiling a dossier. The Bureau's codename for the killer is "Harker."

I skim over the Bureau profiler's by-the-numbers assessment of Harker's make-up: white, middle-aged, male, above-average intelligence. So what else is new? The autopsy reports on the victims are far more interesting. There's a marked similarity in the forensic evidence in every case. Some of this uniformity is due to the manner in which the bodies were mutilated, but that's not the only reason.

Despite the fact the victims vary greatly in sex, age and race, all of the bodies proved so badly decomposed upon discovery it was impossible to tell what mutilations were done before or after death. The only thing the forensic reports say for sure is that each victim was shot then decapitated. The link between the various killings lay within the ballistic report: silver-jacketed .38 slugs were retrieved from each and every body, and it was the Bureau's opinion that Harker himself had manufactured the ammunition.

The fact that the killer could afford to have bullets made using precious metals placed him far outside the Bureau's normal experience. At this point two Special Agents, a man and a woman, were called in to help expand the investigation. Reports written by these Special Agents show a mixture of bafflement and grudging respect for Harker, not to mention an undercurrent of genuine disquiet. However, the agents' apprehension didn't appear to be generated by the acts of the killer they were investigating insomuch as by the background information they uncovered about the victims.

Shortly after the Special Agents filed their reports, a memo from high within the Bureau ordered them to withdraw from the case and to keep the existence of Harker secret from the public and, indeed, all other branches of law enforcement.

This last bit does not surprise me in the least. I've long suspected that select officials within the FBI and CIA, along with their opposite numbers throughout the globe, know the truth about the monsters of ancient legend who walk unnoticed, if not exactly unseen, amongst humankind. It's much easier, and far safer, for those who know the truth to look the other way whenever possible, blaming the growing incidences of missing children and unsolved murders on anonymous serial killers rather than werewolves and vampires. Whether these high-ranking politicos are acting in the best interests of the human race, or under orders from inhuman masters, is another question altogether.

I take the printouts and carefully feed them into the only other technological luxury I have allowed myself: a crosscut paper shredder. As I watch the hard copy of the FBI files turn into confetti, I have no doubt in my mind that the stranger with the white hair and the Bowie knife who shot me is their so-called "Harker." But who he is, and why he's dedicated himself to hunting vampires is another matter… one I intend to get to the bottom of.

***

He stumbled across the first hint of the Blue Woman's existence on, of all things, a computer BBS frequented by minions—those debased humans who had willingly enslaved themselves to the undead.

There were numerous postings from the likes of "NecroPhil" and "renfield236" reporting sightings of a mysterious female who was rumored to be a vampire slayer of great ability. Given that she was often spotted in different cities on the same day, he had assumed the Blue Woman was nothing more than an urban myth; a post-modern *folie à deux*, similar to the mass hysteria that birthed the Satanist Daycare Trials of the last century. Especially, considering how unstable minions tended to be, it was reasonable to assume the Blue Woman was nothing more than a punishing mother projection born of psyches tortured by subconscious guilt.

The minions spoke of her the way children whisper of the bogeyman, and for good reason. According to the reports, the Blue Woman was Anglo, African-American, and Asian. She was tall and short, fat but thin. Some even claimed she was a pre-op drag queen. She was all of these things, yet none of them; all the descriptions were equally valid and equally dubious, since no one who actually laid eyes on her ever survived to tell the tale.

The very mention of the Blue Woman scared the living shit out of those who trafficked with the undead. Knowing the power of myth, he doubted much of what was credited to her was true. But then again, he had also assumed she wasn't real at all until the night before.

He had to find some way of meeting her. Granted, she might not want to renew their acquaintance, considering that he'd put a bullet in her. Still, he had to try. This was the first time he had crossed the path of a fellow vampire slayer. And it was possible she might know something about the whereabouts of Blackheart. He refused to contemplate the possibility that the Blue Woman might have already killed the vampire. He was determined to reserve that pleasure for himself.

***

The moon looks down on the park's carefully maintained nature trails and bike paths with all the warmth and expression of a baked fish. I move through the shadows, heading towards the lake, the liquid heart of the city. As I hurry along, I can make out furtive shadows moving between the trees and shrubbery along the trail. These do not concern me, as I recognize the figures haunting the dark to be more of a distinctly human, and decidedly carnal, nature.

In the moonlight the water looks as black as oil. A huge weeping willow hugs the bank, its verdant tresses dipping into the moonlit water, like a long-haired woman peering at her own reflection. A frog, startled by my passing, leaps into the water with a splash. I part the green curtain and step inside the natural canopy. The willow's inner sanctum is darker than the night outside, not that it makes any difference to my eyes.

"Jen?" I find myself whispering, even though there is no need. *"Where are you?"*

"At your service, as always, dear cousin."

I tilt my head upward in the direction of his voice. Jen is nestled in the crotch of the tree, feet dangling in mid-air, grinning down at me like a later-day Puck. I wonder how he managed to scale the tree wearing five-inch platform heels.

Jen is slight of build, standing no more than five-seven, with graying hair kept in a medusa's coil of braids decorated with ceramic beads. With his heavily mascaraed eyes, matching rouge and lipstick, skin-tight crushed velour pants, and pectoral of gaily painted finger bones about his neck, he looks like a demented transvestite Peter Pan.

"I have a use for you."

"All things have their uses, even those of us trapped between the natures," he replies, smiling flatly.

"I seek a man."

Jen rolls his eyes and grins lewdly. "So those rumors I heard about you are true, eh?"

I choose to ignore his remarks. "He is a stranger to me. He is in his late twenties, early thirties. His hair is long and white and he keeps it in a ponytail. He dresses all in black and favors western clothes. I'm talking Johnny Cash, here, not Garth Brooks. He carries a pistol that shoots silver bullets, a Bowie knife with a silvered blade, and there are silver caps on his boots. I want you to find him and tell him that I wish to parley."

Jen shifts about uneasily. "What matter of man is this stranger?"

"He is a hunter."

His eyes narrow. "A hunter of men?"

"A hunter of those who were once men."

Jen's eyes go from gun slits to open windows. "Have you lost your mind?!?"

"Don't argue with me! Or would you rather go without a protector?"

Jen scowls and quickly looks away, but does not reply.

"Answer me! Do you serve me or not?"

Jen turns back to face me, his voice tight with rage. "You know I *must* serve you. I have no choice."

"That's bullshit! There is *always* a choice."

"Not amongst those born damned."

It is my turn to fall silent. "Forgive me, cousin. I misspoke." I lower my gaze in ritual shame.

Jen nods slightly in acceptance of my apology, but does not look me in the eye. After a long second he finally returns his gaze to mine. "Are you sure this is the course you wish to take?"

There is something in his voice that gives me pause. I stare hard at his face. It is as immobile as a kabuki mask, save for a slight tremor at the corner of his left eye. In the years since we first met, I have learned to read Jen as easily as I once read dear, deceiving Chaz. I can see he is hiding something from me. And the cold black thing coiled in the back of my brain knows exactly what it is.

"You *know* who this man is!" The words drop from my lips like heavy stones.

Jen shakes his head in adamant denial, his braids clattering like wooden wind chimes. "I *never* said such a thing!"

"You didn't *have* to," I reply. "Who *is* he, Jen?"

"Honest, Sonja, I—"

I yank him out of the tree so that he lands on the ground face-first. I bring my boot down hard on the back of his neck, grinding his mouth into the grass. For the briefest of moments I contemplate breaking Jen's neck, but quickly force the thought from my mind.

"Cut the shit, Jen! I'm in no mood! Who *is* he?"

Jen struggles to lift his head, and spits out a clod of dirt before he speaks. "His name is Estes! Jack Estes!"

"What *else* do you know about him?"

"That he's bad news!"

"And I'm *not*?"

Sometimes my loathing of renfields overwhelms me, and when it does, Jen bears the brunt of it. I always end up feeling bad about it, because it's not really his fault. Unlike the human Judas goats who seek out their dark masters, Jen genuinely can't help being what he is. A vampire bit his mother while she was in the early stages of pregnancy, thereby tainting him in the womb. Technically, he's a *dhampire*—sort of a supernatural half-breed, ostracized by both species. In many ways, we have a lot in common.

I remove my foot from his neck and motion for him to stand. "Get up. I don't want you getting off on this any more than you have already."

Jen scowls the grass stains on his crushed velour pants with genuine dismay. "Look at these trousers! Do you have *any* idea what the dry cleaning bill is going to be?"

"I'm sure you can afford it, what with the cash you've been making peddling information to this Estes."

"What makes you think I've got dealings with him? I just said that I knew his name, that's all."

"Come off it, Jen! Remember who you're talking to here. We're *family*, right? We're just like *this*, aren't we?" I hold up my hand and cross my fore- and middle fingers. "You've been acting as a stalking horse for this Estes bloke, am I right? I know you rent yourself out as a double agent to vampires from time to time, so why not another vampire hunter? "

"I'm *not* a stalking horse," he replied petulantly. "I provide consultant work, if you don't mind."

"You can call it synchronized cat-flinging for all I care. All that matters is that you've got a working relationship with this Estes. That means he's more likely to trust you."

Jen fixes me with a cautious eye. "Are you going to kill him?"

"No."

"Is that your final answer?"

***

With its penchant for corpse-pale make-up, heavy eyeliner, black clothing, and eccentrically morbid behavior, the Goth scene is perfect camouflage for vampires and an excellent recruiting ground for minions. And as much as he loathed minions, Estes had to admit they had their uses.

When the pallid little man with the elaborate dreadlocks had first sidled up to him and whispered, "I know what you need," Estes had assumed he was being solicited for either sex or drugs. When he'd attempted to brush his unwanted companion off, the slighter man had smiled slyly, his eyes gleaming like those of a fox in the brush, and pointed at a youngish man with a shaved head and a tinted monocle who was cruising the dance floor.

"That one is hundred and seventy-six years old. He claims to have been a viscount in the Austro-Hungarian court. He lies. I have it on good authority he was a Polish swineherd."

The minion's name was Jen and he claimed to have once served a powerful vampire lord, but had become embittered toward vampire society by his treatment after his patron's demise. Apparently vampires have little interest in taking into their service minions who were not "loyal" enough to follow their masters to the grave. From that evening on Estes had paid to use Jen's considerable knowledge to his own advantage.

Despite their mutually beneficial agreement, there was still something deeply repulsive about Jen, although Estes couldn't exactly put his finger on just what it was. The man was simply intrinsically *wrong* somehow, and he managed to stir an instinctual dislike within Estes. It was the same disquiet humans felt when in the presence of a spider or a snake.

Estes scanned the crowded bar and caught sight of his contact standing at the farthest end of the rail, his appearance as outlandish as usual.

"Jen," he said flatly, nodding his head in polite acknowledgement.

Jen looked up from his drink, his eyes flashing the same feral fire Estes had glimpsed at their first meeting. "What is you want from me, Jack?" he asked, his words slurred by alcohol.

"Information."

"What *kind* of information?" The minion smiled wryly, using an overlong fingernail to stir the ice cubes in his drink.

Estes glanced about, making sure they weren't being watched, and leaned in close. "Have you ever heard of the Blue Woman?"

Jen regarded him in silence for a long moment, and then chuckled humorlessly. "I take it you're not talking about Picasso."

"What has that to do with anything?" Estes snapped. "I'm in no mood for your being clever tonight. Answer the question: yes or no?"

Jen sighed and nodded his head, causing the beads woven into his braids to click like dice in a cup. "Yes, I've heard of her."

"Do you know how I can get in touch?"

Jen eyed him for a long moment, as if deciding whether or not to answer. "Are you *sure* that's what you want? Beware of what you ask for, Jack. You might just get it."

Estes regarded the smaller man carefully. "Are you telling me you can arrange a meeting with her?"

"If that's what you really want, yes."

"You *still* haven't answered my question. *Can* you arrange a rendezvous?"

"Of *course* I can," Jen replied as he sipped his drink. "The Blue Woman and me, we're like this." He held up his left hand. He had somehow managed to wrap his pinkie over his ring finger. "We're family."

"Is that so?" Estes replied, still dubious.

"Would I lie to you?"

"Probably. How come you've never mentioned to me that you know her?"

"You never asked before now."

Estes shrugged. He couldn't argue with him there.

"Is she a genuine vampire slayer?"

"As real as it gets, my friend. She hates vampires more than you do."

"I seriously doubt that," Estes sniffed. "What are you laughing at?"

"You'll find out," Jen said, trying hard to suppress another snicker.

Denny's might seem like an unlikely rendezvous spot for vampire hunters, but think about it for a minute: they're open twenty-four hours and most are conveniently located near major traffic arteries, just in case you have to make that ever-popular quick getaway. Besides, given the clientele that usually occupies the orange and brown booths after midnight, customers like Mr. Estes and me barely merit a second glance from the wait staff.

The parley, as arranged through Jen, is to occur at midnight, but I chose to show up a half-hour early, just in case I'm walking into a trap. I'm not surprised to find Estes already awaiting me, but I am slightly impressed.

He's sitting alone in the farthest corner booth, his back to the wall, dressed much as I first saw him, a solitary cup of black coffee in front of him. Even in repose he's as tight as a steel spring. I have no doubt that he is armed, and I know he thinks the same of me. And he's right, of course.

His eyes follow me as I approach, watching for telltale body language or sudden movement. His gaze flickers to my shoulder. Confusion, as fleeting as a summer cloud, crosses his face.

"May I sit down?" I ask, gesturing to the empty bench. He nods but says nothing. I slide in opposite him. A waitress with a weary expression and sagging pantyhose moves to take my order. I point to my companion's drink and she returns a moment later with a white ceramic mug and a half-empty Bunn pot. The coffee smells of scorched grounds. Neither of us moves or speaks until the waitress has returned to her station behind the counter.

"You are the Blue Woman." It is not a question.

"I have been called that. My name is Sonja. Sonja Blue."

His eyes go back to my shoulder. "I shot you the other night, but you're not wounded. Do you wear a Kevlar vest?"

"No."

The furrows on his brow deepen.

"Look, forget the shooting, okay?" I say, cutting him off before he can ask anything else. "I didn't agree to meet with you to compare notes. I'm here to talk you into giving up this madness. You've been lucky, so far. But that luck will eventually fail you. Despite everything you think you know, you are in no position to truly combat these things."

A flash of anger darkens his eyes. "Who are you to tell me what I do and don't know? I'm hardly a novice on the matter; I've been hunting these creatures for five years! I know if I shoot them with a silver bullet, they die. I know that if I take their heads, they stay dead. I know that if I touch them with a crucifix, they burn."

I shake my head, fighting the urge to laugh. "*Everything* stays dead if you chop off its head. As to burning them with a crucifix, religious icons have no effect on them."

"Mine does," he says, the muscle in his jaw jumping.

I extend my hand. "Let me see it."

Estes casts his searchlight gaze about the diner, then reaches into the interior right breast pocket of his duster and retrieves an ornately detailed antique silver crucifix measuring a foot in length. I take the relic from him, turning it over carefully in my hands. It is weighted so that it can bludgeon as well as bless.

"I bought it from a dealer in rare objects," Estes explains. "He claimed it was a specially designed for use by the Inquisition and blessed by Pope Sixtus IV."

"I know what it is," I reply curtly. "It was used to administer church-sanctioned beatings of heretics and those accused of witchcraft. Breaking bones with a blessed object was believed to pain the demon that possessed those under the Question and guaranteed that no imp could enter the wound after the fact." I return the witch-breaker to him, wiping my hands with one of the paper napkins from the dispenser on the table. "They burn because it's silver, not because it's a crucifix. Not even because it was blessed by a Pope."

Estes stares at the crucifix for a long moment as if truly seeing it for the first time, then carefully returns it to its place within his coat.

"That's exactly what I'm talking about," I say, shaking my head in disgust. "Your understanding of their abilities and weaknesses, while impressive, is seriously flawed. You're good, but you're still just human. There are only a handful who possesses the ability to truly see these creatures for what they are, and most are madder than hatters. I can tell from looking at you that you don't possess extrasensory perception, so I'm assuming your awareness must come from personal contact."

A startled look flashes across his face, as quick as a deer leaping in front of a speeding car, then disappears. "Who told you that?"

I sigh and roll my eyes. People more intense than me wear me out. "Didn't you hear what I just said? Don't get paranoid on me, friend. I don't know a thing about you except what Jen has told me. But give me credit for adding two and two together and not getting five, okay?"

"You say I've been lucky so far. That's bullshit! I've got over twenty kills under my belt. That's more than just luck! You keep saying I'm just human. So what the hell does that make you?"

"Come now, boy," I smile, flashing him a glimpse of fang. "Surely you know by now it takes one to know one."

Estes' hand goes to the concealed holster nestled in his left armpit, but I grab his wrist and pin it to the table with enough force to slosh cooling coffee into the saucers.

"I wouldn't do that, if I were you, Mr. Estes." I keep my voice even and low, as if calming a skittish animal. While I make sure the pressure on his wrist isn't painful for now, there's no way he can lift his hand without breaking his arm. "There are too many witnesses here, for one." I nod to the trio of college students sipping coffee and eating pie two booths over. "Neither of us is interested in harming uninvolved parties."

"Since when has your kind ever cared about harming the innocent?" He spits the words out as if they've curdled in his mouth.

"I am not one of *them*," I reply, trying to keep the anger from my voice. "Didn't I just handle your blessed silver crucifix?"

He relaxes slightly, but remains tense, his brows knit in consternation. "Then what are you, if you're not undead?"

I shrug and let go of his wrist. He yanks it away, studying it cautiously, like a man counting his fingers after a close encounter with a crocodile.

"All I can tell you is that I am Sonja Blue, and I have been a vampire hunter for thirty years."

Estes stops massaging his wrist and tilts his head to one side. "Thirty—? How old are you?"

"Forty-seven."

"You don't look it."

It takes me a moment to realize he is attempting humor. I smile crookedly. "Thanks."

A long, uncomfortable silence falls between us. His eyes flicker over me, trying to decipher the enigma before him via whatever Rosetta Stone he has based his world upon. I skim the surface of his mind, careful not to create ripples that would alert him to my presence. I see hungry, dead eyes and a grinning mouth set in a dark face.

"You're looking for one vampire in particular."

Estes' eyes narrow in suspicion.

"Don't worry. I'm not a mind-reader," I say, lying to his face. "It's just that those who hunt the undead have their reasons, and it's usually revenge. It certainly was in my case."

Curiosity replaces the suspicion in Estes' eyes. "Tell me about it."

I shrug. "It's the same old story. Girl has the world on a string. Girl meets handsome Prince Charming. Prince Charming turns into rapist hell-beast. Girl wakes up from a coma a year later with fangs and a thirst for blood. Girl spends the next twenty-something years trying to track down the bastard who stole her life and future away from her."

Estes leans forward in his seat, his gaze focused on me as tight as a laser. "Did you find him?"

"Yes. More than once, actually."

"Did you kill him?" His breathing has become as ragged as that of an obscene phone caller's.

"Yes."

"How was it?"

I avert my eyes, looking out the window into the parking lot. "Dangerous. Frightening. Violent. Exhilarating."

He gives a tiny sigh and leans back in his seat. He looks like a man who has satisfied some urge better left secret.

"Look, Estes," I whisper sharply. "The world you think you know is a lot darker than even you can imagine. It's a nightmare country, where a little knowledge is as dangerous as complete ignorance. So far you've played the holy fool, strolling towards the precipice, happily unaware of your own blindness. The path you've chosen is dangerous beyond human comprehension.

"That is why the Holy See disbanded the witch finders elite. Once they learned mankind shared the planet with shadow races that had been preying upon humans since the first ape stood upright, they were unable to live with the knowledge. Many went mad, some committed suicide, and others surrendered themselves to the control of those they were once sworn to oppose. They learned the hard way that it's impossible for humans to be hunters of monsters without becoming monsters themselves.

"As for me, I've slain hundreds of vampires. And I've murdered countless humans. Many were servants of those I battled. Others were — if not exactly innocent— certainly not guilty of any crime worthy of death. Yet, I killed them all the same. That's why I'm asking you to stop. If you value your humanity, you'll surrender this madness and get on with your life."

The muscles in Estes' jaw work as if he's biting on a bullet. "Even if I wanted to do that, I can't. Not yet."

One of the diners in a nearby booth stops eating her scramble skillet and stares at us, fork frozen halfway to her mouth, a look of fearful disbelief in her eyes. We've been overheard, if not exactly understood.

"Let's take this discussion someplace a little bit more private," I say, tossing a crumpled ten onto the tabletop.

We stride out of the restaurant and into the darkness beyond its glass doors. I motion for Estes to follow me as I head down a side street, away from the lights of the main drag. He hesitates, and then falls into step alongside me.

"Tell me about yourself, Mr. Estes."

"You don't want to hear my story."

"On the contrary. I want to know as much about you as I possibly can. There are so few vampire hunters; surely we must share some things in common."

Estes shoots me a look from the corner of his eye, trying to decide if I'm making fun of him. After a long moment, he reaches inside the pocket of his duster and withdraws a pack of unfiltered Raleighs.

"Mind if I smoke?"

I raise an eyebrow in mild surprise. "Isn't that an unusual brand for someone your age?"

Estes grunts something like a laugh as he lips his cigarette. "Old habits die hard. It's what they used to smoke in the bughouse. "

"You were in an asylum?"

"Yeah," he sighs, lighting his smoke with a chrome Zippo pulled from yet another pocket. "Sixteen years, total. Although I only remember six of them." He takes a long, hard pull on the cigarette, blowing the smoke out through his nostrils. "So…where do you want me to start?"

"How about from the beginning? That's where most stories start."

"I was conceived at Woodstock. At least that's what I remember my mother telling me. My memories of my mother and father are kind of jumbled up with what I learned about them, so I'm never a hundred-percent sure if I'm remembering something that really happened to me or something I read about later on.

"Despite how it might sound, my parents weren't blissed-out hippies living in a commune in Upstate New York, making beeswax candles and throwing pots. My father was Frank Estes, a concert promoter and record producer who got his start booking acts for West Coast nightclubs. My mother, who was ten years younger than he was, met Dad while working as a dancer at the old Whiskey-A-Go-Go.

"Like I said, I don't remember a whole lot about my parents. When I try to picture their faces, the features are distorted and distant, as if I'm looking at them through the wrong end of a pair of binoculars. I know my father was tall, had a mustache and a tan, and that my mother was young and pretty, with long blonde hair that hung down to her waist. Whether these are true memories or impressions I picked up from the photo albums the doctors showed me, I couldn't say for sure.

"Anyway, Dad was more of a hipster than a hippie. He might have smoked pot and hung out with musicians, but he was out to make a buck, not change the world. He had an eye for talent and trends, and he got his first big break by booking a series of tours for some of the British Invasion bands.

"In 1970, he simultaneously became a father, a husband and a record producer. I still have their wedding picture: my mother was wearing a white fringe go-go outfit with white vinyl knee-boots and carrying a bouquet, and Dad was in a white satin tuxedo with wide velvet lapels. I'm in the photo, too, as a month-old infant, held aloft for the photographer by a shit-faced Keith Moon.

"Dad named his new label Jack Music. I don't know if he called the company after me or vice versa. The first couple of bands he signed did okay, but they didn't set the charts on fire. Then in 1972 he sank a lot of money into developing and promoting an acid rock group called Crushed Velvet that ended up going nowhere in a hurry. By the time 1973 rolled around, Dad was on the verge of bankruptcy.

"That's when my father acquired a business partner and the company's name was changed from Jack Music to Blackheart Records. I don't remember much about what was going on back then, since I was only three years old, but I do recall my father always seemed to be away on business of some kind. Dad didn't take my mother with him when he went on his trips, so I spent most of my time with her. I guess before I was born it was different between them; I don't know.

"Whatever it was my father was off doing, it provided the good life. We had a five-bedroom house up in the hills, an Olympic-sized swimming pool, a private tennis court and an in-home movie theater. I guess you could say we were living large."

Estes paused to drop the cigarette onto the pavement, grinding it under a silver-tipped boot. Although he was looking at Sonja, his gaze was fixed on another time, another place.

"It's funny what we remember," he said dreamily. "The names and faces of friends blur and fade like chalk sketches on a sidewalk, while a commercial jingle for breakfast cereal remains etched in acid. I read in a psychiatric journal how all the kindness and love shown to a child can be cast in perpetual shadow by a solitary cruel act. The truly horrible thing is how that single, thoughtless act ends up defining who that child is and what he becomes more than any of the good and positive things that have ever happened to him, before or since. And, God help me, if I'm not the poster boy for whatever the hell they call that little syndrome.

"Like I said, my memories are indistinct... except for the night my family was killed. Every move they made, every sentence that was uttered in my presence, it's all branded onto my cerebral cortex. I can close my eyes and see it as clearly as a movie."

He shut his eyes and stood perfectly still for half a heartbeat, his features suddenly seeming much younger than they had a moment before. Then he remembered himself and his eyes snapped back open.

"I was excited my father was coming home. He'd been away on one of his business trips. I don't know where he went, but it was out of the country. I was especially eager because I knew he was bringing me back a present. It was getting late and Dad still wasn't back from the airport yet. My mother was anxious; she kept getting up and pacing the rumpus room. I was trying to watch TV, but she kept walking in front of the set. She was chain-smoking, too, something Dad didn't approve of."

Estes smiled crookedly and his voice changed timbre and tone, becoming deeper and gruffer; a child's imitation of adult speech: "'I spend enough time in smoke-filled bars, I don't want to come home to it, too, damn it!' Yeah, Dad was anti-tobacco before it was PC." The smile slid from Estes' face as suddenly as it had arrived. "I remember the doorbell ringing and Mom hurrying off to answer it. At first I thought it might be Dad, but why would he have to ring the doorbell? After a couple of minutes Mom came back into the rumpus room, turned off the TV, and told me it was time to go to bed.

"I said I wanted to sit up and wait for Dad, but she got mad and told me to get to bed right that instant. I knew better than to argue with her when she sounded like that, so I went upstairs to my room and put on my Scooby Doo pajamas. I lay in bed for a long time, waiting for Mom to kiss me goodnight and tuck me in, but she never came. So I snuck out of my room and crept out into the hall to see what was going on.

"The living room and dining room in our house had these open, cathedral-style ceilings, kind of like an atrium, so I could see most of what went on downstairs by peeking through the upstairs banister. I lay there on my belly, the synthetic fibers of the shag tickling my face, and stared down at my mother as she paced back and forth, leaving a cloud of cigarette smoke in her wake. She kept looking at the front door, like she was expecting something horrible to walk through it.

"Just then I heard the jingle of keys and my father crossed the threshold, a garment bag draped over one shoulder and a suitcase in one hand. He was dressed in a denim leisure suit and he looked like he hadn't shaved in days. That was my cue. I jumped to my feet and hurried down the stairs, squealing with delight.

"I was half-way down the stairs when my mother moved to block the foot of the stairs, her arms spread wide. 'Jack! What are you doing up? I told you to go to bed, young man!'

"I was baffled. I couldn't figure out what it was I had done wrong. Normally Mom let me stay up late to welcome Dad back from of his trips. I wasn't the only one confused by my mother's behavior. Dad put down his suitcase, staring at her quizzically.

"'What's up, Gloria? Is something wrong?'

"'You have a visitor, Frank.' She turned her back on him as she spoke, refusing to look him in the face. 'He wants to see you. Now.'

"I looked in the direction my mother was walking and saw a strange man step out of the of the dining room. He was an African-American in his early thirties, dressed in a matching black turtleneck sweater, corduroy slacks with flaring bells, and a floor-length black leather coat. His hair was in a neatly groomed natural and his eyes were sealed behind sunglasses that shone like volcanic glass. His skin was purple-black, with an undertint of rose, like an aubergine. He seemed to radiate a halo of danger that hung about him like smog.

"'Hello, partner,' he said to Dad, smiling with the confidence of a man who has the exploitation of others down to a science.

"My father's face visibly blanched under his George Hamilton tan. 'Blackheart,' he croaked. 'What're you doing here?'

"'You don't seem very pleased to see me, Frank.' Although his voice was, on the surface, silky and soothing, it did not completely obscure the malice that lay underneath.

"My father tried to smile, but ended up looking like a man trying to strangle a scream. 'Of course I'm glad to see you, man—I'm just, uh, a little surprised that's all.'

"'No doubt.'

"He motioned for my father to join him in the living room. 'Come, Frank. We have much to discuss.'

"My father and the man he called Blackheart passed out of my field of vision. My mother picked up Dad's suitcase with one hand and, gripping my shoulder with the other, marched me back upstairs.

"'You get in bed and stay in bed, Jack! I don't want to see you up again tonight, do you understand me?'

"I couldn't figure out why Mom was being so strict. I hadn't done anything to make her that mad at me. It seemed that, for some reason, Mom didn't want me to see or talk to Dad. Normally, I would have done as my mother said and gone straight to sleep. But I was stinging from the injustice of being chastised for no reason and deprived of the present I knew was in my father's suitcase.

"I waited until I heard my mother's footsteps head downstairs, then I got out of bed and, careful not to be seen, tiptoed down the hall to my parents' room.

"The master bedroom was large, with one wall devoted into His and Hers closet spaces. The accordion-fold door on my father's side was partially open, and I could see his suitcase resting inside. Even though I knew if I got caught going through my father's things, I would get the spanking of my life, my desire to discover what my father brought me was so keen I could not resist the temptation.

"I crawled inside the closet full of dry-cleaning and garment bags, doing my best to avoid tripping over the clutter of Italian shoes and hand-crafted cowboy boots that littered the floor. I crouched beside the suitcase and frowned at the elaborate series of snaps and locks that held it shut. This was going to be more difficult than I imagined. As I crouched there, my father's empty suits looming above me like phantom sentinels, my attention was diverted by the sound of someone entering the room. Panicked, I drew farther into the shadows. From my hiding place I could see the door to the master bath was standing ajar, angled in such a way that its full-length mirror reflected the interior.

"My view was momentarily obscured by my father, mother and the man called Blackheart as they passed by my hiding place. My father moved like he was sleepwalking, his face slack and eyes glazed. Blackheart followed immediately after him, his arms folded casually across his chest, the corners of his mouth twisted into the approximation of a smile. My mother hung back, chewing on her thumbnail.

"Without looking either left or right, my father stripped off his clothes. Save for his groin and buttocks, which were frog-belly white, his skin was the color and texture of a well-seasoned catcher's mitt. Apparently oblivious of his audience, he leaned forward and turned on the taps of the bath.

"Blackheart flipped the lid shut on the toilet, making himself comfortable on the shag cozy. He removed his sunglasses and regarded my father's naked body with something too ambiguous and uninvolved to be considered contempt. His voice was deep and resonant, easily heard over the roar of the bath water.

"'I'm not doing this because of the money, Frank. What's a few hundred thousand to someone like me? I've thrown more money away in one day than you've skimmed in two years. No, it's the *principle* of the thing. I can't let others think you've gotten away with screwing me over. It looks bad. And appearance is *everything* in my circle.

"'I'm sorry it had to end this way, Frank. Really I am. But you brought it on yourself. Those who cross me discover I don't do things by halves. He who raises his hand to me, loses his hand by me. He who would steal from me, I take everything from. Is that not so, my sweet?'

"The last part Blackheart addressed to my mother, who was standing in front of the lavatory basin, her eyes as wide and blank as buttons. My father showed no sign of hearing anything Blackheart said as he silently climbed inside the tub. Displaced water sloshed over the rim of the old-fashioned claw-foot and splashed onto the tile floor. My mother jerked her feet away as if the water spreading towards her was a magma flow.

"'I'm actually doing you a favor, Frank. I could have resolved things in a far messier fashion, but I actually like you, in my own way. I'm letting you out easy. Far easier than you deserve. Don't you agree?'

"For the first time my father seemed to respond to the other man's words. He turned his head in Blackheart's direction, revealing a face as rigid and expressionless as a mask, yet something flickered in the depths of his eyes that might have been comprehension.

"The thing that was supposed to be a smile disappeared from Blackheart's face and his eyes took on a red glow, as if reflecting the light from a lonely campfire. 'Hurry up. I don't have all night, Frank,' he growled.

"My father turned slowly back around so that he was once more facing the faucets. He reached into the toiletry caddy anchored to the lip of the tub and with an exaggerated, deliberate movement retrieved the old-fashioned chrome-handled straight razor my mother had given him for Father's Day the year before. His fingers trembled slightly as he locked the blade into position.

"After such leisurely motions, the killing stroke, when it came, was surprisingly quick. My father opened his own throat from ear to ear in a single pass, without a second's hesitation, sending blood arcing nearly two feet before it splashed down into the warm bath water. His death spasm sent the razor flying across the tile floor, spinning in sharp circles until it came to rest against the doorjamb.

"During all this, I remained crouched silently in my hiding place, like a fawn in a thicket, too frightened to speak or move for fear of giving myself away. But the sight of my father's lifeblood jetting from his severed throat and the thump of the razor striking the door caused me to make a tiny little squeak of horror.

"Blackheart turned his head towards the mirror, not looking at me but letting me see him. The corners of his mouth once again lifted in that smile-that-was-not-a-smile, and a crack appeared in the middle of the mirror, as if it had been struck by a phantom hand.

"Whimpering in terror, I tried to burrow into my father's winter clothes for protection, but it was no good. I had been found out. The louvered doors jerked open and a pair of hands as hard and strong as steel bands snatched me from my hiding place.

"'What have we here?' chuckled Blackheart. 'Looks to me like a little boy who doesn't do as he's told.'

"I saw my mother's pallid face peering over Blackheart's shoulder, staring at me with eyes as wide and unblinking as those of a doll's. I called out to her and she looked from me to Blackheart and back again, but did not say or do anything.

"'There's no use in crying for your mother, whelp,' Blackheart snarled. 'Your father is dead and your mother lost to you. Your life is mine now.'

"I kicked at him with my slippers and hammered at him with my little fists, but my efforts were worse than useless, and I knew it. I sobbed in angry frustration, desperate to transcend my helpless, child-flesh with some grand, heroic act. The sight of my impotent struggling seemed to amuse him greatly, and his wry smile widened and became a grin, exposing yellowed, dog-like fangs. I went rigid with terror and screamed as only a child who has seen the face of the bogeyman himself can shriek. My shrill cry seemed to wake my mother from her trance and she snatched me from Blackheart's grasp, trying her best to shield me with her body.

"'Don't hurt him! Please, don't hurt my baby!' She was sobbing so hard her words came out in strangled gasps.

"Blackheart fixed her with a stare as cold as snow. 'Where you are going, no child can follow,' he said flatly. 'Give me the boy.'

"She took a step away from him, her voice acquiring a harder edge. 'I'll go with you of my own free will, but only if you leave my son alone.'

"Blackheart sneer was as sharp as broken glass. 'Girl, you are mine no matter what.'

"'You said yourself that it's better if I *want* to go.'

"Blackheart's features lost their monstrosity, once more resuming the semblance of a human being. 'You are right, my dear. I much prefer that you surrender of your own volition. It makes things so much *easier* for me.'

"'Then give me your word that you won't hurt Jack.'

"'Such concern,' Blackheart said, clucking his tongue in reproach. 'Far more than you ever showed poor Frank.'

"'Frank knew what he was getting into.'

"'Did he?' Blackheart looked at me then my mother. 'Very well, Gloria. You have my word that I will not harm the boy. Now put the brat aside and come to me, woman.'

"I whimpered as my mother lowered me to the floor. I didn't want to let go of her, and she had to pry my fingers loose from her blouse. She wiped the tears from my cheek and smoothed my hair. The last thing I remember her saying to me was 'Hush, sweetie. Don't cry.'"

Estes paused long enough to take a deep breath, struggling to keep control of the terrified five-year-old buried deep within him.

"The next thing I knew, a light was shining in my eyes and there were men and women in white suits peering down at me. Although I didn't know any of them, they all seemed familiar, somehow. Then I became aware that my body was... different. Somehow it had become taller, heavier, bigger... hairier.

"It was several days before Dr. Morrissey broke the news that I had spent the last ten years in a catatonic state. For the better part of a decade my pupils had responded to light, but I did not react to visual stimuli, and nor did I speak. If led by the hand, I walked. When food was placed in my mouth, I ate. When a straw was put to my lips, I drank. But, left to my own devices, all I did was sit and stare, oblivious to my surroundings and conditions, like a doll with a pulse.

"My return to the world of the living was due to an experimental drug therapy championed by Dr. Morrissey, who oversaw my recovery. There was a lot to catch up on. After all, I closed my eyes as a kindergarten student and the next time I opened them I was fifteen years old.

"Dr. Morrissey kept me isolated from the other patients while I underwent a battery of tests to see whether or not I had sustained neurological damage during my 'retreat from reality,' as he called it. To everyone's surprise, I was utterly sound, although, understandably backward in my social and academic skills. After all, I had yet to attend first grade.

"Although I emerged with my motor functions and mental abilities intact, there were still lapses in my memory. I knew my name was Jack Estes, and that my parents' names were Frank and Gloria, but I had no recollection of the events that led to my shut down."

"I know how it feels," Sonja interjected, her voice tinged with sympathetic understanding. "After I was attacked, I was found lying in the gutter. I died for a few minutes on the operating table, but they managed to kick-start my heart again and give me a complete transfusion. I was in a coma for nearly a year. When I woke up, it was as if I was hollow. I walked around looking for things that would fill me up. The whole time I was in constant fear someone would see through my ruse and expose me for the fraud I was."

Estes allowed himself a small, relieved smile. "That's exactly how I felt! *Exactly!* It was really disorienting to suddenly be able to look adults in the eye, instead of having to crane my head up to look at them. And everything was suddenly within arm's reach and scaled for my use. There's so much gradual adjustment that occurs while you grow up, nobody really notices it much. But in my case, it was as if I'd aged ten years overnight.

"I kept asking Dr. Morrissey where my parents were. He was afraid I might withdraw again if I was told the truth, so he told me that my parents were alive but in another country. After two weeks of constant inquiries from me as to when they would come to see me, Dr. Morrissey finally told me that my father was dead and my mother was listed as missing, but presumed dead.

"Upon hearing the news of my parents' deaths, I cried like the little kid I used to be, not the teenaged boy I had become. Then Dr. Morrissey asked me if I remembered what had happened to my mother. The next thing I knew orderlies were pulling me off him. Every stick of furniture in his office except maybe the desk was smashed into kindling. I was sedated and stuffed into a straitjacket.

"After that, I was put back into the wards. It was weird. I didn't like being in gen-pop at all. Most of the patients reeked of spoiled milk, piss and world-class body funk. What made it even weirder was how all the loonies and retards and nurses knew me by name, but I didn't know any of them.

"Using hypnosis therapy, Dr. Morrissey attempted to tap into my buried memories, hoping to discover what was triggering such violent responses in me. While I was strung out on sodium pentothal I related to Dr. Morrissey the exact same story I just told you. But Dr. Morrissey thought Blackheart was a means of projecting negative emotions onto someone besides my father, whom he was convinced had murdered my mother before committing suicide in front of me. It was all a defense mechanism generated by an immature mind unable to deal with the horror it had witnessed.

"As much as I wanted to believe Dr. Morrissey's explanation, deep down I knew that he was wrong and I was right. No matter how often Dr. Morrissey tried to talk me out of my story, I refused to accept his version of events. Finally he was reduced to prescribing electroshock, hoping it would break me of my 'persistent delusions of vampires.'

"I can't really blame him for giving me the juice. After all, Morrissey was a man of science. Vampires were not permitted to exist in his world, at least not the kind I claimed to have seen. After the third round of electroshock treatments, I realized my only hope of escaping the Institute with my mind intact was to go along with the doctors. Once I started to play ball with them, the electroshock was discontinued and I was removed from the wards and given my own room. But the laugh was on them: because I never once stopped believing that Blackheart was real. Not for one moment.

"After so many years spent in limbo, I became obsessed with physical activity. The Institute had a gym for the use of the staff, and I was allowed full use of it. What was at first therapy to strengthen my muscles from years of disuse became a regimen of calisthenics and bodybuilding. One of the orderlies even taught me how to box. But it was not just my body that cried out for exercise. After a decade in eclipse, my mind was hungry for information. Like a man left to wander in the desert, my thirst for knowledge was overwhelming. Once I mastered the alphabet, I was a voracious reader, leapfrogging from *Go Dog Go* to *A Tale of Two Cities* within months.

"On my twenty-first birthday I was released from the sanitarium. The doctors said I was sound of mind and body. I even had a piece of paper to prove it. I was 'cured,' if indeed I had ever been ill. I had a sizeable inheritance at my disposal, thanks to my father's investments and the various offshore bank accounts he had opened in my name.

"Now that I was free to go wherever I wished and to do as I pleased, I decided to find out more about my father's business dealings with Blackheart. I was hoping it might shed some light on where I could find the man who had killed my parents. I was already aware of the fact that Blackheart had loaned my father money to bail out the label. When I went through the records that had been warehoused following the review of the estate, I discovered that my father's company was being used to launder money and distribute narcotics... mostly heroin and cocaine. Somewhere along the line my father began to skim the take.

"I don't know why Dad would do something so incredibly self-destructive. Maybe he wanted to be free of Blackheart's control, or perhaps it was simple greed, fueled by egomania and cocaine. I don't know. Even if Blackheart had been a garden-variety mobster, it still was an incredibly foolish thing for a man with a family to do.

"Still, I do not think my father would have attempted such a thing if he had any idea of Blackheart's true nature. I cannot believe my father, flawed as he might have been, would have knowingly visited such horror upon his loved ones.

"Now that I was free from Dr. Morrissey and the other arbiters of mental health, I set about learning as much as I could about the occult, reading every book on the subject of the undead I could get my hands on.

"I joined various cults and covens, in hope of enlightenment, but they proved to consist largely of bored suburbanites and deluded frauds. I traveled the globe in search of answers, and managed to find a partial manuscript that was once a training manual for the witch finders elite you spoke of, and I was able to translate enough of it to get a grasp of their techniques for identifying and tracking down those suspected of being undead.

"I even taught myself metallurgy, since silver bullets and silver-edged weaponry are not mass-produced. I turned myself into a weapon dedicated to eradicating the loathsome monsters that prey upon the human race. I shall not rest until I have brought down the monster who destroyed my family, this I swore on my father's grave."

Sonja sighed and shook her head. "That was real, um, *dramatic* of you. But at least I know where you're coming from. But what do you want from me?"

"I want you to help me find the vampire who killed my father."

"Uh-uh! No way!" She shook her head vigorously, holding her hands up as if fending off a crushing weight.

"You've been hunting these creatures far longer than I have, and it's clear you know them on a entirely different level than I do. Surely you must know something about him...."

"How can I help you when I've never heard of this 'Blackheart' in the first place? And even if I *did* know anything as to his whereabouts, I *still* wouldn't tell you! Has nothing I've said gotten through to you? You're on a suicide mission, buddy! You're young; you still have years ahead of you. Quit this madness, try to forget the monsters, and find yourself a nice young woman, or man, if that's your fancy, and settle down and live your life. God knows I would do it in an instant if I could, but that option was taken away from me a very long time ago."

Estes' eyes grew as dark as a storm cloud and he spoke with the curt, clipped tones of the indignant. "I thought, being a fellow vampire hunter, you would be willing to extend me professional courtesy. Now I see I was wrong to rely on anyone but myself in this matter. So long, Ms. Blue."

Sonja watched Estes turn sharply on his heel and stride off into the darkness, his duster billowing out behind him like a pair of bat wings. The man was clearly unstable—she could see it in his aura, which pulsed about his head like a magma pool. But there was no denying the attraction he held for her. She wondered if moths felt the same eager anticipation as they danced about the flame.

The lobby of the building is brightly lit, with marble floors and minimalist décor that manages to be upscale and sterile at the same time. It's one in a chain of extended-stay housing complexes that caters to Fortune 500 executives. Before I cross the threshold, I scan the corners for video cameras, spotting a small box just inside the front door aimed at the elevator bank. I step back and close my eyes, sending out a low-level telepathic signal tuned to a precise mental frequency in order to locate an individual, not unlike the echolocation used by bats to navigate their ways through caves. After a long second I receive the answer to my ping. He's on the penthouse floor.

I quickly withdraw the mind probe. Although I'm tempted to peek inside his mind to see what he has in store, I decide against it. While Estes might not be a natural-born sensitive, the drug and electroshock therapy he underwent as a teenager seems to have activated dormant esper talent. That would explain some of his success at spotting and hunting down his prey. Only poets, drunks and madmen can see into the Real World, and Jack Estes is certainly no Shelley.

I circle the building, checking to see if it has an exterior fire escape, but it's too new and too tall. I duck around back, scoping out the service entrance. I'm in luck. The security guard is seated on an upended plastic milk crate, quietly enjoying a blunt as he contemplates the early morning sky. I step out from behind the industrial-strength dumpster and move towards him, hands in my pockets. He lifts his head in surprise, his eyebrows rising quizzically. I reach inside his mind and massage the occipital lobe, effectively rendering myself invisible to his mortal eyes. With another mental shove he doesn't even register me lifting the plastic keycard off the clip on his belt. I stroll past him and into the nerve center of Estes' building. I head straight for the service elevators, which, unlike those open to the public, lack surveillance equipment.

The elevator doors open silently onto the penthouse foyer. Like the ground floor lobby, it manages to be tastefully appointed while betraying absolute no sign of individuality.

The double doors of the penthouse boast an electronic lock, and I slip the magnetic keycard into the slot. The light atop the lock blinks red then turns green, and I push the door open. I stand in the doorway and smile humorlessly before taking a single, deliberate step forward.

I look about the cavernous living room with its luxurious carpets and expensive, modern furnishings. Estes is nowhere to be seen. Everything is angles and highly glossed surfaces; designed to be looked at and never used. It is not a home, but merely a place to stay. I find it far too exposed for my tastes. I prefer keeping a low profile, and I usually doss down in raw industrial spaces, since I have little need for most human comforts.

I pause to inspect a wall-sized bookcase, only to find that the books aren't real—just spines pasted over two-by-fours.

My eye is drawn to the only sign of disarray in the entire room: a jumble of old vinyl forty-fives atop a stainless steel and glass coffee table. I pick up the first record, studying the logo dominating the left side of the label: a line drawing of a heart pierced by a knife, the hilt to the right, and the blade to the left. I paw through the singles until I find another, earlier recording, with the name "Jack Music" printed in Art Nouveau script on the label. I put it aside and return my attention to the pierced heart logo. Something tells me that the symbol must hold some meaning to the vampire Estes called Blackheart. I carefully set aside the forty-five and resume my survey of the room. My gaze stops at the oaken doors at the far end of the room.

Upon entering the darkened room, I am instantly bathed in an artificial dawn. The light reveals a smallish antechamber lined floor-to-ceiling with full-length mirrors. I stand in the middle of the room, surrounded by my twins, shaking my head at his naïveté. Vampires avoid mirrors, not because they cast no reflection, but because they see their true selves. They see what they once were and what they have become.

Once, not too long ago, it used to frighten me to look at myself in the mirror. But I've learned to accept what I see. A multitude of Sonjas reach out in my direction, but all I touch is silvered glass.

I reach out and push one of the mirrors. A latch clicks and the camouflaged door swings inward. The bedroom is as sparsely furnished as the rest of the apartment: a king-sized mattress resting atop a walnut frame, with matching nightstand and dresser. At the foot of the bed is a stack of wooden cubes, piled one atop the other like children's blocks. As I move closer, I can see that the cubes are all painted black and have glass fronts, like shadow boxes. Inside each cube is a human skull with oversized canines. There are at least thirty cubes.

When he strikes, he's as silent as a cobra in the nursery, yet I can hear his rage and fear howling in the back of my head like an angry monkey. His obsession is so intense, so personal it threatens to overwhelm me with its stifling heat. I'm startled by its strength and its familiarity, as if accosted in a dark alley by an old acquaintance. I see the flash of the Bowie knife's silver blade in the corner of my eye. I turn and meet his upward thrust, my crossed hands forming a V to arrest the blow. I grab his wrist with my right hand, easily forcing it backwards. Estes' eyes grow wide, and he valiantly struggles to keep from crying out in pain.

"Let go of the knife." I try to keep my voice as even and unthreatening as the situation allows. "Let go or lose the hand."

His eyes flicker to my face, trying to decide if I mean what I say. The knife drops to the carpeted floor with a dull thump. I let go of his wrist and give the knife a solid kick that sends it flying into a far corner of the room. Estes stands and stares at me, massaging his bruised wrist, his confusion sounding like fuzz-tone feedback in my head.

"So," I say, as I finally turn to face the wall of shadow boxes. "This is your trophy collection, huh?"

Estes gestures at the boxes, his proud smile reflected and replicated in the glass panes. "I took a correspondence course in taxidermy." I nod but say nothing, trying not to betray my thoughts as I review the trophies on display. Most of the denuded skulls are those of adults, although I spot at least a couple juveniles amongst the spoils. But those two specimens are the least of my concerns.

Estes watches me intently, like a journeyman art collector eager to have his collection vetted by an expert. I marvel at what would compel a man to place such grisly trinkets at the foot of his bed, so that they are the last things he saw before going to sleep and the first things that greeted him upon waking.

"I take them with me wherever I go," he says, his eyes glinting like a bared blade. "They serve to remind me that the evil I fight against is mortal, in its way." He taps the glass of one of the boxes. "Recognize this one?"

I glance at the freshly peeled skull, the bone gleaming as white and smooth as a billiard ball. Carefully wrapped about the skull, like a python coiled about an idol, is a bright red braid.

"What do you think?" Estes asks, unable to keep the self-satisfaction from his voice.

"You need more help than you realize."

Estes' face falls like a cake. "What do you mean?"

"I'll admit you're good. Better than any man alive, I dare say. But that isn't enough. You've got to be the *best* if you want to stay alive long enough to nail the bastard who did your old man. The problem is you're *human*, Jack. You can't spot them every time, not the way I can." I tap the sunglasses covering my eyes. "You *think* you know what to look for, but you don't see the big picture. You simply *can't* see it. I don't give a shit whether you believe me or not. After all, you're the one with the agenda. But I can tell you one thing..."

I punch out the glass on the third box from the left and remove the skull sealed inside, my fingers hooked into its eye sockets like a bowling ball. Estes puts ten feet between us, drawing his gun. I ignore the muzzle pointed at my head and hold up the trophy.

"*This* one wasn't a vampire."

"That's bullshit! It's got fangs!" he retorts.

I take one of the over-pronounced canines between my thumb and forefinger and give it a hard twist. It snaps off in my hand, revealing a perfectly normal, human tooth underneath. "They're *falsies*, made from the same dental acrylic used for caps and crowns, the colors mixed to match the shade of the natural teeth, and cemented in place with the bonding agent that keeps movie stars' pearlies so white and even. If you'd just paid attention to the details when you were boiling this 'trophy' of yours, you'd have realized this head belonged to some pathetic wannabe, not a vampire."

The sneer disappears from Estes' face and his hands begin to tremble. "You're lying." His voice sounds like he swallowed a bottlebrush.

"I wish I was," I reply, and, to my surprise, I really mean it. "But I'm giving you the straight shit, man. If you keep on this way, you'll be nothing more than a serial killer. Assuming you aren't one already."

"*Get out,*" he snarls, staring down at his hands as if they were somehow blameless of the crime they have committed.

The moment the door closes behind me there is a shout of raw, animal pain, followed by the sharp crack of breaking glass. The shattering mounts, crash upon crash, until it grows into a final explosion, followed first by silence, then the sound of sobbing.

I pause, deciding whether I should simply go and leave this man to the hell he has built for himself. After a moment's hesitation, I reopen the door.

Estes kneels amongst the ruins of his collection like a penitent, his bleeding hands clenched atop his thighs. My boot heels crunch through the shattered glass as if walking through sharp snow. He looks up at me, his eyes red and raw as wounds.

"*Show me,*" he whispers, his voice reduced to a pained rasp. "Show me how to *see*."

My smile is that of a mentor who knows her pupil is destined for great things—and an early death.

According to the online booking agency, the next flight to New Orleans departed at five-thirty in the morning. Sonja grunted and pulled out a wallet full of credit cards, each with a different name on them. After a moment's consideration she selected one and purchased two first class tickets.

"We better leave for the airport right now," she said, checking her watch. "We're cutting it close if we want to make the flight."

"But I'm not packed."

"You're dressed, aren't you?"

"Yes."

"Then you're packed."

"What about weapons?"

She paused to think for a second, tapping her chin with a fingertip. "You're right. We'll need backup. Better bring a few hundred rounds of ammo and another gun, besides the ones you're toting. Do you have a backpack?"

"How do plan to smuggle a backpack full of guns and ammo past the metal detectors?"

"Relax and leave everything to me."

They caught a cab and headed for the airport, suede backpack bulging with semi-automatic firearms, two hundred rounds of silver-jacketed ammo, a silver-edged machete, and a silver-bladed Bowie knife. Sonja stared out the window, silently watching the strip malls and used-car lots that lined the freeway go by.

As Estes paid off the cabbie, Sonja swung the backpack up onto her shoulders as if it held nothing more than a change of clothes and some cosmetics.

"After we pick up the tickets, we head for the departure gate. When we hit the metal detectors, no matter what happens, act as if nothing is wrong and keep moving."

Since it was early, there was no line for tickets at the air carrier's front desk and they quickly headed in the direction of the departure gates. As they neared the x-ray conveyor and the metal-detector portal, Estes shot an anxious look at Sonja. She merely shrugged and motioned that he go first.

Estes stepped forward, depositing his key ring into the bowl the bored airport security officer held out to him, and moved through the metal detector. There was a beeping sound and the look of boredom on the security officer's face was replaced with one of slight concern.

"Please step to the side, sir," he said, producing a detection wand.

"It's the silver toe-caps on my boots," Estes replied automatically as the security officer waved the detection wand around like a third-rate magician. He wondered how in hell Sonja thought she could get a bag full of weapons past the checkpoint. He glanced over his shoulder in her direction, but she was nowhere to be seen.

"You can go," the security officer said flatly, satisfied Estes was not hiding a gun or knife on his person.

Estes up-ended the bowl, dumping his keys back into his waiting hand. "Thank you," he muttered, still trying to figure out where the hell Sonja could have gone. There was nothing else for him to do but to do as she instructed and act like nothing was wrong and continue on his way.

"See? That wasn't hard, was it?"

Estes gave a startled half-shout, his breath caught in his throat.

"Jesus, Estes!" she snarled. "What did I say about acting natural?"

"What's natural about *that?!?*" he retorted, one hand pressed over his breast. His heart was frantically beating against his ribcage like a trapped bird. One moment she was nowhere to be seen, the next she was walking alongside him. "How the *hell* did you do that?"

"It's called overdrive. It's a means of moving outside the perimeters of human perception. Most Pretenders can do it, if they've got the juice. If a vampire or a demon doesn't want humans to notice them, then they're simply not seen. Just like no one saw me walk around the security check point."

The hair on the back of Estes' neck prickled and his mouth filled with cotton. He glanced about, trying not to look nervous. "Do they give off any sign when they do that?" he whispered.

"Yes," she replied. "But none that *you* can see."

***

After a fifteen-minute delay, they were finally allowed to board the non-stop to New Orleans. They took their places in the First Class cabin, and Sonja secured the window seat. As they left one time zone and entered the next, dawn began to break across the sky. Sonja stared for a long moment out of the jet's windows at the clouds, pink with the blush of the coming day, and then pulled the plastic shade down tight. She removed her battered leather jacket and draped it over her chest as she angled back her seat.

"I'm going to rest until our plane lands. Despite what it may look like, I am *not* dead," she said in an even, conversational tone, in case any of the other travelers might be eavesdropping. "However, I would appreciate it if you could keep the stewardess from noticing I'm not breathing." She stretched back in her seat and, to all outward physical indications, died.

Estes found it rather disconcerting to watch someone go so completely still. Even in deepest REM sleep, people breathed, or muttered and shifted about; but Sonja was as silent and motionless as a department-store mannequin. He realized she had placed the jacket over herself not for warmth, but camouflage, as it hid the fact her ribcage was not moving up and down.

Two hours later, the stewardess came through the cabin to tell the passengers to return their seats to their upright positions for landing. Sonja, who seconds before had been as cold as a stone, jackknifed her seat upright like Max Schreck's Count Orlock rising from his coffin in *Nosferatu.*

Upon touchdown on the tarmac, they waited stolidly as their fellow travelers emptied into the narrow aisle. Sonja walked several steps ahead of Estes as they made their way through the airport; her demeanor was that of woman nursing a world-class hangover. As they passed the luggage carousels, the tourists and business travelers glanced nervously in their direction, like gazelle that find themselves sharing a waterhole with a pride of thirsty lions.

"Where to, Cap?" asked the cabbie. He lifted an eyebrow as he caught a glimpse of Sonja and Estes' clothes in the rearview mirror. "Lemme guess—French Quarter?"

Sonja leaned forward and handed the driver a scrap of paper. He glanced at the address, then back into the rearview mirror, mild surprise and a touch of alarm in his eyes.

"Okay, lady, if that's where you wants to go," he replied, flipping on the meter.

Sonja dropped wearily back against the seat, her shoulders slumping as if she had suddenly grown very old. She grimaced as the sunlight fell across her face, but said nothing.

"Where are we going?" Estes asked, after a few minutes.

"Someplace safe," she replied, her voice drained of energy. "Where I can rest undisturbed."

"I thought you said you could move about during the day."

She gave him a withering look. "Just because I *can* doesn't mean I *enjoy* it. Besides, going into overdrive takes a lot out of me."

Estes turned his face to the world outside the cab window, retreating into a silence as complete as her own. Maybe if he didn't look at her he could forget she wasn't human.

Instead of heading into the city, the driver took an old two-lane highway that winded its way along the levee that shielded the surrounding suburbs from the Mississippi River. Eventually the apartment complexes and condominiums that ringed New Orleans like mushrooms gave way to shotgun shacks and roadside vegetable stands.

The cab turned down a gravel side road and passed through a double column of river oaks that grew so closely together their upper branches formed a canopy, draped by yards of Spanish moss that fluttered in the humid breeze like tattered lace curtains. At the end of the verdant tunnel was an antebellum mansion that must have been a wonder to behold a century or so before. Even in its current state of genteel ruin, with its peeling paint, sagging veranda and dusty windows, it was still an impressive edifice.

As the cab came to a halt at the foot of the drive Sonja reached into her pocket and withdrew a couple of hundred dollar bills. "You did not see us. You did not drive us out here."

"You don't have to tell me twice, lady," the cabbie replied and pocketed the money.

Sonja got out of the cab and trudged up the wide porch steps that led to the front door.

The cabbie cast an uneasy glance in the direction of the rotting mansion. "You folks gonna be alright out here?"

"We'll be okay," Estes replied.

The cabbie shot Estes a look that told him he didn't believe a word of it. "Good," he grunted. "Cause I ain't comin' back out here. Ain't *nobody* gone come out here, 'specially after dark." With that he threw his vehicle into gear, kicking up a spray of gravel in his wake.

As Estes neared the house, he heard a musical sound, like wind chimes. A collection of glass bottles, ranging from humble soda pop containers to old Milk of Magnesia bottles, blue as the sky over Eden, dangled from a nearby tree on lengths of string. With every breeze, they jingled like the pendants on a crystal chandelier.

Estes turned and followed Sonja up the steps. She was leaning forward, peering through the rusty screen door into the dim interior of the house. In the shade of the porch she appeared to regain some of her previous vigor.

"I knocked, but no one answered," she said. "They're probably around back."

"Who's probably around back, if you don't mind me asking?"

"Papa Beloved and his grand-daughter, VéVé. This is their house." Sonja walked along the veranda, motioning for him to follow. Their boot heels made a hollow sound on the worn boards.

The backyard of the house was in far greater disrepair than the façade; with weeds growing around a cluster of defunct automobiles situated a stone's throw from the steps. An old-fashioned laundry wringer squatted nearby, surrounded by a Jacob's ladder of wet clothes.

An young African-American woman dressed in a simple white cotton shift, her head hidden by a plain white kerchief, was bent over an aluminum wash tub atop a wooden bench, scrubbing a pair of overalls with a boar bristle brush, singing under her breath. She was an attractive figure of a woman, despite the dark splotches that covered her *café au lait* skin.

"Hello, VéVé," Sonja said quietly.

The young woman stopped what she was doing and squinted up at them. She drew her hands from the soapy water, her squint intensifying into a frown.

"Sonja?"

"Hey, VéVé," Sonja said, obvious affection in her voice.

"Lord, girl!" the other woman said, hastily wiping her hands dry on the hem of her apron. "We better be getting you inside!" VéVé hurried forward and grabbed Sonja's elbow, steering her through the back door into the house. Estes followed them into a large, airy kitchen with a wood-burning stove squatting in the corner like a household god.

Sonja paused to glance about the room, a quizzical look on her face. "Where's Papa Beloved?"

"Gran'daddy passed on," VéVé replied simply. "It's just me now." She pushed open a swinging door that lead to what had once, long ago, been a fancy dining room. The tables and chairs were no longer in residence, but a crystal chandelier, its pendants swathed in cobwebs, still hung from a hook in the ceiling.

Unlike the kitchen, the rest of the house's interior was gloomy, the shades drawn against the light. The furnishings were spare and the carpets threadbare, but the place was otherwise tidy, save for the ever-present dust that large old houses generate. VéVé steered Sonja through the front parlor and headed up the wide wooden staircase that led to the second story.

The second floor was easily just as gloomy and twice as warm as the first. Sweat instantly leapt from Estes' forehead and armpits as he struggled to breathe the humid air.

"Here. You can stay in my room," VéVé said, pushing open the door nearest the stairs.

VéVé's bedroom was filled with antiques that had never been retired from active service. A walnut chiffarobe large enough to house a family of three stood against one wall, the growling griffins carved into its top board frozen in eternal sentinel, and a colorful hand-made quilt was folded across the footboard of the whitewashed iron bedstead. Without a further word, Sonja collapsed across the bed. The springs squealed in rusty protest as her weight struck the sagging mattress.

"She'll be okay here," VéVé said quietly.

Estes studied the warped and mildew-stained chintz paper clinging to the walls. "Won't she be too hot up here?"

VéVé shook her head. "She don't feel the heat no more than she feels the cold." She turned to look at Estes for the first time. "You must be new to her if you don't know that."

"We met a couple of days ago," he replied. "My name is Jack. Jack Estes."

"You must be thirsty, Mr. Estes. Go sit on the porch. I'll bring you some lemonade."

***

Estes sat on the glider on the front porch, listening to the chains squeal in polite protest as he rocked gently back and forth, and stared at the magnificent oaks that lined the drive. It was not hard to imagine the mansion's original owner seated on the exact same porch, sipping mint juleps and fanning himself with the brim of his planter's hat as he looked out upon his domain.

"Wonderful view, ain't it?" VéVé set a serving tray with a sweating pitcher of lemonade and a pair of glasses onto a nearby table. Now that he was able to get a good look at her, Estes realized what he had first mistaken for splotches on her skin were actually markings of some sort. There were dozens of them, scattered about her body like freckles.

"Are those tattoos?" he asked, pointing to the filigreed anchor on the top of her right hand as she took a seat beside him.

"No, Mr. Estes," she said with a gentle smile that told him she was used to being asked such questions. "They ain't tattoos, they's birthmarks."

He lifted and eyebrow and tried not to choke on his drink. "Is that a fact?"

As she flashed him a dazzling white smile, Estes realized for the first time how young his hostess truly was. "Sonja didn't tell you much about us, did she?"

"No, she didn't. To tell the truth, I didn't even know we were coming to New Orleans until a few hours ago. How is it you know each other?"

"How is it she knows you?" VéVé said, no hint of hostility in her voice. "My guess is she just kind of crossed over into your life, unintentional like. That's just her way, though. Her life bumped into mine a long time ago. She knew Papa Beloved even longer. He wasn't my actual gran'daddy, you know. Not by blood. I don't know who my real folks was. He treated me as his own, though, and that's what counts. He was a powerful *houngan*."

Estes' eyes lit up as he finally realized where he had seen the marks covering her body before. They were the ritual symbols associated with Haitian voudou.

"Your grandfather was a priest?"

"Yes. As I am a priestess. He was respected for his wisdom and th' strength of his mojo. Some said he got his power because his mama conceived him while she was possessed by one of the loa."

"So how did he come to know Sonja?"

"She deals in occult artifacts. Papa Beloved was one of her customers. That's how they first come to know each other. Then, after she gave me to him, they got to be fairly close friends."

"She *gave* you to your grandfather?"

"It ain't what it sounds like. Only reason I'm alive an' kickin' is on account of her. Twenty years ago, while in Haiti, Sonja stumbled across a ritual in a graveyard. The worshippers were 'bout to up an' sacrifice a little-bitty baby to the cannibal spirits. *I* was that baby. Sonja saved me from the knife and, recognizin' me as marked by the loa, turned me over to Papa Beloved, who raised me as his own. That's why she'll always have a safe harbor here at Mojo House."

"You know what she is, then."

VéVé nodded. "Prob'ly better than you do."

"I must confess I find her baffling. Can I trust her?"

VéVé took a deep breath and sighed. "Trust is a very personal thing. Whether you decide to give it is totally up to you. But in order to understand Sonja, you got to realize she got two hearts. I ain't talkin' real ones, mind you. I mean spiritual-wise.

"One heart is good, the other is dark, and they fight one another for control every moment she's awake. Most of the time, the good heart wins out, but not *every* time. When the dark heart wins out, she does *horrible* things. That's why she fights so hard to control it. She's afraid the dark heart is poisoning the good heart, slowly corrupting it from the inside out.

"She came here instead of going into town because the last time she was in New Orleans, the dark heart won out and she did some terrible things. Folks was killed. The police might still be lookin' for her." VéVé fell silent for a long moment, staring out at the verdant green of the lawn, and then loudly clapped her hands. "I reckon you must be as tired as Sonja, Mr. Estes. We ain't got no air conditionin', I'm afraid, and I doubt you could get any sleep inside, what with the heat. So I'll fix you up a hammock on the shady side of the house. It ain't much, but at least you'll be comfortable."

"That would be most kind of you, Miss, um, Miss—?"

"Just VéVé. You wait here. I won't be a minute," she said.

Estes resumed rocking gently back and forth in the glider, sipping lemonade and listening to the chiming of the bottle tree. When the screen door slammed shut he glanced up, expecting to see VéVé. Instead, a tall, muscular African-American man, naked save for a pair of tattered white canvas pants, was slowly making his way across the lawn towards a pair of shade trees, a web hammock draped across one arm.

VéVé stepped out into the porch and stood watching from a distance, her arms folded in the manner of an overseer. Curious, Estes moved to join her.

"I thought you said you lived here alone?"

"I *do* live alone. Levon ain't alive at all. Are you, Levon?"

Levon slowly turned in the direction of her voice. His dark skin had an oddly ashen tinge and his eyes were milky and gray, like those of a baked fish. It was impossible to know whether he was capable of answering the question posed to him, since his lips were sewn shut with coarse black thread.

"When Papa Beloved passed on, he left me everything that was his—which included Levon," VéVé explained. "I don't normally hold with *zuvembies*, but I must admit that sometimes they *do* come in handy."

***

Estes must have been far more tired than he realized, because he managed to fall asleep in a hammock, surrounded by voodoo practitioners and zombies, almost instantly. When the pressure on his bladder finally awakened him, he was surprised to find the sun hanging low in the sky. After relieving himself on a nearby tree, he headed back inside the house.

VéVé was in the kitchen, chopping okra, the aroma of simmering greens and fatback heavy in the air. She glanced up long enough to nod hello then resumed her task. "Sonja should be up an' about within the hour. Soon as y'all are ready, I'll have Levon drive you into the city."

"Are you sure that's such a good idea?"

"Don't see why not. Car's registered, the insurance is paid up and Levon got his-self a driver's license. He's doing better than most folks 'round here."

"I am sorry to hear of Papa Beloved's passing."

Sonja was standing in the kitchen doorway. Neither VéVé nor Estes had heard her approach, although the floorboards of the old house groaned with the slightest step.

"He had the cancer in his belly," VéVé sighed, wiping her hands on the apron tied about her waist. "By the end, death was a mercy." She dumped the chopped okra into a large white enamel bowl and placed it inside the 1950s-era Frigidaire. "So—what's your business in N' Orleans?"

"I came to see Malfeis."

VéVé grimaced as if she'd bitten into a sour persimmon. "That devil? Better be careful, girl."

"Don't worry, " Sonja said, hooking a thumb in the direction of Estes. "I've got someone to watch my back."

"Him? He ain't got the sight."

"That may be true, but he's a quick study," Sonja said, a muscle in her lower jaw pulsing as she spoke. "He knows what's out there, even if he can't see it all the time."

"Seems to me that's what they say about crazy folks, too," VéVé replied. "No offense, Mr. Estes."

"None taken."

VéVé shook her head in resignation. "I know better than to tell you not to do something; it only makes you more determined to do it. So's I best send y'all on your way." She opened the cellar door and shouted down into the blackness. "Levon! Go fetch the car! You drivin' Miz Sonja and Mr. Estes into the city!"

There was a sound like a bag of cement being dragged across a dirt floor and a few seconds later Levon emerged from the lightless depths underneath the house. Estes' skin crawled as the zombie's lifeless eyes fell upon him. If Levon noticed his ill ease, it did not register on his face. They followed at a distance as the zombie shambled out the back door towards the garage.

VéVé stood in the gathering dark, staring up at the mojo tree as the bottles swayed slowly in the humid breeze from the river, then plucked free a small blue perfume bottle, its stopper still tightly wedged in its narrow neck. She turned and handed the tiny vial to Sonja.

"If y'all are going to see Malfeis, you best take this along. Just in case, mind you."

Sonja nodded and palmed the bottle, placing it in one of the pockets of her leather jacket.

There was the sound of gravel crunching under tires and a vintage 1950s Cadillac convertible rolled towards them out of the evening gloom, its headlights off, Levon seated behind the wheel.

"Levon!" VéVé snapped, her tone that of a drill sergeant. "Turn on them lights! How many times do I have t'warn you about that?"

The Caddy's headlights blinked on, bathing the trio in artificial light. Sonja automatically lifted an arm to shield her shaded eyes from the glare, a feline snarl rumbling in her chest.

"Levon will drive y'all as far as y'all want. Just make sure you tell him to drive back to Mojo House when you're done or I'll have to come lookin' for him."

"Thanks, VéVé," Sonja said as she opened the rear passenger door of the Caddy. "You've grown into a fine *mambo*. Papa Beloved would be proud."

VéVé threw her arms around Sonja, hugging her tight. Estes quickly looked away, only to gaze directly into Levon's cold, gray stare.

"C'mon, Estes," Sonja said as she slid into the back of the car. "The way you're gawking at Levon you'd think you'd never seen a walking corpse before."

Estes climbed in beside Sonja as the Caddy began to roll forward.

"To the French Quarter, Levon," Sonja announced loudly and distinctly, as if speaking to someone hard of hearing. "You got that?"

The zombie slowly inclined its head, indicating it understood the command.

"Watch out, N'Orleans!" Sonja crowed. "Dead man drivin'!" She turned to Estes and grinned, briefly flashing fangs as white and sharp as a panther's.

The sight of her fangs triggered a surge of revulsion that filled Estes' stomach with bile. As the car headed up the drive, he looked back over his shoulder and saw VéVé standing in front of Mojo House, her white cotton dress ghostly in the gathering dark.

Every time I come back to New Orleans I marvel over how everything is different, yet nothing has changed. This mercurial constancy makes the Big Easy a genuinely schizophrenic city, which may explain why so many Pretenders seem to gravitate here.

Over the years the French Quarter has gone from inner-city neighborhood to grungy tenderloin to high-dollar tourist Mecca, all the while remaining the hub of the city. Over the years the seedy strip clubs and live sex shows that once catered to the dock workers have slowly been replaced by upscale eateries, souvenir shops and antique stores aimed at the tourists that flock to the Quarter's narrow cobbled streets in search of a good time.

However, despite the Chamber of Commerce's best efforts, a few of the old dives still survive on the streets farthest removed from the hurly-burly of Jackson Square. Our destination tonight is one of these remaining dens of iniquity.

Levon drops us off at the foot of Canal, near the glittering pavilions of the riverboat casinos permanently anchored at the old docks. I stand on the curb and watch the *zuvembie*, fifty years dead, start to pilot his way back to Mojo House. Within seconds the taillights of the Caddy are swallowed by the evening traffic.

"So—who's this Malfeis VéVé has such a low opinion of?" Estes asks, glancing uncomfortably at the inebriated crowds thronging the streets.

"He's an information broker."

"You mean he's a snitch."

"If you want to keep wearing your tongue on the inside of your head, you won't call him that within earshot. Mal's been around a *long* time, and he knows a *lot* of people, living and otherwise. If anyone can recognize your bogeyman, with as little as we have to go on, it's him."

I focus my attention on the steady stream of faces wandering the haunts of the Vieux Carré. The majority are wide-eyed tourists, come to gape at the famed wrought-iron balconies and ancient burlesque queens of Bourbon Street, mixed with the dips, hustlers, pushers and con men drawn by the wealth and carelessness of the out-of-towners. However, they are not the only predators trawling the streets of the City That Care Forgot.

I spot an incubus lounging in the doorway of a bar catering to gay men. New Orleans has always been a magnet for carnal demons of all sexes and preferences. This one fixes me with a murder-green eye and rumbles a *basso profundo* growl that only Pretenders and bull gators can hear. His prehensile penis stirs in the pouch of his leather pants, rising to the perceived challenge like a fakir's cobra. I carefully maneuver Estes and myself out of striking distance; those bastards can squirt venom up to twenty feet.

A *vargr* leaning on a wrought-iron balcony railing watches our passing with open hostility. My gaze locks with the werewolf's, causing the hair on his scalp to rise as he bares rottweiler-sized fangs in my direction. The rank odor of dog piss fills the air.

Estes walks alongside me, mercifully oblivious to the horrors surrounding us. I feel a sharp pang of envy. There's no price I wouldn't gladly pay to be so blissfully ignorant of the hell that I live in.

As we near our destination, I begin to feel anxious. Walking into The Monastery is always dangerous, but this time I'm dragging a human along for the ride. As we turn the last corner before reaching the bar, my train of thought is not only derailed, but sent flying off the trestle into a hundred feet of icy water.

***

"Sonja—Sonja, are you listening to me?"

He felt like an idiot for having asked, because it was obvious she was off in that world of hers again, staring intently at something only she could see. The way she broke off in the middle of a sentence to stare at passersby, or even nothing at all, reminded him a little bit too much of some of the inmates back at the Institute.

He followed her stare and was surprised to discover that what had snared her attention this time was visible to the human eye, although most of those wandering the French Quarter in search of good times were doing their best to pretend it wasn't there.

The homeless man lay on his side in a nest of old newspapers, his back against a crumbling brick wall. He was dressed in mismatched running shoes with no laces, grimy brown twill pants, and a large overcoat that was far too warm for the sub-tropic climes of southern Louisiana. His features were obscured by a mass of dark, greasy ropes that might charitably be referred to as hair, and an equally matted beard, making it impossible to guess his age. The street person had strategically placed himself so that passers-by had to take a step around him in order to keep from treading on his outstretched arm. His callused hand held a paper coffee cup, which every so often he would twitch, causing the collection of loose change inside to rattle.

Sensing he was being watched, the homeless man reared up from his bed of old news, scanning the surrounding area like a radar dish. His gaze met Sonja's and something passed back and forth between the two, although neither spoke. After a long moment Sonja visibly shivered and, freed from her temporary catatonia, resumed her hurried stride. It was all Estes could do to keep up with her.

"Do you know him?"

"What?" she replied, sounding distracted.

"That bum. Do you know him?"

"It's not a bum. And, yes, I know it."

Estes wanted to ask more questions, but before he could, Sonja ducked through the door of a nearby bar. Estes glanced up at the sign hanging over the threshold, which read, in faux-Old English script, *The Monastery*.

The only light inside the bar came from the votive candles placed at the converted pews that served as booths. Decaying plaster saints peeked out from various nooks and crannies like spying gnomes. Behind the bar was an antique walnut hutch, atop which was perched a disfigured Madonna and Child with painted-on eyes. The ancient jukebox next to the confessional-cum-phone booth played Led Zeppelin's *Kashmir* through fuzzy speakers. The hulking bartender turned slightly to follow their passage, his eyes gleaming with predacious curiosity.

Although the bar appeared empty, Estes could not shake the feeling that the heavy shadows that filled its corners were endowed with reptilian life. And that it was watching them.

***

Malfeis occupies his usual spot in the back booth, dressed in the skin of a middle-management type from Iowa who once yearned for a promotion and a newer, prettier wife. He grins as I approach, throwing gang sign in welcome.

"Sonja! Long time no see, girlchick. "

"Hello, Mal. I never figured you for the Casper Q. Milquetoast type."

Malfeis studies the sleeves of the nondescript gray suit over the top of his wire-rim spectacles. He wrinkles his nose, causing the glasses to rise slightly. "This one *is* a tad underwhelming, isn't he? I should change into something a bit more dynamic, given the occasion."

His eyes roll back like a toad swallowing a bug, revealing green-tinged whites. His skin ripples like a horse ridding itself of flies, and a tall, dark-haired man in his thirties, dressed in a double-breasted suit fifty-five years out of date, replaces the mousy middle-management office drone.

With its thick eyebrows and strong chin, Malfeis' new face could easily be that of a matinee idol, if not for the cruel set of the mouth and the coldness in the eyes.

"Mengele was one of *yours*?" I can't help the hint of admiration in my voice.

"Why so surprised, *liebchen*?" Mal smirked. "You didn't think that the good doctor escaped Nuremberg and evaded Mossad for all those years thanks to sheer luck and strudel, did you?" He gestures to the empty pew opposite him with a surgeon's nimble hands. "Please, be seated, my dear."

I slide in opposite the demon, doing my best not to actually come in contact with him under the tabletop.

"I see you have company," he smiles, nodding at Estes. "Breaking in a new renfield, are you?"

"Tone down the smarm. He's *not* a renfield," I reply tartly.

"That's what you *always* say," Malfeis chuckles knowingly. "Far be it from me to argue. Now, what is it you need, girlchick?"

"I'm trying to track down a vampire."

"Aren't you always?"

"Are you interested in doing business or not?"

"My, aren't we touchy...." Malfeis chuckles, shedding the war criminal's skin in favor of that of a woman in a fringed flapper sheath and bobbed hair who wanted to marry a millionaire. "Would you feel more comfortable speaking woman-to-woman?"

"Cut the crap, Mal! Can you help me or not?"

"Depends," she grunts, sticking an ivory cigarette holder between painted lips. "I'll need some specifics."

"African-American. Male. Probably a Noble. He was active in the early 1970s under the name Blackheart, but I doubt it's his permanent tag. Trafficked in hard drugs and was involved in the music industry. Ring any bells?"

Malfeis morphs into an elderly man in Bermuda shorts and a Madras shirt who dreamed of retiring to Florida in style. He frowns for a couple of minutes, tapping an aimless tune on his dentures. "Sounds familiar."

"He may use a sign: a heart with a dagger through it."

Mal's brushy gray eyebrows arch and the rheumy blue eyes twinkle in recognition. "Ah! *Him!* You were correct in guessing he's a Noble. And while he's black, he's more African than American. Rumor has it he's *strega*."

I can't keep from groaning. "Are you sure?"

"More than most rumors I spread."

"What else do you have on him?"

"You know the rules. That's all you get for free, girly-girl," the demon grins, popping his dentures like castanets. "What have you got for me in exchange?"

He's got me. I entered his turf and asked him a question. That means I have to provide him with something of commensurate worth—at least as demons judge such things. And in Mal's case, he has a jones for artifacts impregnated with human evil.

"Estes!"

Estes steps forward a little too quickly for Malfeis' liking. The demon's face spins like a roulette wheel before settling on the visage of a Russian gangster. Estes gasps in astonishment, as Mal hasn't bothered to veil the transformation from mortal eyes.

I hold out my hand, trying to ignore the thunderstruck look on my companion's face. "Give me the witch-breaker."

Estes sounds like a man who has woken from a doze only to find himself strolling down the middle of a busy highway. "The what?"

"The crucifix," I explain.

Estes reaches inside his duster and retrieves the inquisitorial torture device. Mal's eyes light up and I can see the bastard's trying his best not to drool. "My-my! That's a fine piece you're packing, pilgrim."

The demon reaches for the witch-breaker, but I jerk it away. "Now—about that information...."

Malfeis takes a deep breath and drums his fingers against the tabletop. His eyes don't leave the witch-breaker. After a long moment he sighs and nods his head.

"Very well. The one you are looking for is Lord Noir. Although he's Old World, he's been operating out of North America for the last century. He's generated several aliases and he currently owns several 'gentlemen's clubs' across the country. He's headquartered in Atlanta."

"Thanks, Mal."

"As they say: Anything for a friend."

The demon grins, his features redefining themselves into those of young man with shoulder-length blond hair pulled into a ponytail and three rings in his right ear and one in his left nostril. It is a face I know all too well from my dreams. And my nightmares.

I bring the witch-breaker down on the demon's right arm, snapping it like a piece of balsa wood. Malfeis' stolen face opens its mouth in a wail of inhuman pain. Before he or his flunky behind the bar has a chance to react, I grab the demon by the throat, digging my fingers deep into borrowed flesh.

"Let him go!"

"Now, now, Sonja—mustn't play rough!" Malfeis sputters as he tries, unsuccessfully, to pry my hand away.

"I said let him go, you bastard!" I bellow, shaking him for emphasis.

"He's mine by right!" Malfeis squeaks out through purpling lips. "He came to me for a favor and asked its price. The bargain was made!"

"He *didn't* know the rules!"

"Ignorance of the Infernal Laws is no excuse—"

I tighten my grip on Malfeis' larynx. I'm in no mood for his glib banter right now. The demon's face sheds its semblance of humanity, dissolving into a cross between the features of a mandrill baboon and a wild boar. A clawed hand swipes at my face, sending my sunglasses flying. I reflexively lift my arm to shield my eyes, letting go of Malfeis' throat. The demon loses no time putting distance between us.

"*Have you lost your mind?*" he growls, human speech somehow finding its way out of his tusked snout. "Coming in here, on *my* turf, and physically attacking me?"

"I've put up with double-crosses, even triple-crosses from you, Mal. But this will *not* stand!" I bare my fangs in ritual challenge. " Judd's not like the others in your collection! You and I both know he had no idea what he was getting himself into when he asked for your help. Either give him up or die by my hand. Which will it be?"

"You *are* mad!" Malfeis turns and motions to the devil behind the bar. "Willie! Take 'em out!"

Suddenly Estes' back is pressed flat against my own, his guns drawn and pointed at the bartender, who is reaching for something under the register.

"Keep your hands where I can see them!"

The bartender glances in Estes' direction with his third eye, trying to decide whether or not he's a threat, and then slowly returns its claws to the top of the bar.

"You're in the wrong, Sonja," Malfeis growls, his features melting into those of a middle-aged African-American man with thick black dreadlocks hanging about his head like furry snakes. "To know a thing's name gives one power over that thing. That is the Law. He gave me his name of his own free will. He is mine, to use as I see fit."

"Fuckin' protean! Goddamned face-dancer!"

"Now-now! There's no need for racial slurs!" Mal replies, sounding genuinely offended.

I pull my switchblade. Its silver edge gleams like a wet tooth in the dim light of The Monastery.

"Here, now, girlchick—let's not do something we'll both regret!" Malfeis says, an alarmed look in his eyes. "Put away the knife...."

"Give him up."

Malfeis growls in angry defiance. A fang the size of a man's little finger pushes past his lips. "Kiss my rosy red baboon butt!"

I lunge at the demon, hissing a ritual challenge as I unsheathe my fangs. The knife blade cuts a silver arc through the air, centimeters from Malfeis' face. The demon leaps aside like a housecat dodging a strike from a snake.

Before I can move closer again, a creature resembling an anthropomorphic octopus detaches itself from the shadows lining the wall and grabs me from behind. Its bulbous, sac-like head hangs low between its shoulders like a partially deflated balloon and its eyes are the size and shape of clenched fists, reflecting the cold, submarine stare of a shark. It has several tentacles, each tipped with a razor-sharp spur, the undersides of which are lined with grasping suction-pads that cling to my flesh like lampreys.

The octopoid wraps a living noose around my throat, yanking me off the ground. I struggle to free myself, but my feet only make contact with empty air. Estes swings one of his guns away from the bartender towards my attacker, but the creature is far smarter than it looks; it dangles me in front of itself as a living shield while lashing out with its other tentacles.

Estes blinks in pain and a long, bright red line appears across his cheek. After a long moment, the line begins to weep blood. If Estes stays within reach, the octopoid's spurs will slice him to confetti. He has no choice but to make for the door and hope he gets a clear shot before the monster snaps my head off like a Barbie doll's.

Estes edges his way up the bar towards the doorway of The Monastery. Malfeis and his attendant demons follow him, the octopoid holding me aloft like a grotesque lantern. I kick at the air, clawing desperately at the tentacle wrapped about my neck like a thuggee's garrote. My face is dark with congested blood, my eyes starting from their sockets. Something like blood is seeping from my nostrils and ears, and foam flecks the corners of my mouth. It's not a pretty picture, and believe me, it feels a hell of a lot worse than it looks.

"Let her go!"

The demons exchange grins as they close in for the kill, amused by Estes' show of bravado.

"*Again* with the demands!" snorts Malfeis, who is wearing the exterior of a flabby white male dressed in a loud plaid polyester leisure suit with white buck loafers. "Give me that! *Do* this! *Don't* do that!" His smile grows larger, sharper, and meaner as his mouth stretches from ear to ear. "*Who* do you people think you are?"

Estes makes a desperate lunge towards the door, but his way is blocked by a hulking, foul-smelling figure standing just inside the wide flaps of scuffed, translucent plastic that keeps the bar's air conditioning from pouring out into the street. Estes instinctively recoils as the thing steps towards him, uncertain of which threat he should open fire on first.

The shark grin on Malfeis' borrowed face abruptly disappears and the bartender's third eye starts from its socket. The octopoid makes a sound like a backed up toilet disgorging a week's worth of sewage, then drops me on the floor.

Mal holds his hands up, grinning nervously. "Hey, man—we're cool! We don't want any trouble here, okay?"

Estes lowers his gun and stares at the bedraggled street person standing in The Monastery's doorway, baffled by the demons' reaction to a bum with newspapers stuffed in his shoes. Of course, being human, he cannot see things for what they truly are.

The seraph stares for a long moment at my bruised throat and the blood leaking from my nose and ears, then looks at the three demons. A spark ignites in the back of its eyes, filling them with a golden glow, as if someone carrying a torch was climbing up the stairs from a dark cellar. With great deliberation, it takes a single step towards the demons.

The seraph opens its mouth and a trilling noise, like that of a thousand crystal wind chimes, issues forth. It's both beautiful and ominous, like the chanting of Kyoto monks. The octopoid makes a sound like broken plumbing and, tentacles waving in panic, disappears in a cloud of shadow.

"No! Fido—stop!" I croak, lurching to my feet. Bloody spittle flies from my lips as I force the words from my bruised larynx.

The seraph halts and turns to regard me. I feel its thoughts pass through my mind, like minnows darting through swiftly moving water.

"Please, Sonja—make it go away!" Malfeis begs, on the verge of tears.

"Why should I?" My voice sounds like someone had used a floor stripper on my throat. "I ought to let it sing you and your toadies straight back to Hell."

"*No!*" Malfeis wails in panic, wringing his talons. "Not that! I'll do *anything* you want—just make it leave!"

"Give it up, then."

"Deal." The demon looks around, a sour look on his face. "I'll need something to put it in."

"Here—I think I have something that'll do the trick." I reach inside my jacket and pull out the little blue bottle VéVé gave me before we left Mojo House.

"It'll do," Malfeis says with a resigned growl. He unplugs the neck of the perfume bottle, raises it to his lips, and spits out the name. He then quickly stoppers the bottle and hands it to me. "There you go," he sneers. "Are you *happy* now?"

"I'm fuckin' ecstatic." I hold the bottle between thumb and forefinger so I can squint at the tiny glimmer of light within.

"We square now?"

"Yeah," I answer grudgingly, returning the bottle to my breast pocket. "I guess so."

"*Then get that fucking thing out of my bar!*" Malfeis shrieks, stabbing a clawed finger at the seraph.

"C'mon, Fido—let's clear out of this shit hole."

Fido glances at me, then back at Malfeis.

"Yeah, I know," I sigh. "But a deal's a deal."

The seraph obediently steps back and falls in behind us. The golden glow in its eyes gutters out as it returns to being a rank-and-file vagrant who wanders the streets in search of spare change and Thunderbird. I reach into my jeans pocket and hand the seraph a crumpled dollar bill. It quickly stuffs the money into its overcoat; nodding its head to a rhythm only it can hear, then simply turns and walks away.

"Who was that?" Estes whispered, eyeing the seraph's retreating back.

"Something I used to know."

"A friend?"

"No. But not exactly an enemy, either. It's too complicated to go into right now."

"That's alright. I don't think I could handle any more information to-night...."

Estes trails off, staring at a clutch of approaching tourists as if by sheer willpower he can somehow see beyond their cargo pants and divine whether they harbor monsters within. I can't decide whether the look in his eyes is suspicion or madness. Perhaps there's no difference.

Part Three

Rage in the cage

And piss upon the stage

There's only one sure way

To bring the giant down

Defunct the strings

Of cemetery things

With one flat foot

On the devil's wings

Living Dead Girl, Rob Zombie

With its Kennedy-era strip malls, yuppie boutiques, and gentlemen's clubs, Atlanta's Cheshire Bridge Road presented an overall picture of prosperous, well-scrubbed depravity. The numerous strip joints,, triple-X boutiques and jack shacks that lined the busy street were nondescript ranch-style buildings lacking visible windows and with little to distinguish one establishment from another, save for their signage. In the case of Dolly Dagger's, the roof boasted a blood-red heart pierced by a glowing pink dagger.

"Are you sure this is the place?" Estes asked, squinting through the windshield at the stuttering neon.

"What did you expect? A gothic castle with a drawbridge and a giant spider's web spun across the entrance?"

Estes flinched. Although he tried hard to avoid looking foolish in Sonja's eyes, it seemed he managed to say something stupid every time he opened his mouth.

"Have you ever dealt with a brood before?"

Estes shifted uneasily. He could tell from her tone of voice that she was about to unveil another hither-to unseen portion of the world he thought he knew.

"What's a brood?" He didn't want to ask the question, but at the same time he knew he needed to know the answer. As much as these glimpses of what Sonja called the "Real World" intrigued him, they also made him extremely anxious. He had thought his view of the universe was jaundiced, but listening to Sonja made him feel like a sleepwalker wandering a minefield. "They're a collection of undead Made by the same vampire. His posse, if you will. That's not counting whatever other hired muscle he might have working for him."

"Why would vampires need paid assassins?"

"I'm not talking thugs. Usually vampires as old and as powerful as this Noir have a couple of non-humans on the payroll, to provide back up in case of daylight attack. Mostly they use ogres."

Estes thought of the monstrosities he had glimpsed in New Orleans and did his best to suppress a shudder. "What about werewolves?"

"What about them?"

"Don't they work for vampires as servants?"

Sonja made a snorting noise. "Vampires and werewolves get along about as well as lions and hyenas. *Vargr* and *enkidu* are both very efficient predators of humans, which makes them rivals, not comrades in arms. But since our man's *strega*, there's no telling who or what he might have in his employ."

Estes frowned. "I thought you said he was a vampire."

"He is. But *strega* are a certain kind of vampire. I guess you could call them a subspecies. You see, most undead are created when a vampire drains a human enough to kill them. Vampires themselves call the process Making or being Made. But that's not the *only* way to become undead—it's merely the most common.

"*Strega* are those who've chosen to become vampires via damnation. They embrace the ways of the vampire while still alive, voluntarily surrendering their humanity by consuming human flesh and blood while observing necromantic rituals involving the defilement and mutilation of innocents. Provided they haven't been decapitated or cremated before hand, *strega* rise three days after their mortal deaths.

"Gilles de Rais, also known as Bluebeard, was one such *strega*. So was the Countess Bathory. Dahmer would have become one, if the pathologists hadn't sliced his brain up like a deli platter. *Strega* are very powerful, because they're Made in no image but their own and so have no master they have to obey. Many of them also have unique abilities—ones your standard undead don't—such as a limited tolerance to sunlight and silver. It's even rumored the more powerful of them can use magic to cause their enemies to literally sweat blood.

"In any case, the differences between the damned and the undead are enough to keep them from trusting one another, which is saying something, given how the Ruling Class is constantly warring among itself. As for me, the couple of *strega* I've run into over the years were extremely dangerous."

"Are you trying to scare me off?"

"I just want to make sure you're truly committed to going ahead with this plan of yours before we go wading in up to our hips."

He shifted in the car seat, clearly eager to get started. "Why shouldn't I be?" After all, this is what I've spent my entire adult life working towards."

"I realize that," Sonja replied. "I just want to make sure you understand that once you enter the door of that club, there's no going back, mentally as well as physically."

"I understand."

"Do you?" she sighed.

A block-shaped man dressed in a white linen suit and a black turtleneck stood at the entrance to Dolly Dagger's, collecting cover charge. The bouncer's skull was wide, flat and hairless, his lower jaw jutted forward like an ape's, and when he fixed his tiny, piggish eyes on Estes, the vampire hunter felt a chill travel up his spine and lodge itself in the back of his skull. It was a feeling he was quickly learning to associate with what Sonja called "Pretenders"—inhuman creatures that wore the semblance of men and women.

The bouncer glanced first at Estes, then at Sonja. "Twenty dollar you," he said in a thick, vaguely Slavic accent, stabbing a finger shaped like a Vienna sausage at Estes. "Woman no pay."

Estes dutifully peeled a twenty from the roll in his pocket. The bouncer snapped it up with surprising dexterity for someone with hands the size of a catcher's mitt. He grinned knowingly at Estes, flashing an array of inward-curving yellow teeth, and motioned with his blunt head to the claret-colored curtains hung just inside the open door.

They pushed past the heavy velvet partition and entered a large, dark room that, except for a low stage that dominated the middle of the floor, looked no different from any other nightclub in the area. The dim, mirrored interior was lit by the footlights that ran along the runway and a collection of colored baby spots that hung from the exposed rafters like nesting bats.

On one side of the main room a deejay was simultaneously spinning CDs and working the lighting board from a raised booth. On the opposite side was a large, well-stocked bar.

"Gentlemen's clubs, adult entertainment centers, sports bars: I don't care what you call them. You've seen one titty bar; you've seen them all," Sonja muttered under her breath. "Still, I have to hand it to this Noir fellow for hitting on a perfect means of hiding in plain sight."

"Are you sure this is the place?" Estes asked as he scanned the tables and booths. "I don't see him anywhere."

"Oh, it's the place, alright. The ogre at the door is proof enough."

"So *that's* what he was," Estes said, genuine wonder in his voice. "I *knew* there was something not right about him."

"Good. You're picking up on the vibe. But don't get cocky. Ogres have the poorest camouflage skills of all the Pretending kind. That's why they hire themselves out as muscle."

Sonja turned her attention to Dolly Dagger's employees, peering over the tops of her glasses at the wait staff. "The aura on the deejay reads like a schizophrenic's MRI, but he's otherwise human," she said in a stage whisper. "Probably a renfield."

The ogre they had spotted at the door was now seated near the curtained-off VIP rooms reserved for private lap-dances, glowering at Sonja with imbecilic malice.

"You got any armor-piercing rounds in your little arsenal?" she asked, keeping her tone as casual as possible.

"No. Why do you ask?" Estes replied, startled by the question.

"Ogres don't possess significant psionic powers or magic, but they're incredibly strong and damn hard to kill. I know from personal experience their skin is as thick as rhino hide. I think you ought to be aware of that, in case you have to open fire to get out of here."

A dancer writhed on the stage to the accompaniment of overamplified, electronically enhanced music, spreading her legs so that the men assembled along the periphery of the stage could get a better look at her exposed sex. The Dagger's clientele largely consisted of unexceptional, middle-aged men wearing khakis and polo shirts and a splash too much aftershave. Although most of them were seated alone at the tables or in chairs that faced the runway, they did not look at each other as they drank their beers and mixed drinks.

Estes noticed a woman working the register behind the bar. Although her back was to the room, her face was reflected in the mirror, revealing her to be around thirty years old, with long, dark hair that fell in tangled curls like the mane of a wild pony, and a smattering of freckles across the bridge of her nose and cheeks. Compared to the outfits worn by the dancers, her loose-fitting smock and dark leggings were practically demure.

His attention returned to the woman on the stage, who was now easing herself up and down one of the brass poles. She was young, with long blonde hair the color of raw honey and creamy white skin as smooth as marble. Estes felt an ache building in his groin and tried to look away, but his eyes were drawn once more in her direction.

He had spent his adult life in pursuit of creatures that exploited human weakness to their own ends. Lust, sex, need—those were the most potent weapons in the enemy's arsenal. Although he knew more than any other man alive the horror that might lurk behind the mask of beauty, he found it impossible to take his eyes off the dancer on the stage.

As Sonja moved towards the bar, the woman at the register turned and faced the room, planting her hands in the small of her back to ease the weight placed on her spine by her swollen belly.

Sonja halted in mid-stride, taken aback by the sight of the heavily pregnant bartender. Vampires detest expectant women nearly as much as they do sunlight and silver. So why in hell was one doing working at Dolly Dagger's? She dropped her vision back into the occult spectrum, but the bartender still came up clean. Whatever else she might be, at least she was human....

Estes watched as one of the dancer's admirers placed a dollar bill on the edge of the stage. The dancer swung her head in time to the music, allowing him to catch a fleeting glimpse of her face before her hair obscured it once again. Although he did not quite recognize her, there was definitely something familiar about the woman on the stage. Estes stepped closer to the runway, hoping to get a better look as the dancer slithered her way towards the proffered bill.

The man who placed the money on the stage leaned forward in his seat, his eyes burning with a lust that seemed inappropriate from someone dressed in Dockers. The blonde stooped to pick up the money and stroked her admirer's face with her free hand, then carefully folded the dollar bill and inserted it between his lips and slowly pulled it out with her mouth. Her admirer stared up at her, his forehead dripping beads of sweat as if stricken by a sudden bout of malaria.

Sonja experienced a small stab of alarm as she turned to speak to Estes, only to find him standing at the foot of the runway, staring up at the dancer gyrating on the stage the same way a starving man looks at T-bone steak. She was surprised by the jealousy his attention to the dancer sparked within her, and quickly pushed it out of her mind.

The dancer laughed and tossed her head back in amusement. As she turned in Estes' direction, he was finally able to get an unobstructed view of her face....

Sonja sighed and massaged her temples as an ashen-faced Estes turned on his heel and fled the club. She had suspected this might happen, although not so soon. She gave the dancer on the stage a final, disparaging glance before following her traveling companion outside.

Estes looked a lot like his mother.

***

Estes felt dizzy and the world kept tilting under his feet, so he leaned against the rental car and vomited onto the asphalt. He visibly started as Sonja appeared at his elbow. Although he knew she was inhumanly quick, he cursed himself for leaving himself so open.

"You okay?"

Estes nodded, wiping the bile from his lips with a trembling hand.

"That dancer. The one on stage. She's..."

"Your mother," Sonja finished the sentence bluntly, but not without sympathy. "I thought she might be here."

Estes laughed, but it came out with a painful, choking sound. "I don't know *why* I'm so surprised. The last time I saw her she was with Noir. It just never occurred to me she would be... she would be..." He tried to say the words, but they would not come out of his mouth.

"One of them?" Sonja finished the sentence, speaking the words he could not.

He nodded gratefully and looked away.

Sonja leaned on the hood of the rental car, folding her arms across her chest. "Look, kid, I told you there was no going back once we stepped inside that club, but that's not exactly true. Granted, there's no way you can forget what you saw tonight. But you can still hand it over to me to finish. There's no disgrace in that. I'll bring you the bastard's head on a platter, if that's what you want." Estes shook his head, shame spreading across his neck and shoulders like hot oil.

"*No!*" He slammed his fist hard enough to put a dent in the hood of the car. "I haven't come this far to get cold feet! She's *not* my mother—my mother died twenty-five years ago!"

Sonja looked at him for a long moment before speaking. "It's one thing to tell yourself that—another to accept it. I'll let you take down Noir. You deserve that much satisfaction. But I beg you; let *me* kill her."

"She's my responsibility, Sonja."

"No, she's *not*. Believe me, you don't want to do this." Her voice was so horribly sad, yet her eyes were impossible to read. "Killing someone you love is like driving a nail through your own heart—not hard enough to finish you off, but deep enough to ruin you for life. Look, Jack—I'm *not* human." She said it gently, as if reminding him of a minor, indelicate fact. "I do not have to live with the things I have done—I simply have to exist. And existing is far different from living. Ask any street person. Whatever crimes you've committed pursuing your vendetta, I won't let you add matricide to them, even if it is once removed."

Estes shook his head as if he could somehow make her words fly out of his ears. Grief was bubbling up from underneath his anger, threatening to render him defenseless. He could not allow that to happen. He looked Sonja straight in the eye—but all he could see was his own contorted, angry face reflected in her sunglasses.

"If you can do this, so can I."

"That's what I'm afraid of."

Noir loathed the Twenty-First Century.

Granted, it was just beginning, but the era was already showing signs of being tiresome, what with humans constantly prattling on about computers this and digital that. It reminded him of all that blather about steam power and pneumatics during the Industrial Revolution.

Humans were so insanely proud of their little discoveries, but inherently blind to their darker applications. Little had changed since the first grunting upright ape set the savannah ablaze while dragging a burning branch back home to his tribe. It was up to Noir and others of his ilk to realize the *true* potential of the computer age, then orchestrate a way to benefit from the damage and despair it would spawn. Still, it was difficult for him to become excited about the prospect of stalking victims in cyberspace. It was all so… bloodless. What was the point? Where was the sport?

So much had changed since he had first fought his way free of the shroud: kingdoms had risen and collapsed; religions died only to be reborn in different skins; new worlds were discovered, conquered and reconquered. So why should he bother mastering the nuances of modern technology, language, etiquette, and dress when it all was going to change in a few years, anyway?

Why bother indeed? He knew the answer to that question all too well. It was far too easy for one of his kind to become anachronistic. Vampires had to stay up to date if they wished to avoid detection. That was why he affected dreadlocks and black silk suits instead of a turban. There used to be a day when Nobles prided themselves on staying current, but now most of them seemed content to remain walking museum pieces. He had seen Count Tenebrae on the streets of London just last year, dressed like he was planning a night out with Wilde and Whistler. In the old days, such blatant anachronism in dress would have been equivalent to signing your own death warrant, but not anymore.

Perhaps, in his own way, he was guilty of the sin of anachronism as well. There was no denying that things had changed for the better for his kind. The days of existing in fear of vampire hunters and the witch finders elite were long gone. But still, old habits died hard.

He had seen kings beheaded, martyrs torched, Popes strangled in their baths, cities burnt until the sky was so thick with soot there was no telling day from night. Some of the most dangerous men known to history had once been amongst his confidantes and enemies, and yet he endured: eternal, if not unchanged.

He was born in the Holy Land, in the city of Tyre, in what was once known as the Kingdom of Jerusalem. His father was a second-generation crusader baron, his mother a former slave who occasionally served her Christian masters as healer and sorceress.

His father's father had been the third son of a rural petty-baron in the north of France, who realized it was better to soldier in the name of the Lord and risk death by heathen hands than to squat in a chilly castle and munch turnips in the vain hope his elder brothers and their progeny might succumb to the plague, and took up the cross and followed Hugh of Vermandois across the Alps.

His grandfather fought with great bravery and precious little mercy, emerging from the slaughter of Jerusalem looking as if he had been dipped in blood. Man, woman, child, it made no difference to him; his ruthless *sangfroid* in battle became legendary amongst his fellow crusaders. In reward for his service, Noir's grandfather was granted a baronage by King Baldwin and presented with a *goules* shield bearing a two-handed sword in argent, point down, piercing a human heart in white. He was also given the surname Coeur de Neige: "Heart of Snow." In France, Coeur de Neige had been the surplus son of a lesser noble, but under the baking sun of the Transjordan he became a man of means whose counsel was heeded in the Court of Lieges. Using his new status to its greatest advantage, the fledgling baron married the niece of Raymond of Saint-Gilles, Count of Toulouse and Lord of Tripoli, thereby cementing his place in the emerging aristocracy of Outremer, as the crusader kingdoms were then known. Noir's father, the first of his line born to the title, arrived in 1130.

Noir's mother, Lisha, often claimed the blood of Hannibal flowed in her veins. As a boy, she would regale him with tales of her family having been descended from the royal wizard-priests of Moloch and, more recently, the master hunters who captured and sold African elephants and other wild beasts to the Romans for the spectacles at the Circus Maximus.

When Noir's father, the younger Coeur de Neige, first laid eyes on Lisha, she was a slave. Years before, while traveling to Mecca, her family's caravan had been set upon by brigands, who slaughtered her relatives and sold her into slavery. Fortunately, Lisha had proved herself not only beautiful, but also skilled as an herbalist, and she was bought by a wealthy Frankish baron who was more interested in curing his gout than sating his lusts.

Coeur de Neige was visiting the old baron, who was a friend of his late father's, when he fell ill with a fever. Lisha nursed him back to health, spending weeks at his bedside. When the old baron died a year later, one of his last acts was to grant Lisha her freedom. Coeur de Neige quickly brought her within his retinue as apothecary and concubine. Noir was born three years later, in 1161.

He was the first of four children, and the only one to survive past infancy. Although born on the wrong side of the blanket, his childhood was a comparatively happy one, as his father proved favorably disposed to him. The baron lavished a great deal of time and attention on both Noir and his mother, making sure they wanted for nothing.

Along with making sure Noir was taught the finer points of horsemanship and combat, Coeur de Neige saw to it that his son was schooled in both Latin and French, so that he might serve as steward to the house.

Lisha made sure that her family's traditions were passed along to her son, as well. She schooled the boy in how to recognize, harvest, and dry the various herbs and plants used in any respectable apothecary, and upon his reaching the age of thirteen, they graduated from the potions and pills of the healer to darker knowledge. It was then that Noir discovered that his mother was indeed heir to ancient power.

Although it was within Lisha's power to summon siroccos, call down cyclones, and visit unimaginable plagues upon her enemies, she never once did any of these things. Even though she could curdle the wombs of those who spited her so that they produced hare-lipped fools, she never lifted her hand to curse them. It simply was not in her nature to do so, despite the degradation and injustice she had suffered throughout her life.

Some would say that his mother was a woman of kind heart and good intentions. Noir thought she was weak.

When Noir turned eighteen, Coeur de Neige presented his illegitimate son with an emblazoned shield depicting a two-handed sword in argent, point sinister, piercing a human heart in sable. This was the closest his father ever came to publicly acknowledging him. Noir was proud to have been given arms and promised to serve Coeur de Neige as loyally as any vassal knight. And for nearly ten years, he was as good as his word.

Coeur de Neige soon discovered that his son was an adept diplomat with a keen eye for the interests of the family. Given the tenuous situation of the crusader states, having an intelligent aide whose loyalty was assured by blood was handy indeed. Coeur de Neige's trust in his son was so absolute, he appointed Noir his steward and left him in charge while he traveled to France and claimed the northern barony of a great-uncle who had died without issue. For the better part of a year, Noir served in Coeur de Neige's stead, settling issues amongst the tenants and filling his father's seat at the Council of Lieges.

During his father's absence, five galleys were brought to the Port of Aïlet on the backs of camels. This bizarre fleet, manned by Outremer warriors thirsty for Muslim blood and treasure, sailed the Red Sea, ravaging the coasts as far as Aden. A group of knights even went so far as to try to seize Medina. After a year of such raiding, Saladin's navy destroyed the Frankish fleet and had the prisoners put to death at Mecca, much to the Mohammedans delight.

The man behind such outlandish piracy was Reginald de Châtillon, Lord of Krak Montréal and the Port of Aïlet. He cared little of a man's pedigree, provided he was ready with a sword and willing to die for Christ and kingdom. Noir admired the crazy-brave Châtillon, who was the type of man whose personality could easily sway Popes and kings and incite men into taking up arms against insane odds.

The smell of a new crusade brewing in the Holy Land brought Noir's father, the fifty-five year old Coeur de Neige, back from France. And when he arrived, Noir was stunned to discover his father had a sixteen-year-old wife. Her name was Mathilde and she was her husband's second cousin on his mother's side, as well as being directly related to Eleanor of Aquitaine. The baron, who was getting on in years, had succumbed to pressure from his Frankish cousins to produce a legal heir, one whose pedigree as a European and a Christian could not be questioned.

One of the grounds for agreement to the marriage, as put forth by Mathilde's family, was that Coeur de Neige renounce both Lisha and Noir and turn them out of his service. Which he did as easily as another man might change his boots.

Lisha was aggrieved by the turn of events, but she did not allow it to destroy her. For years she had been setting aside the pieces of jewelry and other finery the baron bestowed upon her, and lost no time in securing a villa on the mainland. Noir, on the other hand, was not so well prepared, either financially or emotionally, and found himself turned out into the world with nothing but the clothes on his back, a sword, and a bastard's shield. It was his mother who made him the gift of a fully outfitted horse, a set of arms, as well as a page from her household staff.

Thus caparisoned, he traveled to the fortified castle of Krak Montréal and pledged his sword to Châtillon's service, knowing that he would soon have the chance to prove himself in battle to his new lord.

In 1185 Saladin attempted to take the Krak Montréal, only to meet with a stalemate. A truce was signed between Saladin and Châtillon, but Reginald, ever the daredevil, broke it by raiding a caravan and carrying off the sultan's own sister. This final insult was all that it took for Saladin to declare holy war and invade the Kingdom of Jerusalem in earnest.

Saladin's troops blocked the main road to Tiberias and sent a small force to attack the town, hoping to lure the crusaders into the open. Coeur de Neige's kinsman, Count Raymond of Tripoli, urged the King of Jerusalem not to fall into Saladin's trap, even though his own wife was within the threatened city. As the evening wore on and tempers flared, Châtillon, who was never a friend of Tripoli, accused Raymond of cowardice and treason and prevailed on King Guy to change his mind. For once, Châtillon's vaunted brashness did not hold him in good stead.

The next day the forces of Jerusalem underwent an exhausting march in grueling heat and spent the entire night without water. To make matters worse, Saladin's men set grass fires that filled the air with choking smoke that added even further to the troops' thirst and disorientation. Finally, with the smoke from the grass fires pouring into their faces, the foot soldiers broke ranks and fled, disrupting the cavalry. The bravery and dedication of those marshaled on the shores of Lake Tiberias was not enough to overcome Saladin's army, who swarmed them like locusts on a field of ripe wheat.

The Christian forces were annihilated; the king, the grand master of the Templars and Châtillon were captured, and only a handful of knights escaped. By all rights, Noir should have died with his comrades on the lakeshore, but he somehow managed to stagger from the chaos of the battlefield with the help of his page.

By the time they reached his mother's villa, Noir had no more blood in him than a mouse. He vaguely recalled tumbling from the back of his horse upon entering the courtyard. Although Lisha was deeply afraid for her son's life, she did not allow herself to become distraught. She kept her head, ordered that he be prepared for treatment, and sent a runner to Coeur de Neige to inform him of his son's condition.

Lisha knew Noir was dying, and that no mortal medicine could save him. She set aside her dried herbs, powdered rhinoceros horn and pickled tiger penises and turned to the ornately worked rosewood chest with the golden lock she kept in a special hiding place in her workshop.

As a boy, Noir had seen the contents of the rosewood chest only once, for the things locked inside it were rare and wondrous indeed, used only in the direst of emergencies. Lisha took from the box a glass jar sealed in beeswax and wrapped in a rosary. Inside the jar was something black and shriveled that looked like a bloom of fungus, but was actually the heart of a vampire.

Utilizing specific elixirs and rituals, Lisha boiled the heart down into a vile broth the color of tar. As her son lay dying, she forced the noxious brew down his gullet with the aid of a funnel. Within seconds of being fed the odious concoction, Noir breathed his last.

Although the life had fled her son's body, Lisha showed no outwards signs of grief or sorrow. Instead of ordering her servants to anoint his body and wrap it in a winding sheet, she told them that within three days time he would arise from the dead. The servants thought her mad, but none dared go against her orders.

On the second day following Noir's death, Baron Coeur de Neige arrived at the villa. Although he had not so much as spoken to Noir since renouncing him, the baron lost no time in riding out from Tyre with an escort of Knights Templar once he learned of his bastard son's condition. Upon his arrival the servants quickly filled the baron in on how Noir's death had unhinged the Lady Lisha's mind.

The baron was outraged when he saw his son's body still sprawled on his deathbed, his brow naked of the priest's unction. Coeur de Neige demanded to know why Noir had not been given last rites. Lisha stated that their son was not truly dead, and that he would rise on the evening of the third day as surely as Christ had rolled back the stone, but this blasphemy angered the baron even further.

Lisha attempted to explain what she had done, hoping he would understand the desperate measures love had lead her to take. Instead, Coeur de Neige turned upon the woman who had shared his bed for twenty-five years and, denouncing her as a witch, plunged a dagger into her belly. She died at his feet.

The Templars who accompanied the baron saw that Noir's mortal remains were administered the last rites. Now that the body was officially consecrated, Lisha's remaining servants sewed Noir into a shroud and took the corpse to be buried in a nearby churchyard. Satisfied that all was as it should be, Coeur de Neige headed back to Tyre, where his young wife and infant son awaited his return.

Of course, Noir awoke on the night of the third day, just as his mother had said he would.

Upon his resurrection, Noir found himself somewhere dark and close, his arms crossed over his chest and tied into place by strips of soft cloth, with a great weight bearing down upon his entire body. He tried to open his eyes, but something cold and metallic lay atop the lids, keeping them in place. He tried to cry out in alarm, but his mouth was filled with cotton.

Marshaling all his strength, he managed to tear his arms free, pull the cotton batting from his mouth, and knock the coins from his eyes. He clawed at the shroud with nails that were far longer and stronger than any he had possessed in life, struggling upward like a swimmer desperate for air. Loose earth fell into his eyes and open mouth as he struggled to escape the claustrophobic darkness. The moon of Islam hung in the sky as he wriggled free of his grave like a snake shedding its skin.

He wandered forth from the churchyard, dazed and empty-eyed, like a statue suddenly transformed from marble into flesh, dressed in nothing but the tatters of his burial shroud, his hair filled with grave dirt. Like every new resurrectant, he was operating by instinct alone, shuffling towards those things his living brain had deemed family, as they would be the ones most likely, in their grief, to cast aside caution and throw open their doors to such a shocking apparition.

A mile from the churchyard Noir came upon a solitary pilgrim huddled in one of the shelters built along those roads that lead from the seaports to the Holy Sepulcher in Jerusalem. The pilgrim awakened suddenly, startled from his pious dreams by the smell of death. Upon seeing the horror looming over him, the pilgrim cried out to his god to deliver him, but there was no salvation to be had in the Holy Land that night.

Noir attacked the pilgrim like a man fresh from the desert drinking from a skin of water. After he had drained the pilgrim dry, Noir's senses returned to him, at least enough to realize he must cover his nakedness if he wished to continue his journey unnoticed. After stripping his victim of garments, he set out anew, this time not to feed mindlessly, but to find his mother, for Noir knew that whatever change had been worked upon him must have been her doing.

In escaping the grave, Noir discovered he had also escaped the frailties of the human condition. His eyes now could see as clearly in the night as they once did during the day; he could smell all manner of things he never had before, things such as fear; he could hear the faintest rustling of a mouse amongst the dry grasses along the road, or the slither of an asp hidden amongst the rocks. But the biggest change of all was the need, unlike any he had ever known as a mortal man, located just below the pit of his belly and just above his loins, which called for the blood of the living.

As Noir drew closer to his mother's villa, he saw that no lights were burning in the windows. He found this strange, for he knew Lisha often sat up late into the night, working on her various potions and spells. As he approached the outer walls, Noir caught a familiar scent rising from the nearby dung heap, a stink he had come to know all too well on the battlefield: the odor of decomposing human flesh.

There was what looked like a scarecrow, thrown by a careless farmhand, atop the heap. Upon closer inspection, Noir recognized the body as that of his mother. He could identify her only by her hair and clothes, since the dogs and vultures had been at her. A rage so great it manifested itself as calm broke within his breast.

Noir strode into the courtyard, kicking open his mother's padlocked workshop. The servants appeared, awakened by the noise, torches in hand, swords and cudgels at the ready. The majordomo demanded to know who he was and what business he had with them at such an hour. When Noir turned to face them, they gasped aloud, crossed themselves and offered up prayers of protection to Allah.

Noir demanded to know who had slain his mother and ordered her body cast out with the offal. At first the servants were too frightened to speak, but at last the majordomo said it was the work of Baron Coeur de Neige, who believed the Lady Lisha had poisoned their son in order to avenge herself against him for marrying the Lady Mathilde.

Upon hearing this, Noir burst into laughter, which made the servants gathered before him shiver in their boots. What an egotist his father was! The baron saw all things done by others as somehow relating to him; he could not fathom how Lisha's actions could be fueled by love, not hate.

Indeed, the Lady Lisha had not robbed the baron of his posterity, but presented him with a son who could never grow old, never die—one who could stride the world forever! And this was how he repaid her?

Two nights later, in the city of Tyre, Noir entered his father's house, moving like a shadow through the inner court with its splashing fountain and carefully tended rose garden. He found his father's wife alone in her chambers, her attention focused on a piece of embroidery. She looked up from her handiwork as he approached, her brow furrowed in confusion for a long moment, before her eyes grew wide in recognition.

Her gaze cut quickly to the far side of the room then back to where Noir stood. He followed her furtive glance and saw the peaked crown of a cradle, swaddled in white gauze to keep biting flies away from the occupant's tender flesh. Noir smiled, and his father's wife cried out in horror and flung herself at him, desperate to put herself between her child and the demon in her bedchamber.

Noir grabbed her by the heavy braid hanging down her back, jerking her out of his way as he would a hound on a leash. The Lady Mathilde fell to the stone floor as Noir snatched up his infant half-brother, dangling the child like a rabbit in a butcher's stall.

The babe opened its maw, revealing bare, pink gums, and issued a cry as thin as gruel. Noir shook his head in amazement that his father would chose to turn him aside in favor of such weak meat.

The Lady Mathilde, seeing the look in Noir's eyes, crawled on her belly and placed herself at his feet, promising she would give herself to him, to do with as he saw fit, if only he spared her son. Noir looked down at his groveling stepmother, her eyes swollen and made red by tears, and with a smile dashed the child's skull against the wall.

Noir then took his father's wife as she lay on the floor, stricken dumb by fear and grief. He was cold as death inside her, causing her to find her tongue at last, and she cried out to her savior to deliver her from the devil's embrace. As the last flicker of sanity and hope fled her eyes, Noir buried his fangs in her neck and took from her that which he truly lusted after.

Sated on Mathilde's blood, Noir sat in the dark and awaited his father's return to his family. As luck would have it, he did not have long to wait.

Baron Coeur de Neige entered the room dressed in a long shirt and soft slippers, carrying a taper to light his way. Hidden in the shadows, Noir sneered at the sight of his father tiptoeing towards the bed, calling out his wife's name in a singsong voice like a smitten schoolboy. The baron nearly dropped his candle when he stumbled across the Lady Mathilde's corpse sprawled on the floor. At the sight of his wife's body, the baron made a noise somewhere between an angry roar and a pained sob. He looked about wildly, searching for the assassin he knew had to be lurking nearby.

"Hello, Father," Noir said, stepping from his hiding place. "Did you miss me?"

Coeur de Neige stared for a long moment, unable to believe his eyes. When he finally spoke, his voice was little more than a whisper. "I saw you buried. You're dead."

"No, Father. I'm far from it. But I will tell you who *is* dead: my mother, for one, as well as your other, lesser spawn. But as for your pretty little wife… once her incubation period has passed, she will return to this world, but as *my* bride, not yours. And while I may be a bastard, I am not a cruel one. I will not slay an unarmed man; I am giving you a fighting chance, which is more than you gave my mother."

Noir removed the dagger from its sheath at his waist and tossed it to Coeur de Neige. It landed at the baron's feet, the pommel towards his hand. The baron quickly snatched up the weapon and buried it to the hilt in his son's chest, skewering his heart.

The baron took a step back and wiped the back of his hand across his lips, expecting Noir to collapse onto the floor. Instead, he stood and stared at his father, a mocking smile on his lips, the dagger jutting from his chest like a bothersome thorn.

Coeur de Neige crossed himself with trembling hands as his son pulled the blade free. Noir grinned, baring his new, sharp teeth so that his father could see them..

"You are not my son, but some fiend dressed in his shape, sent by Satan to torment me!" Coeur de Neige cried, his voice made hoarse by horror.

"Believe what you like, father," Noir replied. "It will make no difference in Hell." And with that Noir drove the dagger pulled from his heart into the baron's own. Coeur de Neige fell to the floor at his son's feet, his face set in a rictus of terror.

Thus Noir began his existence by obliterating his paternal line; assuring there would be no others of his blood, save for those of his Making. Still, he did not completely sever himself from his past, as he took the name Coeur du Noir, after the bar sinister coat of arms presented to him by his late father.

Still, avenging his mother's murder by committing patricide was just the beginning of what would prove a long and contentious existence. Noir quickly discovered he was not the same as other vampires. Having been Made through sorcery rather than by another of his kind, Noir lacked the patronage and protection that came with being part of an established brood, which meant he not only had to worry about detection by humans, but challenges from other vampires as well.

Realizing his disadvantage, Noir approached different Nobles and offered his skills as a necromancer if they would accept him into their service. But in undeath, as in life, a man is judged by what he is not, not by what he is. And, in the Ruling Class's bloodshot eyes, Noir was *strega*, not *enkidu*, and therefore not to be trusted.

Since the Nobles would not have him, Noir set about creating his own brood—one fashioned not only of those he Made, but other solitaires who did not fit the *enkidu* definition of "normal." And in time, Noir watched those who once snubbed him as a freak fall into extinction, while he continued, surrounded by his little family of oddlings.

He had spent centuries wandering from country to country, moving through the kingdoms of mankind like the shadow of a bad dream. For those who knew how to look, his will and whims were visible in the histories of a dozen peoples, like a vast tapestry woven from bloodied thread. But that was part of a time long past, in a world so different from the one he now dwelt in, it might as well have taken place on Mars.

Where once he commanded princes like pawns on a chess board, now Noir satisfied himself with manipulating the city councilmen, business executives and government officials who frequented establishments such as Dolly Dagger's.

While many Nobles turned up their noses at posing as a member of the "lower orders," Noir had discovered it was far easier to avoid detection by pretending to be a shady businessman rather than posing as a member of the aristocracy. Blackmail, hot cars and credit card theft might seem prosaic for one of his station, but it was nothing more than window dressing. Humans expected a certain amount of mystery from someone involved in the underworld. If they thought you a villain, they would never suspect you of being an actual monster.

Not that Noir had to worry about being hunted down by vampire hunters. Once humans stopped looking for vampires in abandoned houses and deserted churchyards, the undead were free to move about unnoticed. However, the threat from members of the Ruling Class was still very real, and a good portion of Noir's time and energy was spent guarding against attacks from rival Nobles eager to boost their status. There was any number of scheming *enkidu*, including that bastard Tenebrae, who were more than eager to eat his heart.

The office intercom buzzed. It was three o'clock in the morning; the bar was closed and it was time to review the night's receipts. Noir mimed opening a lock and the office door swung open of its own accord.

The sight of Lady Madonna's gravid belly caused a prickle of disgust to travel up Noir's spine, but he forced himself to smile at her nonetheless. As loathsome as her condition was to him, she had proven herself extremely useful to him time and again, and that, in the end, was all what truly mattered.

"What do you have for me, my dear?"

Lady Madonna placed the cash box onto the table for his inspection. "The house made three thousand, counting door and bar receipts."

Noir gave the contents a cursory glance, then pushed it away. "How did the girls do?"

Lady Madonna responded by tossing three wallets, two sets of car keys, and one diamond-studded Rolex onto the desk. Noir quickly thumbed through the plastic, ferreting out the department store and gas cards.

"We'll unload the cars on DeMarco. He's always in the market for rolling steel," Noir said, tossing the gutted wallets into a nearby wastebasket.

Lady Madonna laced her hands across her swollen belly, which he had come to recognize as a sign of ill ease.

Noir turned to face his lieutenant, raising an eyebrow as he spoke. "Was there any trouble tonight?"

"I'm not sure. There was someone here earlier who looked like trouble. A woman. Black leather jacket, jeans, boots. Whatever she was up to, she didn't stay long. She couldn't have been in the club more than five, six minutes, tops."

Noir reached out and touched Ygon's mind with his own. The ogre's thoughts were as thick as compost, but nowhere near as fertile.

Ygon.

The ogre looked around, trying to locate the source of Noir's voice.

I'm in the office, moron!

"Yes, milord?" Ygon vocalized his response in order to form cogent enough thought patterns, otherwise all Noir picked up was pictures and scent patterns.

Bring me the surveillance tapes from the main floor.

"As you command, milord."

A few minutes later Ygon entered the office carrying a set of VHS tapes in one hand like they were dominoes. He handed the cassettes to Lady Madonna, who inserted the first one into a video player built into the bookcase. The thirty-two inch video monitor set flush into the wall behind the desk suddenly blinked on. Lady Madonna hit the Play button on the remote control and the silver snow on the screen dissolved into the interior of Dolly Dagger's, as shot from a hidden camera just inside the front door.

The surveillance cameras had not been Noir's idea, but a holdover from the establishment's previous owner. Still, they proved to be a useful bit of technology; especially those cameras mounted behind the mirrors in the VIP rooms.

Lady Madonna pointed to the time code running in the far right side of the screen: twenty after midnight. Noir leaned forward, steepling his fingers as he watched the playback. There is no way to read auras on videotape, so he had to use other physical cues to decide whether or not the woman was human. Judging from her build and her clothes, it was easy to dismiss her as an off-duty dancer checking out the club before an audition. But there was something in the way she handled herself.... She moved like a woman who knew she was being watched, but not for the usual reasons.

"She's trouble alright," Noir said, nodding thoughtfully.

He followed the trouble as she moved towards the bar, came to a sudden halt, and then turned toward the runway. The camera angle, however, did not allow him to see exactly who or what she was looking at. A couple of seconds later she exited the bar, clearly in pursuit of someone off-camera.

"One thing is for certain; she didn't come alone." Noir snapped his fingers impatiently. "Where's the other surveillance tape?"

Lady Madonna popped out the first tape and fed in a second, fast-forwarding until the timer read 12:20. This time the camera angle was facing outward from the stage.

"There. There she is." Noir pointed to the trouble crossing into the camera's field of vision, headed towards the bar. She was in the far background, but still visible on the tape. He watched the trouble come to a sudden stop, then turn. The colored lights from the stage flared off her mirrored sunglasses. It was relatively simple to trace her line-of-sight to a man standing at the foot of the runway, staring up at one of the dancers.

Although the lust in the man's eyes was familiar enough, he was not the type of customer the Dagger tended to attract. Noir was tempted to label the stranger a renfield, until he saw a silver belt buckle shaped like skull winking in the lights from the runway. No. Whatever this man in black might be, he wasn't the human servant of a vampire. Still, Noir could not shake the feeling that he recognized the man's face. That was one of the curses of having existed for nearly ten centuries: after a while, *all* faces were vaguely familiar.

As the man in black stared at the dancer undulating on the stage, the lust abruptly winked out of his eyes, to be replaced by a look of horrified recognition. The man in black turned and ran out the door, the trouble following on his heels.

Most interesting.

"Who was working the stage during that shift?"

Lady Madonna checked her clipboard. "Gloria was on from midnight to a quarter after one."

It took Noir a minute or two to place the female. He had acquired so many brides over the centuries, their names and faces tended to blur together. He had a clearer memory of her previous owner than he did of her. Then again, that was almost always the case, since the vast majority of his brides once belonged to former business partners foolish enough to betray him. Some would say he was endlessly repeating that final, Oedipal act between his father and himself, but Noir saw it as going with what he knew.

"Have her brought to me. She was recognized tonight—I want to know by whom."

"As you command, milord."

Noir took the remote control from Lady Madonna, rewinding it back to where the trouble turned to face the stage. For some reason, he felt the same thrill of excitement he used to experience when he was on the run from the Inquisition.

Something told him things were about to get interesting again.

Despite the city being a sprawling metropolis, the smell of honeysuckle still somehow perfumed the warm night air. From her spot on the hotel balcony, Sonja saw fireflies clustered like fairy lights in the trees of a nearby park. Normally she didn't get to enjoy such views while she was working, since she usually hunkered down in abandoned warehouses in the less desirable parts of town.

She reached inside her jacket and removed the bottle VéVé had given her, holding it between thumb and forefinger. Although it glowed like a blacklight bulb, it remained cool to the touch. The sight of Judd's captive soul burning with such fierce purity triggered despair within her as deep and profound as first love.

She brought the bottle to her ear and heard an almost imperceptible buzzing, like that of bees sealed in a mason jar. She strained to decipher what, if anything, the sound might mean. Did he know she was there? Did he know he was free of Malfeis? Did he know he was dead? Did he know anything at all? Or did he exist in a place beyond words; beyond even the thoughts that words represent?

She had loved Judd as she had loved no one else in her existence. Unlike Chaz and Palmer, Judd was neither a psychic nor one of the death groupies drawn to vampires. He was simply a handsome young man who found her attractive and enjoyed her company. Of course, it being around someone like Sonja was not a good thing for someone like Judd. She had tried to warn him off, but part of her enjoyed being mistaken for normal; she had not been able to bring herself to tell him the truth about the things she was capable of, and the Other had turned that weakness against her.

Judd had cared for her, and the Other had repaid his affection by breaking his mind and using his body to sate its base lusts. The Other raped both his body and his soul, and when it was through, his mind was like a broken toy hastily glued back together. For all their physical adaptability, humans have psyches as delicate as Christmas ornaments. It was impossible for them to glimpse the Real World without it warping them in some way. In Judd's case, his ordeal twisted him so that he craved the psychic domination of the Other. So she killed him, dismembered his body and fed it to alligators. It was the only humane thing to do.

For years she had carried the guilt of Judd's fall from grace locked within me. She had believed that the Other's ravaging of his psyche and his flesh was responsible for the damage to his soul. But now it was clear to her that that Judd had gone to Malfeis, seeking her whereabouts. And, in asking the demon where he could find her, he had, innocently and unknowingly, bartered away his soul. The thing she had killed was just a husk. Everything that truly made Judd who he was, his kindness, his empathy, his sense of humor, now lay in the palm of her hand.

She stared at the glow trapped within the tiny bottle and wondered what would happen if she removed the stopper. Would Judd's soul shoot out like a bottle rocket, or ooze out like dry-ice fog? Maybe it wouldn't even realize there was a difference between inside and out, like a tiger raised in captivity that continues to sit in its cage after the door has been thrown wide. Her fingers closed on the stopper, then fell away. She lacked the courage to set him free—at least for now.

Sonja could hear Estes bumping around inside the room. She retired from the balcony to find the door to the honor bar sitting wide open. Miniature bourbon, tequila, whiskey and gin bottles littered the tabletop.

"How do they expect a man to get drunk with these damned things?" Estes snarled, shaking the last few drops of Johnny Walker into a tumbler filled with half-melted ice and Coca-Cola.

"You seem to be making a go of it," she replied. "Oh, and for your information, I don't intend to hold your head while you blow chunks."

Estes fixed her with a drunken glare. "I expect *nothing* from you—except what we agreed upon."

"That's cool. It's your death trip, man. I'm just along for the ride." She dropped onto the settee and picked up the remote control, pointing it at the color TV nested in the faux armoire. The screen blinked on like a giant's eye, revealing the black and white figure of a man dressed in a baggy suit with a little cloth heart pinned to its breast. The man's face was painted like a clown's, with twists of hair sticking up through a bald wig like a crown of thorns.

"What's this?" Estes asked, his voice slurred.

"He Who Gets Slapped."

Estes frowned at the screen, his brow knitting. "Why isn't there any sound?"

"This was made before films had soundtracks. You know about the old silent movies, don't you?"

"No," he replied flatly, dropping onto the settee beside Sonja. "I've never even been to a real movie theater. I've only watched them on TV and video players."

"That's right—I keep forgetting you were—"

"Raised in an insane asylum?"

"I was going to say 'catatonic for ten years,' but, yeah, that's what I meant."

"My knowledge is full of gaps. Blind spots, I guess you could call them. I was taught how to read and write, I was tutored in American history, basic math, biology… but I never went to school. And once I was released from the Institute, well, I was only interested in learning those things that would help me track down vampires. I never experienced growing up, not the way I saw it on television: I didn't go to the movies, didn't hang out after school, didn't read comic books or play video games. I know I *should* have been doing all those things, because I saw kids my age doing them on TV, but I never got the chance. How about you? Did you ever get to be a kid?"

"Yeah, I guess so. But I wasn't me back then, I was someone else."

"But you can remember *being* her, can't you?"

"Enough to hurt."

"Did you play video games?"

"They weren't invented yet." She turned to search his face. "You honestly don't remember anything from before that night?"

Estes shook his head sadly. "Just blurs. They're more like dreams than genuine memories. Every time I try to examine one, it dissolves. It's like trying to catch soap bubbles with your bare hands."

"You resent your childhood being taken away from you."

He took a deep breath and then slowly let it out. "Yeah, I do. Funny, I couldn't bring myself to admit that to myself before now. It always sounded kind of selfish. Avenging my parents seemed so much more noble."

"I understand where you're coming from—I was angry for a very long time. For years I thought I wanted to kill the bastard who made me a vampire because he raped me. But it was more than that. I was angry because my life had been stolen. I'll never get to grow old, have children, or even truly die. All of that was taken away from me. I know there are people out there who would gladly sacrifice everything they own and are to be like me. And all I want is to be able to age, die, and stay dead. And it makes me angry that such simple things have been denied me. I've tried to get a handle on that anger, tried to make myself its master, not the other way around."

"Have you succeeded?"

"I'm getting better. But I still have my bad nights. Sometimes I feel like I'm watching myself from a great distance, as if everything I say or do is happening to someone else. Other times it feels like I've been dropped down a mineshaft: I can't see, hear or feel anything but the darkness surrounding me. I tear at it and rage against it, just to make sure I'm still there. Then there's the times when everything in the world is going on all at once inside my mind: babies crying, women screaming, men cursing. It's like having a short-wave radio in your head that you can't turn off; all you can do is adjust the volume up or down. When it's *real* bad, everything I look at, every sound I hear, every thought that churns inside my head hurts like hell. If it gets too loud, the only way I can have some bloody peace and quiet is to kill every living thing within striking distance."

"Jesus..." Estes' face contorted in genuine pity. "I had no idea..."

"But, you want to know *why* it hurts so much? *Because I haven't surrendered yet.* No matter how good succumbing to the darkness might feel— and it *does* feel good, that's the terrible thing about it—I refuse to give in. Still, every so often I weaken and allow the Other to escape. That's why I know how good it feels to surrender in the first place.

"Giving in to the Other is better than sex, better than drugs, better than liquor—because it makes the pain stop. But every time I give in, I lose a little bit more of my self, my humanity, if you will, to the vampire inside me. You see, I died on the operating table. Just a little bit, mind you—only for a minute or so. But when I died, I became a bridge between the land of the living and that of the dead. The Other is mine, yet not of me. We're like Siamese twins joined at the medulla oblongata. It roams at will inside my mind, like a wild animal pacing its cage. It's always with me, no matter what."

"Is it with you now?"

"Yes."

"Do you know what it wants?"

"Yes," she replied matter-of-factly. "It wants to kill you."

Estes nodded his understanding. There was no fear in his eyes. "Is there any way of getting rid of it?"

Sonja shrugged her shoulders. "How can I escape when there is no place to run from? When my rage overwhelms me, it's like the whole world is bathed in blood and fire. Sometime I know what's going on but am unable to stop it, as if I'm riding in the backseat of a car, unable to grab the wheel. But most of the time I black out, like a drunk on a bender. I never know what it's done... what *I've* done... until I come back to my senses. But I *do* know the fucker likes to hurt people who are close to me, and because of that, I'm dangerous to be around. I've learned to keep my contact with others to a bare minimum."

"What about, you know, blood?" Estes asked, his cheeks burning as if he'd just questioned her about her sex life.

"I feed myself with black market plasma. The only time I allow myself a fresh drink is in self-defense, if you will."

"What does it taste like?" There was an excited tremor in the back of his voice Sonja decided to ignore.

"It tastes like blood. But I will admit there is a difference between fresh and bagged. The bagged stuff is cold and stale. The hot red straight from the vein is fresh, vivid, and alive. And it's good—no, what am I saying? It's fucking *great!* In that regard, I'm no different from any of the suckers I hunt. Believe me, no junkie has hurt for a fix the way a vampire lusts for fresh blood.

“Blood enables vampires to ignore the pain of being an unnatural thing in a natural world, and they will do whatever it takes to sate their need; whether it means luring their grieving widow into a blizzard, snatching a baby from a stroller, or trawling for johns in subway stations. But no matter how much they feed, it’s never enough. That’s what makes the bloodlust so terrible. It isn’t a hunger for food, but for something else: something that isn’t there and never can truly be replaced. Where I’m different from the others is that there’s one other thing that feels as good as blood —and that’s killing vampires.”

***

Frank was the night auditor of the Peachtree Park Hotel. He liked the graveyard shift, since he could work in relative solitude and catch up on his light reading. The hotel’s bar closed at midnight, which normally left the lobby deserted.

“Excuse me—sir?”

Frank glanced up from his copy of GQ at the attractive, dark-haired young woman standing on the other side of the reception desk.

“Yes, ma’am?” he said, automatically. “May I help you?” As he got to his feet, he couldn’t help noticing that the woman was very pregnant, her belly riding low on her hips.

“I need the room number of a guest who is staying here. His name is Estes.”

Frank frowned. Someone had called ten minutes before, asking whether or not there was a guest by that name registered at the hotel. When he offered to put the call through to the room, the caller had hung up without another word. However, Frank distinctly remembered the caller as being male.

“I’m sorry, ma’am, but we’re not allowed to give out the room numbers of our guests.”

“But he’s my husband,” the pregnant woman said quickly, a look of distress crossing her face.

“I’m sorry ma’am, but I still can’t help you. I can place a call to his room, though, and *he* can tell you his room number…” He pushed the house phone resting atop the desk towards her.

The pregnant woman laced her hands protectively across her belly and grimaced as if she was going into labor on the spot. “No, you don’t *understand.* He—he’s here with another woman. He *promised* me he wouldn’t see her again. He promised on the life of our *baby.*” Her voice cracked and she began to cry, her belly trembling like a bowl of Jell-O with each sob.

Frank cringed. He hadn’t felt this guilty since he’d accidentally backed over the neighbor’s cat with his Toyota.

“Ma’am… please don’t cry. *Please…*” He sighed and rolled his eyes in surrender as her slender shoulders began to shake even harder. “Okay! *Okay!* I’ll check the register.” He turned to the computer and tapped on the keys. Within a half-second, the name and room number of Jack Estes flashed onto the screen. "Mr. Estes is in Suite 1432. But, please, don't tell *anyone* I told you. It would mean my job."

The woman he assumed to be Mrs. Estes dried her tears and favored him with a wan smile. "Thank you, sir. And my child thanks you, too."

Frank's gaze inadvertently dropped to the woman's midsection. And for the briefest second he could have sworn the child inside her had maneuvered itself so it could press its ear against the inside of her stomach.

***

"You know, Sonja…You're the only person I've ever met who understands," Estes motioned with one hand to include not just the room and its furnishings, but the world itself. "*You* see what *I* see. You see even *more* than I do. You don't think I'm crazy, do you?"

"Just a little," she said with a shrug. "But not in a bad way."

"When I first came to my senses, back at the Institute…Dr. Morrissey was my lifeline. He was my father and my mother rolled into one, you know? He was the man who unlocked my mind and set me free. I thought I could tell him everything. But when I talked about Blackheart, he didn't believe me. Oh, he said he believed *I* believed I was telling the truth. But *he* didn't believe. He kept insisting I was creating false memories to hide the truth from myself. He said I created Blackheart to take my father's place.

"When I insisted I was the one who was right and he was wrong, that I *wasn't* lying to myself or anyone else, Dr. Morrissey's attitude toward me changed. When he scheduled me for electroshock, that's when I discovered I was *truly* on my own.

"Up until the day they wheeled me into the electrotherapy room and stuck that rubber stopper in my mouth, I still trusted others as a child does. But my ability to trust was burned out of me with the first surge of electricity.

"It was a bitter lesson, but I quickly learned that no one was going to believe me, no one was going to help me, and no one was going to plead my case. If my family was to be avenged, it would have to be by my hand, and no other's. From then on I learned to hide what I really thought and lie to others about what I knew to be true.

"I was robbed of everything—my parents, my childhood, my place in the world. I could never be like the people I see on the streets, the ones who are happy and simply going about their business. I told myself that I didn't miss those things, because I had never known them. But that's not true. Maybe some needs must be satisfied if we are to live as human beings."

His hand dropped onto Sonja's knee, its warmth and weight oddly comforting. She knew she should remove it, but it had been so long since she had last been touched by anyone in something besides anger, she allowed it to stay.

Estes leaned in closer, his breath redolent of alcohol. She had feared this might happen, but now that it had, she was actually relieved. She hated worrying about things that had yet to happen.

"You scare me, Sonja," Estes whispered, his voice as raspy as a file. "I look at you and I see something I should kill. But I can't, because I also see someone who has been where I've been, who has seen what I've seen. I never thought I would ever be able to relate to anyone else, or find anyone capable of understanding what I've gone through—until I met you."

His lips grazed Sonja's cheek, sending an electric shiver down her spine, while his warm, masculine smell generated a pulsing ache between her legs. If Estes noticed how cool her flesh was against his own, he didn't show it. Sonja closed her eyes, trying to block the sight of the carotid artery pulsing inches from her mouth. It would be so easy to pin him to the sofa and sink her fangs into his exposed throat....

As he cupped the pale weight of her right breast in his palm, she gasped aloud, opening wide her mouth. Her fangs ache to be unsheathed from their hiding place in her gums. The urge to plunge her canines into his throat and make the sweet, hot red that pulsed within his veins her own was t unbearable. She quickly turned her head away from his and growled a warning.

Estes made a strangled noise and jumped off the sofa as if it was on fire, Sonja's sunglasses caught in his numbed fingers. Sonja raised a hand to her eyes, shielding them as best she could. Although the only light in the room was from the television, it might as well have been the high beams from a car shining directly in her face. Estes went white around the lips and nearly fell over his own legs as he hurried for the john, a hand clamped over his mouth. The door slammed behind him just as his strangled groans exploded into violent retching. The scene was bad and headed for worse if she stayed around. She snatched her sunglasses from where Estes had dropped them on the floor. She needed to put some distance between them before things got completely out of hand.

As she turned to close the door of the hotel room, she glanced at the television one last time. Parades of clowns were marching by Lon Chaney, each slapping him viciously in turn. The last clown in line snatched the silk heart pinned to Chaney's costume and hurled it to the sawdust of the center ring, then gleefully jumped up and down on it. Although Chaney's painted face was fixed in a rictus of pained hilarity, his eyes shone with tears of madness.

"Idiot," she whispered, to no one who could hear.

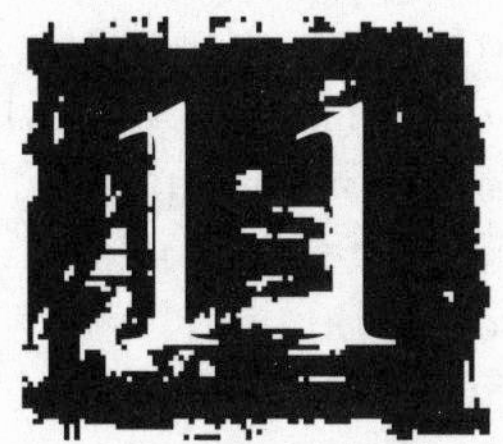

It is that time called "morning," even though it seems more like night than day. The streets are deserted, save for the occasional taxi and stretch limo bearing those on their way to all-hours clubs located in Midtown. I walk past the shuttered restaurants and shops lining Peachtree without really seeing them, a lonely figure on foot amongst the towering bank buildings and executive office blocks that loom overhead like black glass monoliths. A carload of inebriated college students speed past, leaning out of the open passenger windows while hooting like baboons.

There's an edge of desperation to these after-hours revelers, as they chase after parties while the city winds down around them like a clockwork toy. In another hour or two the taxis and limousines will glide back to wherever it is they go during the day, to be replaced by boxy vans making dawn deliveries to restaurants and hotels, before the crush of commuter traffic turns the wide, empty boulevards into temporary parking lots.

A limo pulls up to the curb beside me, its sleek surface as shiny as a beetle's carapace. I see myself reflected in silvery glass as impassive and unreadable as my own mirrored gaze. The rear passenger window slides down, revealing an older, heavyset man with a bad comb-over. The tie of his business suit is loose and the collar of his shirt is smeared with lipstick. An attractive young woman with unfocused eyes is seated beside him, smiling vacantly at nothing in particular, CK1 coming off her in waves.

"Hey, baby," the john leers. "Wanna party?"

The john's companion leans across him to address me. "Yeah—y'wanna party, honey?" She takes one look at me and the coked-up smile disappears.

I instinctively take a step back from the curb when I realize I've been made. Most humans can't pick up on my vibe, unless they're drunk or messed up on drugs. And the party doll qualifies on both levels. "No, thanks," I reply.

"Your loss, baby," the john says, with a shrug. The window glides back up as the limo pulls away.

I continue walking. I have no destination in mind, merely somewhere I'm headed from. I still haven't decided whether or not I should go back. Part of me wonders whether I did the right thing, walking out like I did. That's probably the one thing humanity fears worse than death: deciding whether to take action or do nothing. So many people spend their lives in perpetual stasis, just so they never have to figure out for themselves what to do—or not do, as the case may be. It's so much easier to allow things to happen to you, rather than take action. I could have fucked Estes; it would have been the easy thing to do. Instead I walked out of the room. But why?

Was I afraid of getting too close? Was I scared of weakening my control over the whole situation? Over Estes? Or was I afraid it would change things between us, and not for the better?

No. Although all of those are good answers, none of them are true. My reason for leaving had nothing to do with the fear of intimacy. I left because I knew I was about to kill him.

Still, there's no denying I wanted him to hold me; that I *needed* to be held. After a while, I hunger for the heat of intimacy. When you're isolated from others, even the most fleeting of physical contact takes on great meaning. Humans are social beasts; they aren't meant to exist in a vacuum. The need to belong, to be part of something other than yourself is strong. That's why vampires take human lovers and create broods. After all, *enkidu* society is simply human nature viewed through a dark mirror with a crack down its middle.

I'm lonely. Horribly, painfully lonely. Damn, I miss Palmer sometimes. For all his moodiness, he at least had a funny bone. Estes' sense of humor is sorely underdeveloped. Still, there's something about him that resonates with me, and has done so from the moment I first laid eyes on him. Perhaps what attracts me to him is a different human need, one nearly as basic as feeding one's belly and replicating the species: the need to be understood.

An Atlanta Police Department cruiser turns a corner two blocks ahead of me, and I reflexively head down the next side street. I'm halfway down the block before I realize it is a dead end, cut off by one of the numerous creeks that lace the city like the veins of a leaf.

However, the red taillights glowing in the turnaround tell me I'm far from alone. I recognize the parked vehicle as the limousine with the john and his companion for the night. Judging from the way the limo is bouncing on its suspension, the party is well under way.

As I turn to leave, the rear driver's-side door flies open and the party doll tumbles out onto the street, accompanied by a stream of curses. She gives a frightened cry as she hits the pavement. I watch as she struggles to pick herself up off the ground, but the best she can manage is crawling on her hands and knees.

The john climbs out of the limo after her, his pudgy face contorted in rage. The crotch of his expensive suit is covered in vomit.

"Goddamn fuckin' whore! You puked all the fuck over me!" He grabs her by the hair like a pony, yanking her head up and back.

"Please, mister… I didn't mean it… I'm feelin' sick…"

"I didn't lay down two balloons of smack for you to give me a fuckin' Roman shower, bitch!" the john snaps, shaking the party doll like a maraca.

This is none of my business. I should simply turn and walk away. But the malevolence radiating from this man draws me closer. Being in the presence of human cruelty is… enticing. It's like walking past a bakery and catching the aroma of freshly baked bread. I feel something stirring in the back of my head, like a shark lured to the surface by chum. Although I know I should leave, I move even closer, surrendering my hiding place in the shadows.

The john turns and glowers in my direction. "What are *you* lookin' at?" He squints for a second and his scowl becomes a lewd grin. "Hey, mama! So you decided you wanna party after all, huh?"

The driver's door of the limo opens and a large man with a neck for a head climbs out. He is almost big and ugly enough to pass for an ogre.

"Get lost, bitch," he growls. "This ain't no business of yours."

He's right. There's no reason I should care about what happens to some fucked up party doll. What difference does it make to me that she's overdosed on smack, Special K, meth and whatever the hell else she's managed to shoot, snort, drop, drink and smoke in the last couple of hours? Why should I give a shit what happens to her, when it's clear she doesn't care what she does to herself?

There's no reason I should give one tenth of one percent of a rat's ass about this woman….

Except for the fact I can hear her dying in my head.

Her death sounds like a short-wave radio being moved randomly up and down the dial, dragging in a distorted jumble of words and music, growing weaker with each passing moment.

The party doll's turning blue, her pupils reduced to pinpricks. I turn my attention to the driver, trying my best to sound non-threatening. "She's of no use to you. Leave her here and I'll call 911."

"And give them my license number? I don't fuckin' think so," the driver replies tersely. As I look into his thick, brutal face, I think how easy it would be for me to kill him.

The john lets go of the party doll and nervously wipes the back of his hand across his lips. "Shit. I think she's dying." He turns to the driver, his voice rising in panic. "Nobody can know about this!"

The driver looks first at the john, then at the dying party doll, and finally at me. I can see the thoughts forming in his head as if it was made of glass. The john is a wealthy executive. If the driver helps get rid of the hooker, plus any witnesses, he'll be sitting sweet. He motions for the john to get back in the limo.

"But what about her—?" The john points at the party doll sprawled in the gutter.

"What about her? Just get in the fuckin' car!" The driver stabs a thick finger at me. "You, too, bitch!"

I look down at the party doll. The signal coming from her is weak, but distinct. There are no more voices in her head, just a melancholy tune, like a music box playing unheard in a deserted attic. She turns her face to me and I see a flash of the girl she should have been in her eyes, like a ghost glimpsed at a dusty window. And then the music stops.

As I stare at the dead girl sprawled at my feet, I'm reminded of another young woman who had been tossed into the gutter from the back of a stranger's car. That girl's name was Denise Thorne, and she died in the streets of London's East End over thirty years ago, after being violated in every way possible. As the life drained from her torn veins, Denise had watched the world turn from Technicolor to sepia as a terrible sea change overtook her, body and soul, transforming her from a human girl into… me.

As the memories of Denise's last breath echo within my skull, I feel a cold, hard rage flowing up my spine, raising the hair along the nape of my neck.

"I *said* get in the car, bitch!"

I move so fast the driver doesn't realize he's been hurt. His right hand clutches the lapel of my jacket, but he can't seem to tighten his grip. He frowns at the thin red line that has appeared about his wrist, like a bracelet made of crimson string. His fingers suddenly spasm and jerk, like the legs of a dying spider, as his hand bends back at an impossible angle, then falls off his wrist.

The driver's eyes bug out like a squeezed bullfrog's as he clutches his wrist with his remaining hand, the blood shooting out between his fingers like water from a hose. The smell is ripe and red, thick with terror-born adrenaline, and it's more than I can resist. I leap onto the driver like a child greeting her father from work, bearing him down to the pavement with such force that spinal fluid sprays out his ears as his head makes contact with the pavement.

Although he's technically dead, the driver's blood still bears the heat of a living heart. His stolen vitality rushes through my system, restoring my energy and heightening my senses to the brink of rapture. As I drink, I experience a deep satisfaction accompanied by a dire trembling, as if breaking a week-long fast while riding a roller coaster. I get to my feet while wiping my mouth on the back on my hand. I feel much better now that the blood lust has been fed. It's easier for me to think. I stare down at the driver's thuggish face, rendered impotent by death. A glimmer of amazement can be seen in his cooling eyes, as if still surprised by his inability to escape the fate dealt him.

The john is still cowering in the back of the limo, his Mack Daddy, bitch-slappin' fantasies long since dissolved into pants-wetting terror.

"Hey, stud—y'wanna party?" I purr, sliding across the seat.

The john opens his mouth but all that comes out in a strangled noise. His face contorts painfully as he clutches his chest with hands as gnarled as tree roots.

"What's the matter, tiger?" I sneer. "Am I too much woman for you?"

The john gasps and flails at the upholstery. He kicks the wet bar, sending a bottle of tequila and a couple of crack pipes flying. Judging from the open bottle of Viagra lying on the floor of the limo, I'm probably not the only reason for his throwing a thrombo. I watch the john struggle against the inevitable for a few more moments, before growing bored and leaving in mid-infarction.

I step out of the limo and carefully remove the party doll's body from the gutter, propping her up next to the dying john. I smooth out her skirt and make sure her hair is out of her face.

I return the driver to his place behind the wheel, propping his left hand on the steering wheel while placing the right one in his lap, palm-up, like a dead white spider.

I glance one final time into the back seat. The john has stopped making noise and his lips are blue. If I wanted, I could dial into his mind to read his last, few dying thoughts, but I have no interest in sullying myself like that. My gaze, instead, lingers on the body of the party doll; except for the dried vomit crusting her lips, she could almost pass for living.

How strange that a woman so hardened by life that she allowed herself to be treated like so much meat could become, upon her death, as delicate as the rarest of orchids. It reminds me of just how fragile humans truly are, and that triggers a twinge of concern for Estes' well being.

I sigh and turn away from the tableau before me, heading back in the direction of the hotel. As much as I would like to run away, Estes is far safer when I am around than on his own.

Man, responsibility's a bitch.

Estes stared at the thin gruel of partially digested food and stomach acid sprayed across the bathroom's sink, toilet tank, and guest towels, his eyes stinging as if they'd been rolled in margarita salt. Although there hadn't been that much in his stomach, he still managed to paint half the room with it.

Normally he didn't drink. It dulled the mind, lowered the reflexes, and made him susceptible to depression. Alcohol helped him forget, but sometimes forgetting wasn't a good thing. Take Sonja, for example. Even though she understood where he was coming from better than anyone in the world, the truth of the matter was that she was not a human being. He had almost succeeded in forgetting that little fact—until he saw her eyes. The whites had been filled with blood, as if the eyeball itself had ruptured, and the pupils resembled something dragged from the bottom of the sea.

The very memory was enough to make Estes' body convulse. It felt like his stomach was caught on a fishhook and someone was trying to reel it out through his mouth.

He leaned forward, peering into the puke-spattered mirror, watching his own eyes, as if he could somehow see into the mind of his reflection. A feeling of panic combined with deep despair came over him, wrapping his heart in layers of regret twenty times heavier than lead. The part of him in denial kept insisting things could be as they had been before; that nothing had changed between him and Sonja. And as much as he wanted to believe that, he knew it was a lie.

Estes looked at the face of the fool in the mirror and saw the devastation in his eyes. This is what he got for letting his emotions get the better of him. In a moment of weakness, he had placed the entire mission in jeopardy. Everything he had worked for since leaving the Institute was on the verge of being undone, leaving nothing but blasted stumps and shifting sand. Without Sonja, his chances of successfully infiltrating Noir's stronghold were slim to none. And he had no one to blame but himself. But what cut him deeper than a surgeon's knife was the knowledge he had made an idiot of himself in front of her. Sonja's opinion had always mattered to him, but until that moment he did not realize just how much.

Stupid. Estes smashed a fist into his head hard enough to make himself stagger. *Stupid, stupid bastard.* The second blow was hard enough to split his lower lip. Fresh blood filled his mouth, replacing the bitter taste of bile.

Moaning in disgust, Estes pushed open the bathroom door and peered out into the darkened hotel room. The only light was that cast by the flickering television. "Sonja?"

He knew there would be no answer, even as he called her name. His mouth now ached as badly as his head, each throbbing to its own beat. Estes rubbed the back of his hand across his lower lip; it came away crimson.

Despite its size, the room seemed close and cramped, as if the walls were closing in on him. He staggered over to the sliding glass door that opened onto the balcony and pushed it open. The curtains billowed inward, lifted by a gust of night air, wrapping him in a gauzy embrace. His claustrophobia abated, Estes unceremoniously crawled into bed.

All he wanted was the room to stop spinning. And, after he passed out, it did.

***

Estes didn't know how long he had been asleep or what woke him up. One moment he was unconscious, the next he was lying on his back, straining to catch the sound of a muted footfall on the carpeted floor.

He raised himself on one elbow, scanning the darkened room for signs of movement. His free hand automatically felt under the pillow beside him, seeking the Bowie knife he kept there.

"Sonja—?"

As if prompted by his whisper, a figure emerged from the shadows clotted at the foot of the bed. Estes, his thoughts still fogged from alcohol and sleep, could not make out much detail, save that his visitor was female, then he saw the glimmer of light reflecting from mirrored sunglasses. He relaxed his grip on the knife's hilt.

"L-look," he stammered, his cheeks flushing with embarrassment. "About what happened earlier… I'm really sorry—I was drunk…"

Sonja shook her head and placed a finger to her lips, signaling him to remain silent. Before he could say anything further, she lifted the blanket and crawled under the covers. As she pressed her naked body next to him, he wasn't sure whether he should be pleased or shocked. He lay there, dumbstruck, uncertain as to what to do or say as she caressed his abdomen, gently brushing the back of her lower arm against his pubic bone. He took a sharp, short intake of breath between his teeth as she unzipped his pants, setting free his erection. He shuddered as her nimble fingers, cool and dry as snakeskin, wrapped about his penis, expertly pumping its length. The speed and force of the climax that overtook him made him roll his eyes back in his head as he arched his back, his hips thrusting upward with each spurt of semen. Shuddering like a winded stallion, he reached out to run his fingers through Sonja's short, spiky hair, only to find them buried, instead, in long, silken locks.

Estes locked the thing masquerading as Sonja in a stranglehold, pressing the tip of the Bowie knife against the soft underside of its jaw. The vampire's face shimmered like heat rising from a summer sidewalk, and Sonja's features were replaced by those even more familiar.

"Is this any way to treat your mother?" Gloria Estes asked, her voice as sweet and sharp as a honeyed blade.

Estes ground his teeth, fighting the urge to recoil from the thing he held in his arms. "You're *not* my mother," he whispered hoarsely. "My mother is dead."

Gloria grinned, displaying fangs better suited for the mouth of a wild animal. "Is that why you ran away when you recognized me? Because I'm *not* your mother? I knew who *you* were the moment I saw you. A mother can *always* tell her own." She gave him a knowing looks. "You've grown into such a strong, handsome man, Jack. If your father had been half as virile as you, I never would have been tempted to go elsewhere for companionship…"

"*Shut up!*" Estes tightened his grip on the hilt of his knife. The anger rising within him was so great it was in danger of sealing off his larynx. "Shut up, or I'll pit you like an olive! I swear it! My mother would never have done what you did to me—*never*!"

"I'm sorry you didn't enjoy it like you seemed to," the thing that wore his mother's skin mother purred. "But I promise nobody will *ever* know. It will be *our* little secret. You're good at keeping secrets, aren't you, Jack? After all, you never told the police *I* was the one who killed your father…"

"I said *shut up*!"

Once Estes had believed he would never see his mother again, and now all he wanted was to kill her. Every word out of her mouth burned him like acid. He wanted her to stop saying things he never wanted to hear. The anger and betrayal and shame buzzed in the back of his head like angry wasps, until the rage drained the color from the edges of his sight, turning the world from color into starkly defined black and white; a world where there was only light and shadow, and only one way to respond to the face of evil.

"*Estes—no!*"

Sonja, the *real* one, this time, was standing in the doorway of the hotel room, her arms held out as if trying to stop an oncoming locomotive.

"Don't do it, man! Let her go."

Estes shook his head in disbelief. "Let her *go*? Are you crazy? She's one of *them*!"

"Don't you think I *know* that? But this is not for *you* to do. You can't kill her—not like this. Not in anger. That's what *he* wants."

The buzzing in Estes' head grew louder, as if someone had turned up the volume in order to drown out her voice. He swallowed and blinked rapidly, bringing the knife closer to Gloria's throat. The vampire made a low growling noise, like that of an angry cat, but did not offer to move. Somehow, Estes knew the screeching inside his skull would not stop until he buried the silvered blade of the Bowie knife into the she-demon's cold, unbeating heart...

Sonja stepped forward, her voice echoing like the ocean within conch.

"Let go of him."

Estes frowned and nervously cast his gaze about the room. "Who the hell are you talking to? There's no one else here."

Sonja acted as if she had not heard him. She stood at the foot of the bed, her arms held straight to her sides, fists clenched tight, staring off into space with an intent look on her face.

Something *pushed* Estes' brain as if an invisible hand was inside his skull and pressing the flat of its palm against his frontal lobes. The screeching inside his head became so loud he forgot everything but the agony reverberating between his ears. He let go of both the vampiress and the knife, and he curled into a fetal ball, wrapping his arms around his head.

Sonja stood transfixed at the foot of the bed, her gaze focused on something only she could see. She did not move as Gloria, pale and naked as the moon, ran past her and out onto the balcony.

As suddenly as it arrived, the feedback coursing through Estes' brain was gone. Sonja's dropped heavily onto the corner of the bed, her shoulders slumping in obvious exhaustion.

"*This* is why I never use hotels," she wheezed.

Estes raised his head and stared at Sonja with angry, accusing eyes. "You let her get away."

"I couldn't let you kill her," she said, gasping as if she'd just dashed up several flights of stairs. "That would be playing into his hands. Besides, I was too busy kicking Noir out of your head to deal with her. Noir wanted you to damn yourself. And in order to do that he had to make sure you killed your mother. Not out of love and mercy, but out of hate and anger. He was even willing to use a little long-range telepathy to make sure you got the job done. I had to run some interference to break his grip."

"That bastard!" Estes spat in disgust. "Did she know that's why he sent her to me?"

"Does it matter? Noir is her Maker. Gloria has as much free will as a piece of furniture; she is his to use or destroy as he sees fit." Sonja motioned to the slowly brightening sky. "It'll be dawn shortly, and I need a rest. It's clear they know where and who we are—or at last who *you* are. *Tête-à-têtes* burn up a lot of energy, and pushing Noir out of your head sapped what few energy reserves I have. I'm going to need everything I've got if we're going to survive the next twenty-four hours. The first thing we do is check out of here and find someplace safe... the sooner the better." She stood up, swaying slightly on her feet. She frowned and shook her head, as if trying to clear it. "Son of a *bitch*—"

"Sonja—what's wrong?"

"The fucking driver must have just dropped something just before I..."

"What are you talking about?"

Sonja didn't answer him, but instead dropped heavily onto the bed, her voice slurred. "Not ready for this... *Ssshit*."

She pitched backward across the mattress and stopped breathing. Estes nudged her, but she remained motionless as a stone. He grabbed her shoulders and shook her as hard as he could, but it was no use. Since it was obvious he was not going to be able to wake her up, he closed the sliding door that opened onto the balcony, locking it behind him. He then dragged a chair into the middle of the room, so he could maintain surveillance of every window and door while keeping an eye on Sonja. Come dusk she would awaken, as would Noir. Until then, it was up to him to keep watch.

Estes mulled over what Sonja had said. It was clear Noir knew who he was—otherwise why send his mother to him? But why not simply command Gloria to kill him, instead of toying with him in such a disgusting manner?

Whether she was intended as an assassin or sacrificial victim, Noir's motive had been to trick him into matricide. Sonja had said something about damnation, but it was not as if he didn't already bear the mark of Cain on his brow. In his own way, he was as foul a murderer as the creatures he was sworn to destroy.

Since the night Sonja plucked the faux-vampire skull from his collection, Estes had wracked his brains trying to remember which one it could have been. There were so many, they tended to blur together after time, which frightened him all the more. Had it been the malnourished Goth punk dressed in the black lace T-shirt and fingerless leather gloves, or the fashionably dressed young woman with the neon-purple hair and Nefertiti eye makeup? Perhaps it was the tall, elegantly attired older gentleman with the shaved head and ivory-handled cane, or the six-foot-plus transsexual with the receding hairline and fullback shoulders in the black wedding dress? He could still hear their voices pleading with him, begging him to spare their lives. Their cries for mercy were mixed with the gunfire that had ultimately silenced them, echoing in his head like a distant cathedral bell, tolling for the dead.

For the first time since setting out on the life he had chosen, Estes felt adrift. He became a vampire hunter because it was the only way to prove that he was truly sane. He knew what he'd seen that terrible night had been real, and that the doctors' glib rationalizations were nothing but lies. So he had made himself into a living weapon, dedicated to the eradication of the horror that had so callously intruded upon his life. But he had never meant to harm the innocent; his mission was to slay vampires, not murder humans.

He had started on this mad journey to prove his sanity, but now he doubted his reason more than ever. He had set out to hunt monsters, only to find that he, himself, had become one. What, if anything, could he possibly do to atone for such sins?

The knock on the door startled him from his reverie. Judging from the light seeping in from the window, it was probably nine o'clock in the morning. There was a second, louder knock, accompanied by the rattling of keys. He moved to the door, gun at ready.

"Who is it?"

"Housekeeping," came the muffled reply.

Estes put one eye to the peephole and peered through the fish-eye lens into the hallway. A woman dressed in maid's whites, her back to the door, was busying herself with a service cart stacked with fresh linens, clean ashtrays, and rolls of toilet tissue.

"Come back later."

"Okay, mister. You need clean towels before I go?"

He glanced back at the bathroom and the vomit-encrusted bath linen hanging over the toilet tank.

"Okay. Just leave them by the door."

As the maid turned to face the door, her arms laden with clean towels, Estes could clearly see that she was in the final months of pregnancy.

Suddenly something the size and shape of a refrigerator filled the peephole, driving the door into Estes' face, felling him like an axe.

Ygon sniffed the human male and lifted his lip in a growl, exposing the two-inch tusks jutting from his lower gums.

"Why this one?" The ogre asked petulantly, his voice reverberating like a kettledrum.

"It is not up to you to question his lordship's decisions," Lady Madonna snapped as she rolled the service cart into the room. "Now shut up and put the door back in place."

Ygon grunted and shrugged his wide shoulders as he realigned the hotel room door with its jamb as best as the broken hinges would allow. He had learned not to argue with Noir's lieutenant over the years.

"His will be done," the ogre growled. "But I still do not understand why we should bring the man if it is the woman his lordship wants."

"We are to capture the male so that the female will follow."

Ygon scratched his skull, perplexed. "But the female is here," he said, jabbing a meaty finger at Sonja's motionless body "Why not take her now?"

"Because this is how Lord Noir said it was to be done!" Lady Madonna replied tartly as she removed a garment bag from the service cart and tossed it to the ogre. "Now stop trying to think and prepare him for travel! Every minute we dawdle, we run the risk of someone finding the housekeeper's body."

Lady Madonna casually shed the white housekeeper's dress, dropping it aside like a snake abandoning its skin, and stood naked in the middle of the hotel room. As she rubbed her hands over her distended belly like a fortuneteller trying to coax the future from a crystal ball, a bas-relief impression of the fetus appeared just below her skin, like a hungry man peering through the window of a bakery. She smiled, as if sharing a joke only she could hear, and removed her clothes from their hiding place underneath a pile of towels on the service cart.

Ygon maneuvered the unconscious human into the garment bag as easily as a father might tuck a slumbering child into bed. As he zippered the bag up, he was careful to make sure there was at least an inch of open space, since Lord Noir had insisted the human not suffocate in transit.

Dead. Alive. It was all pretty much the same to Ygon, at least as far as humans were concerned. However, the ogre had long since learned never to thwart the vampire lord's will.

"All is ready," Ygon growled.

Lady Madonna was standing at the foot of the bed, staring at the vampiress who lay atop the covers.

"Lord Noir is playing with fire with this one," she said, shaking her head in dismay.

"But you said it is not our place to question..." Ygon said petulantly.

"I *know* what I said, you bullet-headed ape!" she snapped, slapping him upside the head. The ogre didn't even so much as flinch. "Now let's get out of here!"

The concierge looked up upon hearing the ping of the elevator doors. Since it was his job to hail taxis, hold baggage and supply guests with information as to nearby restaurants and tourist attractions, the bell always drew his attention, no matter what time of day it might be. During his tenure he had seen every possible variation of man and wife stroll across the lobby of the Peachtree Park Hotel. But he had to admit that the couple that exited the elevator that morning was amongst the odder ones. The woman wasn't that unusual, really, except that her demeanor was extremely hard-bitten for someone so pregnant. Her companion, on the other hand, would have raised eyebrows even in a circus.

Although slightly stooped from the weight of the garment bag he carried over one shoulder, the man was easily seven feet tall, the top of the pregnant woman's head barely reaching his chest. Judging from the width of his shoulders and shaved head, the concierge assumed him to be a professional athlete of some sort—probably a Falcons fullback or a pro wrestler.

The concierge tried to imagine how such a physically mismatched pair managed to have sex, but his mind blanched at the thought. Some things, he decided, were better left unknown.

Estes regained consciousness wrapped in a plastic shroud. He coughed violently, struggling to suck clean air into his aching lungs, his skin covered by a clammy sheath of condensed breath. He found himself free of the fetid darkness, as he was dumped onto a bare concrete floor. The stacks of cardboard boxes and five-gallon plastic containers of peanuts and mini-pretzels lined against the wall told him he was in the basement of Dolly Dagger's. As he tried to get to his feet, a hand the size of a Virginia ham dropped onto the back of his neck.

"Ah. Estes the Younger. It has been some time since we last met." Although the Afro and turtleneck had been exchanged for fashionable dreadlocks and a Brooks Brothers suit, the vampire's face was unchanged since Estes had last seen him.

Estes tried to see if there were any other doors in or out of the room, but the ogre's fingers tightened on the back of his neck, causing him to grimace in pain.

"Do not try anything foolish, dear boy," Noir said, matter-of-factly. A palpable evil, like the stench of rotten garbage riding a hot, dry wind, radiated from his smile. "Ygon is more than willing—and able, I dare say—to tear your head from your shoulders."

"*Blackheart!*" Estes spat the word as if it had curdled in his mouth.

The vampire stepped forward, moving in a stately pantomime of normalcy. "Ah! That name brings back memories! However, I no longer go by that *nom de guerre*. You can call me by the name I took upon my resurrection..."

"Lord Noir," Estes said, finishing the sentence.

Noir paused for the slightest moment; eyebrow lifted, and then grinned like a beast born of distant, hungry jungles. "Did you find that bit of information on your own, or did your mistress tell you? I know you fancy yourself a vampire hunter, but it *was* your mistress who ferreted me out, isn't that right?"

"Sonja is not my—it's not like that between us."

"Oh? You are not her minion?"

"No! I'm—she's my friend."

Noir snorted in derision. "Call it what you wish, my boy! You are hers, of that I am certain. Although, I must say, you have handled yourself fairly well for a human. I saw much within you during our brief *tête-à-tête*."

"Since you're being so talkative, would you mind telling me how long I was unconscious?"

"Less than an hour," Noir replied. "Nightfall will not be for some time. Not that sunlight could ever find its way down here."

"Why did you bring me here? Why not simply have your goons kill me at the hotel and get it over with?"

"You misunderstand, my boy," the vampire lord said with a deceptively easy smile. "Granted, I *am* willing to kill you, but only if you leave me no other choice. No, I brought you here so you could join me."

"What makes you think I would want to do that? You're the bastard who killed my father!"

"*Au contraire*, young Estes. Your father killed himself. Slit his throat from ear to ear."

"Only because you made him!"

Noir nodded his head, as if conceding a point. "It *is* true I danced the silly fool like the puppet he was. But your father's fate was sealed the moment he chose to steal from me. It's as simple as that. It is something of a habit of mine, destroying those who would betray me. I've gotten quite good at it, over the centuries.

"Still, I do not understand why you hate me so. Certainly your father's death was no great loss to you. The man was rarely home, and when he *was* there, did he really have time for you? Isn't hating me simply a safer means of channeling the anger you feel towards the one *truly* responsible for ruining your life? Believe me, I *know* what it is like to want to kill your father. I even know what it is like to *kill* my father! It is not as horrible as others have made it out to be. But in our cause, your vendetta is so unnecessary. I am not the one who destroyed your family, dear boy—your father was."

"You sound just like Dr. Morrissey," Estes growled. "He kept insisting there weren't any monsters in the world, only guilt and shame."

"A wise man, indeed. You should have heeded his words, young Estes. Now that I think of it, you should be *grateful* for all I have done for you. If it were not for me, you'd be just another Southern California Gen-Xer with divorced parents, a problem with alcohol and an inability to maintain a committed relationship. You certainly would not have become the dedicated killing machine that you are now.

"A boy is shaped by his father far more than any other man in his life, and you must admit I have shaped your mind and manners beyond anything Franklin Estes ever could. You are as much my son as his—perhaps more so. When I look into your eyes, boy, I see loneliness without break or pause. You walk in darkness, you live in darkness; your bread is death and your wine the blood of enemies. In that you are as much my son as if you had sprung from my loins.

"You are an orphan, bereft of family and future. I, *too*, know what it is like to be cast adrift and denied your birthright; to be made an outsider against your will. I *know* what it is to walk apart from the common herd. By joining me, you will be part of a family knit far tighter than any born of man and woman. Once initiated into my brood, you will be accepted without qualm or hesitation. You will be brother and son to your mother, just as she will be sister and wife to you. You will be both son and grandchild to me, for I am the fountainhead from which all things flow."

Noir leaned forward, his placing his words chill upon Estes' cheek. "Besides, who do you think you are protecting? Humanity? If your kind can turn a blind eye to the pedophiles and serial killers amongst their number, how much easier is it for them to pretend more arcane predators don't exist? Man lives cheek-by-jowl with monsters, but pretends he does not see them, because it is easier that way. Better to be selectively blind than to see ugly truth—that is the human way.

"Humans are thankless, thoughtless beasts, more apt to turn on those who would save them than those who prey upon them. If you were to walk up to someone on the street and tell them that there are vampires loose in the world, would that person thank you for the warning? Of course not! He would call you insane and try to have you locked up some place where your words would not be heard or believed.

"If the police ever got their hands upon you, would they recognize your handiwork for what it is? More likely they would call *you* the monster and stick you in that rogue's gallery of mass murderers and serial killers your species is so adept at producing. They would look at your past and cluck their tongues about how yet another madman was set loose upon society. *All* your work, *all* your efforts to prove yourself, would be for nothing.

"However, I could use someone like you, Jack. To have a skilled vampire hunter in my service would give me an edge against my enemies within the Ruling Class. Renfields and ogres have their uses, but they are nothing compared to a trained assassin. You can still kill vampires to your heart's content—but only the ones I tell you to. Come now, boy, what say you? Why waste your life and energy on defending a species content to march in lockstep to the slaughterhouse? Better to join my little family than to forever wander the world a pariah."

Estes turned his face to Noir. They were so close their noses touched. The vampire lord drew back, aware that he was being seen not as how he wished to be perceived, but for what he truly was: an inhuman thing.

"I don't know if you're right about mankind or not," Estes replied, his voice dripping with contempt. "But I will agree with you on one thing: you *did* shape my destiny. It was you who forged me into the instrument of your destruction."

All pretense of affability dropped from Noir's face, leaving it as rigid as a plank. "Tie him up. I have grown weary of talking to this fool," he said, with a terse, dismissive motion of his hand.

Ygon grunted and produced a length of clothesline from his coat pocket. Estes gritted his teeth as the ogre trussed him up like a Christmas turkey. Once he was finished, all he could do was lie on his side on the cold, hard floor of the basement.

Noir squatted beside Estes, studying his captive's face with the dispassion of an entomologist watching a mildly interesting species of beetle meet its end in a killing jar. Now that he was no longer pretending to care, Noir's otherness was as blatant as exposed genitalia.

"You love your truth so much?" the vampire lord hissed. "Then you shall have it. I have no real interest in acquiring you for my brood. You are nothing more than bait. It is your 'friend' I want, the one they call the Blue Woman. She will come for you."

"How can you be so sure?"

"Because I know vampires, my dear boy. And a vampire *always* comes to claim those humans who belong to it."

Noir stood up, dusted off his knees with a brisk clap of his hands, and headed back up the stairs, leaving Estes alone in the cellar with only the ogre for company. Ygon shifted his weight from one foot to the other, absently cracking his enormous knuckles, and then dropped down onto his haunches, his arms dangling between his knees like those of an ape.

Estes had not felt so helpless since his resistance to Dr. Morrissey's version of reality had landed him in the Box. At least the Box had padded floors.

After a couple of hours of discomfort, Estes lost consciousness, only to awake with a start. As he tried to reorient himself to his surroundings, he heard the telltale click of high heels on the concrete floor. He tried to look around, but it was impossible to see who was there. A familiar female voice spoke up.

"His lordship needs you upstairs."

Ygon stood up and rolled his shoulders. "As he wills, milady." He nodded to where Estes lay on the floor. "What of this one?"

A pair of women's feet shod in black patent leather entered Estes' limited field of vision. "I am to watch him."

As Ygon clomped up the stairs, the woman rolled Estes onto his back with a kick of her pumps. It was the pregnant maid from the hotel, except now she was dressed in a bright red skintight knit mini-dress that made her look like a candy apple on a stick.

"Who are you?" He whispered hoarsely.

"They call me Madonna. *Lady* Madonna," she replied, sneering.

"You're human, aren't you? How could you do this?" he asked, appalled. "How can you ally yourself with monsters? What about your child? What do you think these creatures will do to it once it's born?"

Lady Madonna tossed back her head and laughed, sounding more hyena than human.

"What do I *think* will become of my child? There's not a moment goes by when I *don't* think of him—or *he* of *me*!" She dropped to her knees beside Estes, staring intently into his face. "How pregnant am I?"

"What—?"

"How many months along do you think I am, you ninny!" she snapped.

Estes frowned, uncertain of where this line of questioning was going. "I... I don't know—seven months, eight?"

"Try three-hundred and sixty." The look of shock that crossed his face triggered another burst of humorless laughter from her. "I've been like this since *1971!* I started out as a dancer, like the girls upstairs; except back then it was just topless, none of this bottomless stuff. Then the guy who owned the club where I was dancing knocked me up. Suddenly I was out on the streets with no way to make a living and too far gone to get a legit doctor to take care of things. I ended up going to this back-alley quack. When I met him, I could tell he was weird, but beggars can't be choosers, right? When I came to, the weirdo was gone, my neck was torn up, and I was still pregnant.

"At first I thought I got burned by some psycho pervert, but it didn't take long for me to figure out that something was different. The baby didn't move around like he used to. During the day he just lay there in my belly, motionless, but the moment the sun went down, he began kicking like crazy. Hell, I couldn't sleep at night anymore he was so active! I also started to get cravings. Not for pickles and ice cream and shit like that. I wanted raw liver and fresh ox blood. I wasn't sure what was happening to me, at first, but I had a pretty good idea it had something to do with the quack biting me.

"I tried to find others like me, you know, thinking I could fit in with them. I didn't know how much vampires loathe pregnant women, though. That was bad enough, but when they realized I was a living human woman with an undead child in my belly, they went ape-shit! If it hadn't been for Lord Noir, we would never have made it to sun-up.

"Lord Noir didn't want to destroy me. He said we weren't an Abomination, but an oddling—just like him. He said oddlings were unique , each special in its own way. That's why the regular vampires hated us so—because we weren't exactly like them. Lord Noir took us in and made us part of his operation. For the first time we didn't have to worry about being found out by humans or hunted down by rival broods. Lord Noir protected and sheltered us as if we were his own. He is our liege and lord; his will is ours. And Lord Noir has willed that you join us." She shook her head in disdain as Estes struggled in against his bonds. "That will do you no good. Even if you somehow managed to free yourself, there is no escaping his will." Lady Madonna stood up and took a few steps away from where Estes lay, then squatted and leaned back, planting her elbows against the floor, spreading open her legs so that he was able to see her naked sex. Estes' cheeks colored and he averted his eyes as best he could, but was helpless to look away.

Lady Madonna began to pant loudly, her breath coming in short, precise gasps, punctuated by grunts of pain, as she labored to expel the thing inside her. Instead of the hours it would normally take, the top of the baby's head crowned between her legs within a matter of minutes. As he watched, Estes realized the reason the delivery was so rapid was because the infant was actively participating in its own birth.

With a sudden burst of frenzied wriggling, its head and shoulders popped free of the birth canal, its tiny, ferret-like nails scraping against the floor. The scrawny creature that emerged, red and slick, from Lady Madonna's womb more closely resembled a skinned rabbit than a human child. It lay motionless for a long moment, then raised its oversized head and opened its mouth, giving voice to a weird, thin cry, like that of a kitten, exposing a pair of tiny fangs in otherwise naked gums.

It wasn't a baby so much as it was a fetus: an unfinished thing, with spongy, pinkish tissue in place of skin and dark-adapted eyes. It flopped about like a landed fish for a few moments, squirming on its back, the garnet-colored eyes open and closing like those of a baby owl in the unaccustomed light. After a few seconds it seemed to orient itself and flipped onto its belly, lifting its upper torso off the ground with its surprisingly well-developed forearms, like an iguana sunning itself on a rock. The fetus's hairless head was unnaturally large in comparison to its stick-like legs and starved-dog ribcage, causing it to wobble and bob like a balloon on a stick. It sniffed the air with a stunted, upturned nose, hissing like a basket of snakes.

"Dear God," Estes whispered in open horror.

The fetus snapped its head in the direction of his voice and made an eager gurgling cooing sound, like a baby who has spotted its favorite toy. Pulling itself along with its clawed hands, it crawled forward, an obscene mechanical doll dragging the umbilical cord behind it like a lap of gut.

"What's the matter, Jack?" Lady Madonna said with a laugh. "Don't you like children?"

The sun is hanging on the horizon by the time I reach Dolly Dagger's. Within a few minutes it will be gone completely. I curse myself for the fool I am; I should never have taken blood from the driver. Although the rush that comes from tapping live victims is immediate, the effects of any impurities in their systems is delayed by digestion, and even then the drugs often don't have the same effect on me that they would on the original user. As late as it may be for Estes and myself, it is still early for the club's clientele, and my rental car is the only vehicle in the lot.

I know the game Noir's playing. These goddamn Nobles always make things far more complicated and dramatic than they need to be. If he wanted me dead, it would have been simple enough for his minions to slaughter me in the hotel. No, he wants to recruit me, so he draws me onto his turf, assuming Estes is my renfield, and I'll come to reclaim him. Well, he's half right about that.

The front door of the club is shut and bolted from the inside. I unlock it with my right boot. Fuck stealth. They know I'm coming, and I know they know I'm coming.

The lights lining the runway are off and the chairs are stacked atop the tables, legs jutting towards the ceiling. My footsteps echo hollowly as I move across the room. I know they're here. I can feel their eyes on me. Underneath the reek of stale cigarette smoke and industrial-strength floor cleanser is another stench, like forgotten gardens left to rot in their own fecundity. It's the smell of the female of species. The silence is broken by a shrill, tittering laugh, like that of a schoolgirl giggling at a dirty joke. I turn to face the runway. There are four of them: the first is a tall, well-built African-American woman with elaborately corn-rowed hair; the second is a slender Korean girl; the third is a redhead sporting EE-cup silicon implants; and the fourth is the dancer I recognize as Gloria Estes. All four are dressed in halter-tops, hot pants and white vinyl go-go boots. They stand in a semi-circle, glaring at me with fevered eyes that shine in the darkness like those of cats. Where the Dagger's unwitting clientele would see four sexy women, I see a quartet of harpies, their features warped out of human semblance by the hatred, greed and despair trapped within them.

"*She's* the one he wants, Foxy," Gloria says, pointing a crimson fingernail in my direction, her voice dripping with envy.

The African-American dead girl nods her head, causing her ceramic beads to rattle like hail on a tin roof. "Lord Noir is eager to have you join him," she said. "But *we* are not."

"He has *too* many brides *already*," the Korean dead girl says petulantly.

"Kim is right," Foxy says in agreement. "Isn't that so, Ginger?"

"There ain't enough of him to go 'round as is," the redhead with the scary tit job drawls. "It's bad enough we gotta share him with that Abomination, now he wants to take *you* in too!"

"Go away, oddling," Kim growls, showing her fangs. "We don't want you here!"

"You ladies have nothing to worry about," I reply. "I have no interest in joining your master's stable. I just want to kill him, that's all."

The foursome fall upon me with howls of outrage, leaping from the stage with their fangs extended and fingers hooked into claws. I throw Estes' silvered Bowie knife dagger-fashion, sending it right through the Korean's ribs and into her heart. She drops to the floor, her limbs drawing in on themselves, like those of a dying spider.

The remaining dead girls freeze, staring at the body of their fellow bride in mute amazement. They lift their heads in unison and gaze at me, bafflement in their inhuman eyes.

"*Silver,*" Foxy whispers in fearful awe. "She can touch *silver*."

"So fuckin' what?" Ginger growls. "I'm *still* going to tear her heart out and eat it raw!"

The dead girl lunges at me, talons extended, shrieking like a band saw on sheet metal. I sidestep her charge like a matador caping a bull, and my open switchblade catches her in the back, severing her spine. The exaggerated weight of her implants causes Ginger's upper torso to swing away from its lower half like a garden gate on a busted hinge.

Foxy and Gloria exchange glances and move to circle me, their eyes narrowed to slits of calculation. They hiss and spit at me like angry panthers, occasionally feinting an attack, but careful to keep outside my reach.

Gloria suddenly leaps onto my back, wrapping her dancer's legs around my waist, raking my face and head with razor-sharp talons. Foxy rushes forward, fangs bared. I turn at the last moment, allowing the vampiress to impale herself on my knife. My fist rises violently, and I pull back the blade in an eruption of viscera.

Gloria's jumps free of my back and bounds back towards the runway as her sister-bride drops to the ground. Blood streams down my back from the numerous gouges and cuts made across my scalp and shoulders. Gloria is crouched in the light rigging, glowering down at me like a treed panther.

"It's not fair," she growls. "He was willing to sacrifice *me* to make you his, and you don't even *want* him!"

"Ain't that just like a man? Now where's Jack?"

Gloria tilts her head to one side. "Who?"

"Your *son*. Where is he?"

"The Abomination has him." She thrusts her lower lip out in an exaggerated pout. "*I* wanted to be the one to Make him, but Lord Noir said no. He said it didn't really matter *who* did it, as long as it was done. That's true. Now my sweet little boy and I will be together again; and *nothing* will keep us apart!"

"Oh, yeah?"

I throw back my jacket, drawing Estes' gun from the waistband of my jeans. Gloria hisses like a frightened cat and turns to flee. I fire once and she drops onto the runway below like a cut sandbag, a silver bullet lodged in her shoulder.

I hop onto the stage and stand over the thing that had once been Estes' mother. I watch as she writhes and yowls in pain, tears of blood welling in her eyes and spilling onto her painted cheeks.

Gloria claws at her right arm with her left hand, helpless to reverse the necrosis spreading through her system, reducing her stricken limb to a mass of rotting tissue. It is only a matter of minutes before the silver contaminating her blood reaches her heart and brain, reducing them to so much bubbling sludge. I lift the gun a second time, aiming it point-blank at the dead girl's head. She turns her face to me and bares her fangs in futile rage. Blood and cerebral fluid are already leaking from her nostrils.

"My master will kill you for this, oddling!"

"He can try," I reply, as I pull the trigger. "They always try."

A piece of Gloria Estes' head splashes onto my left boot. I grimace in distaste and wipe it clean on the back of my right calf.

"I was right about you. You're good. You're *very* good."

I look in the direction of the voice and see only darkness pooled in the middle of the stage.

"Show yourself!"

There's a low, throaty laugh as the coagulated shadows slide away like oil, revealing a tall man with a coffee-colored complexion. Dressed in an impeccably tailored silk suit, with thick, heavy dreadlocks, a decorative walking stick fashioned from a single piece of ivory, and circular wire-rims the color of a billiard shade, his demeanor is one of alert, malevolent elegance.

"Lord Noir."

"You honor me," he says with a slight bow, placing one hand over his heart. "And I trust I have the pleasure of speaking with none other that the infamous Blue Woman?"

I nod cautiously but say nothing.

Noir smiles and leans on his cane, and for a second I almost expect him to break into a little soft shoe.

"Our mutual friend, the young Mr. Estes, told me very little of you, but his mind spoke volumes. You occupy his thoughts a great deal, my dear. I can see why. You are truly extraordinary!"

Noir nudges Gloria's carcass with the toe of his expensive Italian boot, and the body collapses on itself like a rapidly deflating pool toy.

"Such fatal style! Such lethal panache! You have made the extermination of your own kind into an art!"

"She was not of my own kind." Even as I say the words I realize by the way he smiles that he's caught the scent of blood in the water. It isn't good to reveal a weakness, no matter how minute, to a predator like Noir.

"Do not misunderstand me; I have no love for the undead! Those silly women you so ably destroyed were excellent examples of the breed; tiny, narrow minds occupied with the pettiest of jealousies. Their wills were mine to command, but their IQs proved so low it lead them into mischief every time my back was turned. That is why I *allowed* you to slaughter the silly bitches. Their idiocy resulted in their defying my will, and the penalty for such a transgression is death everlasting. I thank you for disposing of them for me."

"I didn't come here to help out with your domestic situation. Where's Estes?"

Noir grimaced as if he had just bitten into a sour persimmon. "Frankly, I do not understand why you are interested in that young psychopath. You have far more in common with *me* than you do with that lout. Granted, we *are* as different from one other as each of us are from the common undead.

"I have a great fondness for variants such as yourself. In the old days, oddlings were usually the result of magic, but nowadays it is science that interferes with the unnatural order of things. No doubt you were given a full transfusion after being attacked—?"

Noir leaves the question hanging, eyebrow raised, waiting for me to fill in the blanks.

"I died on the operating table, but they were able to revive me."

"The miracles of modern medicine!" Noir smirks. "The monsters it breeds! If it weren't for autopsies, the world would be hip deep in the undead!"

"What about Estes? Is he okay?"

"Lady Madonna is with him."

"That doesn't answer my question."

"Fear not. Your friend is in very... capable hands. But enough about Estes! I would much rather talk about what we share in common. Like yourself, I never asked to be this way—"

"*Bullshit!*" It is all I can do to keep from spitting when I speak. "Everyone knows *strega* use sorcery to turn themselves into vampires!"

Noir shakes "While that is true of the likes of Medea and the Bluebeard, I assure you I had no hand in my Making. As I lay dying, my mother fed me a potion brewed from the heart of a vampire, hoping it would save me. But, instead, she damned me.

"Although I did not ask for this existence, I have made the best of it, even though I have been shunned by the Ruling Class of the *enkidu*, who fear me because I am *strega*, and ignored by the Synod because I never underwent the Ritual of Making as the other *strega* have. Like yourself, I am an outsider, struggling to maintain my individuality."

"You're *nothing* like me!" I snort in derision. "You prey on humans to keep your harems fed."

"Come now! I believe you are judging me far too harshly! I do not send my children forth into the night to hunt down victims. Nor do I lure the men who come to this place, or to any of my other clubs, under false pretenses. They flock to these places on their own, like moths drawn to a flame. I do not have to cloud their minds to make them fools. It is my nature to take advantage of the weaknesses of others. Am I to be faulted for doing as I would? And what about you? Do you not prey on humans as well?"

"Only when I can't avoid it—and only with those who deserve it."

"You delude yourself, my dear, if you think you and I are so different! We *both* serve as judge, jury and executioner for those hapless enough to fall into our grasp. You and I are well suited for business together; I could tell it from the moment I saw you on the surveillance tapes.

"It has been a long time since I've looked upon another being, human or not, and felt the thrill of danger. When I gaze upon you, I feel the rush of dread that comes with knowing I am in the presence of something capable of destroying me. It has been decades since I was in the presence of such a force."

I raise my hands to stay the words flowing from him. "Wait, let me guess: You want me to join you as your lieutenant, slaying rival vampires in exchange for leaving your family alone."

Noir laughs so hard I think his dreadlocks are going to come loose. "My sweet Satan, *no!* You don't understand at *all!* I'm not interested in your *joining* me, my dear. I want you to *hunt* me!"

"You want me to *what?*" I have to admit he's caught me; I honestly can't believe what I'm hearing.

"When you have existed as long as I have, things become boring and predictable. There are no risks anymore, and I have become far too comfortable in my routine. Every night I fight off the creeping death-from-within that is the Ennui. I never thought I would come to miss the Inquisition," he said with a sigh. "Ever since the witch finders elite disbanded, it has all been downhill. There is nothing to challenge me. I am in danger of becoming old and foolish, like the museum pieces of the Ruling Class. I need someone to keep me on my toes! And I have decided that you, my lovely, are the challenge I need."

"And what if I refuse to accommodate you?"

Noir smiles at me with only half his face. The result is disconcerting. "That's why I have taken steps to make sure you will be more than eager to pursue me to the ends of the earth."

I get a cold, hard feeling in my chest, as if I've just swallowed an ice cube. "What have you done with Estes—?"

"As I said, he's keeping company with Lady Madonna. But as to his being in capable hands—well, when it comes to Lady Madonna, she's *capable* of just about *anything!*"

I leap onto the runway, switchblade in hand. I want to rip the smirking bastard's dreads off and use them for a mop. "If you've hurt him, so help me—"

The *strega* raises his left hand and says something in a language I don't recognize but don't like the sound of. Then there's a strange pulling sensation in my chest, as if my heart is a toy balloon and someone's yanking on its string. The palms of my hands are damp; I glance down and see blood rising from the pores of my skin like sweat on a summer's day. I blink in astonishment, my vision abruptly turning scarlet as tears of blood well from the corners of my eyes. My ears also fill with blood, muting my hearing as if I'd suddenly stuck my head in a bucket of water. I open my mouth and crimson vomit gushes forth. I'm hemorrhaging as if I've been stricken with instant Ebola. Too weak to stand, I drop to my knees, my eyes rolling back in my skull.

There's a thick, cloying smell of spoiled fruit, of decomposition on a grand scale, and the empty air about me fills with waxen faces, gray as bled-out meat, their glazed eyes beyond all hope and prayer. Some of the faces seem to be exulting, others appear to be in horrible pain, and all of them are dead. These are the souls of those refused access to heaven or hell, condemned to wander the path that leads to neither salvation or damnation, their wails of despair unheard, their misery unseen by all—save for the dying.

I know that if I'm to survive the blood wizard's assault, I have to reach within and call upon the one thing I fear above all else. I have to free that part of me I've worked so hard to master, the living darkness I call the Other.

I close my eyes, sending tears of blood down my cheeks, and turn my focus inward. I drop through a hole in the back of my brain, where it lies in wait, like a trapdoor spider. In a blinding brilliance that is not light, in howling quiet, I hear it breathe and feel its fetid exhalation upon my soul. The choking, acid stench of insanity tells me that I am no longer alone—the Other is in attendance.

You need my help. Again, it whispers in a viscous murmur.

"Yes." There's no lying to the creature before me, as much as I fear and loathe it. The Other knows me far better than any lover ever could.

It turns its face to me, its naked body glowing with unadulterated hatred. *What do I get out of it?*

“You get to keep existing.”

Not enough.

I’ve learned it’s better to barter with the thing than to deny it. By ignoring the Other’s urges, I only make it angry, which prompts it to fight for control of the body that we share.

“You get a kill.”

Still not enough.

“Two, then.”

It’s a deal, it says, smiling in horrible complicity.

I can feel the Other rising from the depths, like a great white drawn to the surface by the splashing of an unwary swimmer. And, God help me, my fear melts away and becomes exhilaration.

The Other tosses back its head and laughs in celebration of its release, shaking itself like a dog, sending droplets of blood flying in all directions. Noir frowns and takes a step back, sensing some sort of transformation has occurred. The Other opens its arms wide, as if greeting a long-lost fellow, and smiles through the gore caking its face.

“So, you want to play rough, huh?”

The Other reaches into its deep, black well of power and roars like a pride of lions, shaking the very foundation of Dolly Dagger’s with its ecstatic fury. Noir staggers backward, clapping his hands to his ears.

The Other continues to advance, purple-black energy crackling about its head like a rotten halo. Its smile widens and becomes a rictus-like grin, displaying every tooth in its head. It grabs Noir with its mind, digging invisible talons deep into the *strega’s* psyche.

Noir howls like a wounded animal, dropping his walking stick as he falls to his knees, blood seeping from his nostrils. Even as he writhes in pain, a look of delight crosses his face.

“You are worthier than I ever *dared* dream possible!” he gasps, wiping the blood from his upper lip. “This is going to be *so* much fun!”

The blood-wizard gestures with his right hand, and a curtain of shadow drops between the Other and its prey. The darkness pours itself across the room, leaving only an empty stage in its wake. The Other snarls in frustrated anger and claws at the fleeing shadow, but its talons connect only with thin air. Noir’s laughter rings out from nowhere and everywhere at once, his challenge echoing throughout the deserted club.

“Catch me if you caaan! Oh, and by the way—I left a little something for you in the storeroom!”

The door leading to the basement was behind the bar. As she stood on the threshold, looking down into the gloom at the foot of the stairs, she spotted a pair of legs sticking out from behind a stack of cardboard boxes, the booted feet tightly bound with a length of clothesline. The sight was enough for Sonja to push herself back into the driver's seat.

"Jack!" she shouted, trying to keep the panic from her voice.

There was a low, throaty moan, followed by the sound of an infant hungrily attacking a rubber nipple. The trussed legs jerked and trembled like those of a calf in a slaughterhouse. Sonja vaulted over the stair railing, sending the makeshift screen flying with a single kick.

Estes lay on his back, eyes rolled back in their sockets, helpless to defend himself against the hideous mockery battened onto his exposed throat. An umbilical cord trailed like a hank of slimy yarn from the vampire-child's beet-colored body, connecting it to the prone figure of Lady Madonna, who lay with her legs spread wide, moaning in an obscene parody of orgasm.

As Sonja watched in horror, a clot of stolen blood slowly pulsed its way up the cord and disappeared between Lady Madonna's thighs.

Disturbed by the intrusion, the fetus raised its oversized head and hissed at Sonja like a feral kitten defending a saucer of milk. Its face was transparent and pink, like a mask made of pig's intestines engorged with blood. Nausea rose in Sonja's throat like floodwater.

Abomination! The Other's voice shrieked within Sonja's head, its revulsion and horror even greater than her own. *Let me destroy it now!*

The Other's rage spread through Sonja like a high fever, licking the inside of her skull with tongues of fire. The hatred the approximation of a child triggered in the Other was as basic and instinctual to the *enkidu* as the fear of snakes is to humans. She could not have turned aside its murderous fury, even if she had wanted to; fighting the Other when it felt itself threatened was as futile as it was dangerous.

Lady Madonna struggled to sit up, groggy as a junkie on the nod. "What—what do you think you're doing—?" she thickly slurred.

The Other brought a boot down on the narrow cord of tissue connecting Lady Madonna to her child-parasite. The fetus squealed angrily and flopped around like a gigged frog, impotently clawing the air as its attacker sliced its lifeline with the switchblade. A spurt of fresh blood—Estes' stolen life force—gushed forth from the severed umbilicus.

The screams from the fetus grew frantic as its skin dissolved into a red jelly and its eyes spurted from their sockets in soft, warm globs. Blinded, dripping melting flesh like wax from a candle, it crawled back to its mother-host, mewling like a lost kitten.

Lady Madonna, however, was no longer able to protect herself, much less her nightmare child. She writhed on the ground like a wounded snake as time, held so long at bay by her symbiotic relationship with her undead offspring, ravaged her body like a school of hungry piranha. Her breasts, swollen from decades of milk, withered into empty wineskins, while her belly deflated like a hot-air balloon.

"My baby!" Lady Madonna wailed, loose teeth falling from her aged gums. "You killed my baby!"

She lunged at the Other, her arthritic, liver-spotted hands hooked into impotent claws. The Other batted aside the crone with bemused contempt.

"It was never a child. It was Abomination."

"He was the only thing I had! *Now* look at me!" She grabbed a snarled handful of gray hair, the heavily wrinkled, empty skin hanging from her upper arms in loose flaps. "You ruined everything, you god-damned oddling bitch!"

"There's nothing sadder than an orphaned renfield," the Other said, clucking its tongue. *"You're better off joining your master."* Placing one hand on Lady Madonna's shoulder, as if offering comfort, the Other drove the open switchblade through her withered breast.

Lady Madonna clutched at the Other's fist, trying to peel its fingers away from the knife hilt. The Other pulled the blade free and Lady Madonna dropped back onto the floor, as boneless as water.

"That's your second kill," Sonja whispered hoarsely as she reasserted her autonomy over their shared flesh. "Now go away."

You know as well as I do I can't go away. I can only go back, the Other said with a malicious sneer. *You'll call on me again, of that I have no doubt. You need me, sister. You need me more than you ever will need anyone else.* With that, the Other folded its malignancy about itself, like a bat wrapping itself in its wings, and dropped down the hole in the back of Sonja's brain.

The relief Sonja felt upon the Other's departure was short-lived. She knelt beside Estes. She had not allowed herself to really look at him until then, and she didn't like what she saw. His color was not good and he was far too still as she removed the ropes from his hands and feet. As Sonja pressed her fingers against the bruising around the tiny puncture wounds on his jugular, a clear, yellowish fluid, similar to snake venom, oozed forth.

She took one of his hands in her own, only to find it as limp as an empty glove. It was as if he had collapsed into himself, like a straw effigy left out in the rain. His skin, already pale, had become as translucent as opal, causing the veins of his face and hands to stand out like nests of snakes. A hard, cold lump filled the pit of her stomach, as if she had swallowed a lead sinker.

"Jack! Wake up!"

After a long moment his lids trembled and lifted, revealing eyes that shimmered like spectral lakes.

"Sonja…" His voice was vague and distant, as if dulled by morphine. He was greatly diminished, as if taken apart and then poorly reassembled. "It… it was so small… it fed… for hours…."

Sonja's lungs filled with a dread as thick and cold as mud, but she forced herself to smile. "I'm sorry it took so long to reach you. You're safe now. I killed it."

"My mother—?"

"I took care of her."

"Thank… you." His eyes moved restlessly, like those of a caged monkey. "Noir? Is he—?"

"He's dead," she replied, a little too quickly.

Estes frowned at her like a judge studying a suspicious witness. The shame crowding Sonja's throat became so great she had to look away.

"You're… lying."

She nodded, unable to meet his eyes. "He used his magic to escape. Took his damned ogre with him. Fuckin' blood-wizard."

"It's not… your fault…" he rasped, his voice as fragile as a moth's wing. "I'm the one… who failed…."

"That's bullshit, Jack."

"I failed… my father… and myself…. Sonja… please… I need you… to do… one last thing…."

Sonja could see he was headed, and she didn't want to go there. "No. It's not going to come to that, Jack."

"You're… lying to me… again…. I can feel… my life running out… it's too late for me…."

"You're going to be okay."

"No… no, I'm *not*… you know what to do… don't let me… become one of them…."

Sonja looked into his eyes and felt death's presence nearby, invisible yet real, like the oxygen in the air between them.

"I think I love you, Jack." The words slipped out with surprising ease.

Estes' lips twisted into something that was supposed to be a smile, but looked more like a grimace.

"I… think… I loved you, too…."

He gasped as if a large rock had been dropped on his chest, his back arching like Ulysses' bow. He clawed weakly at his throat, his eyes bulging from their sockets. Then, as quickly as it began, he dropped back into her arms, lifeless as an empty suit. His head lolled to one side as the spark in his eyes faded like the picture on an old television set.

Sonja gently rocked Estes' corpse back and forth, smoothing the hair from his pallid forehead. It was so much easier to be gentle with the dead than the living, and so unfair. She held him close until the last of his body heat was gone, leaving him as cold as clay in her arms. She didn't want to do what she knew had to be done, but she had no say in the matter. She had promised him he would not rise as one of the undead he had dedicated his life against. It would not be an easy task, or a pretty one.

She stretched his body out on the floor so that he was lying in repose; hands folded atop his chest, and placed the edge of the switchblade against his throat. She shook her head and folded the knife back into its ornate handle. It would be better if she used something more suited to the job.

As she reached inside the breast pocket of her leather jacket to retrieve Estes' Bowie knife, her fingers brushed against cool glass. She removed the mojo bottle and stared at the dancing light trapped within its blue heart.

Maybe, just maybe, it wasn't over yet.

Part Four

It's been a long long long time;

How could I ever have lost you

When I loved you?

Long Long Long, George Harrison

VéVé sat on the front porch glider, her sewing basket in her lap, quietly darning a pair of Levon's stockings. The way she saw it, just because the man was dead didn't mean he had to go walking around with holes in his socks. She paused to rest her eyes from the close work, gazing out at the shady canopy of live oaks lining the drive leading to Mojo House.

Levon lumbered across the meadow-sized front lawn with the push-mower, oblivious to the delta sun climbing its way across the sky. Although the morning air was heavy with the scent of freshly cut grass, VéVé could smell trouble coming on the wind from the river. And, in her experience, the river winds were seldom wrong.

The augury proved itself correct when a strange car suddenly appeared at the mouth of the shell drive, sending up a trail of white dust in its wake. VéVé set aside her sewing basket and got to her feet. Levon let the push-mower drop and moved towards the house with surprising speed, considering his condition. It wasn't until the car came to a halt in the turnaround that VéVé recognized the driver.

"Sonja!" The voodoo priestess exclaimed as she hurried down the front steps. "What the hell are you doing back here?"

The vampire slayer climbed out from behind the wheel of the rental car. In the open sunlight she looked as pale and vulnerable as a grub. "It's an emergency, VéVé," she said, grimacing as the sun cut her eyes.

The other woman frowned as she glanced inside the car. "Where's that nice Mr. Estes you had with you?"

"He's still traveling with me," Sonja replied, popping the trunk release.

Jack Estes lay curled in the boot of the rental as if held in the jaws of some amiable beast, wrapped in a makeshift shroud fashioned from a velvet curtain, with twelve five-pound bags of crushed ice arranged atop his body.

VéVé placed her hand on Estes' chilly brow and quickly removed it, shaking her head.

"My heart grieves for you," she said, sadly. "But, woman, why bring him to me?"

"Because you're the only one who can save him."

"*Save* him? He's deader than a burnt match!"

"Not for long," Sonja replied grimly, turning the dead man's head so that the puncture marks on this throat were visible.

"May the loa protect us," VéVé whispered, crossing her self. "He is *infecté!* Girlfriend, have you gone mad?"

"Maybe. Maybe not. But I *do* know that you are the only who has the power to help me. By the way, could we possibly continue this inside? The sunlight's giving me a killer migraine and Estes needs to be stored somewhere where he won't spoil."

VéVé nodded her understanding. "I'll have Levon take him into the cellar. I'm sure he won't mind the company."

The *zuvembie* leaned into the trunk then paused, studying Estes with eyes as opaque as an oyster's gaze, then lifted the corpse across his back in a fireman's carry.

Five minutes later, VéVé sat at her kitchen table, slowly stirring her chicory coffee as she listened to her guest's story. Now that she was out of direct sunlight, Sonja did not look quite so haggard and her manner was more animated.

"Hear me out, VéVé. I know what I'm going to tell you sounds insane, but I'm convinced it can work. Estes died from a vampire bite twelve hours ago, give or take and hour. That leaves me sixty hours, more or less, to expel the vampire taint before he resurrects. Once he reawakens as one of the undead, he's lost forever."

"Let me get this straight—You want to exorcise the vampire element within him? But how could that possibly save him? He would still be dead."

"So's Levon."

VéVé's eyes widened in horror. "Merciful spirit, woman! You want me to bring him *back*? That is something reserved only for those who were never punished for their crimes while living! Levon was a rapist and murderer who preyed on children. What you suggest is something that is inflicted on your worst enemies, not your loved ones!"

"But Levon is the way he is because he has no soul."

"That *is* true," VéVé said, nodding her head thoughtfully. "Not that he possessed one while alive, from what I've been told."

"But what if you restored life to a dead body—and there was a soul on hand to fill it?"

VéVé frowned. She could clearly see where her friend was going, but was not sure if she wanted to follow her there. "I can't be one-hundred percent certain, but my guess would be that such a creature would be a living thing, but with no memory of who he once was, either physically or spiritually, not unlike those reincarnated in the bodies of infants."

"That's what I hoped you'd say," Sonja said, grinning in relief.

"But you overlooked one thing, honey—I don't happen to have a spare soul lyin' around."

"That's okay," Sonja said, reaching inside her jacket. "I've got it covered." She placed the little blue bottle between them. "How did you know Malfeis had Judd in his collection?"

VéVé lowered her head so that her eye was level with the edge of the table, staring at its glowing contents. "I was hopin' you'd figger things out on your own and get Malfeis to cough up."

"I had to wrestle him for it, and he surrendered with less than good grace. I'll be unwelcome in the Monastery for the next year or two, but he'll get over it. That's the good thing about demons: they're practical when it comes to business. I'm too good a customer for him to ban me for good." She shook her head wearily, a bitter smile on her face. "I blamed myself for what happened to Judd for so many years. Not so much for killing him, which I still don't regret… but for the damage I had done to his spirit. When he came to me that last time, I could tell his soul had been extinguished just by looking into his eyes. I thought I was the one to blame for that—that the Other had corrupted him, turned him into yet another renfield. I had no way of knowing that he had bartered with Malfeis. He damned himself for my sake, and I killed him out of ignorance. I owe it to Judd to rectify my mistake. So—what do you think? Can you pull it off?"

"I don't see why not, provided we can find a way of ridding the host of the *enkidu* before it germinates. Plus, there's the question of decay. If the tissues deteriorate beyond a certain point, he'll be no better than Levon." VéVé got up from her place at the table, her brow knitted like that of a physicist puzzling out a question of quantum mechanics. "I'll need to see what grandpa's books have to say about the exorcism of vampires."

Sonja followed VéVé to Papa Beloved's study, located on the first floor of the house. The room was small, and made even cozier by the floor-to-ceiling barrister-style bookcases that lined the walls. Although born into poverty and illiteracy in the Caribbean, Papa Beloved worked hard to educate himself upon reaching America, first learning how to read and write in English, then going on to school himself in French, German, Greek and Latin. Over the years, he had amassed a sizable collection of rare and unusual books pertaining to the occult. Hands clasped behind her back, Sonja studied the spines of the volumes on display. No doubt the Garden District society ladies whose lawns Papa Beloved once tended would have been shocked to discover the bandy-legged little man with the battered straw hat and sagging pickup truck owned such titles as *The Aegrisomnia*, Legendre's *Le Livre de L'Absinthe*, Von Valkenberg's *Die Grauen Fremden*, and *Il Gospel della Capra*, which was illuminated by the heretical Brotherhood of St. Dionysus during the Middle Ages, and possibly even more horrified to learn he could read them all in their original languages.

VéVé stuck her hand into her apron pocket and fished out a large metal ring bristling with keys. She unlocked one of the glass-fronted bookcases and plucked out several oversized, leather-bound volumes.

"This will take some time," she warned as she lugged the books over to an old roll-top desk. "I'm not as skilled with the dead languages as Papa Beloved, so I must rely on his notes. Why don't you rest a spell?" She motioned to an old leather couch arranged against the only wall space that wasn't occupied by a bookcase. "I won't have an answer for you before dusk, anyways."

Sonja nodded and wearily stretched out on the couch. The moment she closed her eyes her blood pressure dropped like a stone tossed down a well and her body went completely limp.

When she reopened her eyes, it was to find shadows climbing the walls and the room lit by the flickering light of a kerosene lamp. VéVé was still seated at the roll-top desk, hunched over her grandfather's books like a student cramming for mid-term.

"What did you learn?" Sonja asked with a yawn, picking up the thread of conversation exactly where it had last left off.

VéVé turned to face her houseguest, massaging the bridge of her nose with her thumb and forefinger. "I have good news and bad news. Which do you want first?"

"What's the good news?"

"I've found numerous means of exorcising a vampire."

"And the bad news?"

"Most of the texts assume that the *enkidu's* host is dead and is going to stay that way. All of the exorcism rituals call for either total or partial destruction of the host body, ranging from traditional cremation and decapitation to packing the body cavity full of sea salt and driving a spike through the top of the head. However, there *is* one means of exorcising the vampire that doesn't require the destruction of the host body, but it's so off-the-wall I don't even consider it a true possibility...."

"And that is—?"

"Expulsion by the seraphim. According to the Gospel of the Goat, they have the ability to drive forth major and minor demons, including the *enkidu*. Which is all well and good, provided we knew where to find seraphim and then get them to pay attention to us after we found them."

"Maybe that's not as crazy as you think. I have pretty good idea where I can lay my hands on at least one."

VéVé stared at Sonja as if she'd just grown a second head. "Girl, are you *serious?*"

"As cancer."

***

I hurry through the French Quarter, as determined as Orpheus. I don't allow myself to be distracted by the rowdy tourists clutching Hurricane glasses and milling about the Vieux Carré's narrow streets. I also ignore the various and sundry demons, *vargr* and the like mixed amongst the revelers. I have no time for such trifles. I am in search of one breed — and one breed only — of Pretender tonight.

I stand and stare at the patch of empty pavement where I had last seen the seraph Fido. I fight the surge of panic rising from my belly like a bitter tide. Still, if Fido is no longer to be found, there must be other seraphim in the vicinity. They are invariably drawn to hot zones like New Orleans, where demons and the other dangerous varieties of Pretenders congregate.

I toss back my head and throw open the doors of perception, allowing thousands of voices to pour in like competing short-wave signals. I sift through the voices in my head, like a prospector panning for gold, seeking out a particular pattern of thought waves. One by one I tune them out, until all that is left is a sonorous, droning chant, like that of Buddhist monks at prayer. It is the call of the seraphim.

I cut across Jackson Square and Decatur Street, passing within feet of the Café Du Monde's open-air pavilion, where the smell of coffee, fried dough and powdered sugar hangs thick in the evening air. A street performer dressed like a medieval jester juggles flaming batons near the approach to the earthen dams that shelter the French Quarter from the Mississippi River. Honeymooning couples, teenage lovers and pensive drunks stroll along the Moonwalk atop the levee, lost in their own self-contained worlds, oblivious to my passing. I hurry through Woldenburg Park, with its carefully maintained magnolia and crepe myrtles, towards the Aquarium of the Americas. I pass through the Spanish Plaza at the foot of Canal Street, where several garish riverboat casinos have set permanent anchor, without bothering to give their glittering façades a second glance. I find the seraph under the Greater New Orleans Bridge, far from the lights and bustle of the city's tourist district, surrounded by piles of old tires, shattered glass, and trash discarded from the speeding cars crossing the bridge above. The sound of traffic passing overhead is as constant as that of the river slapping against the huge chunks of concrete fill dumped along the bank as a breakwater.

The seraph squats as immobile as a cypress knee before its tiny campfire, dressed in a greasy canvas coat and soiled pants held in place by a length of twine. Its hair is wild and matted as a bison pelt, filled with twigs, scraps of old food and other detritus, and it smells of urine and body odor. The only hint that the creature hunkered before me isn't exactly what it appears to be is its skin, which shines like rotten wood in the dim light.

I move forward cautiously. This is not a seraph I am familiar with, and I am uncertain of my reception. I have to fight more than my own unease. The Other doesn't like being near seraphim, no matter how wretched they may seem. This particular specimen agitates the Other as much as Lady Madonna's freakish little vampire-baby, but it seems more interested in flight than fight this time. It's all I can do to keep from turning on my heel and fleeing back into the darkness. I pause to take a deep breath and steady myself as best I can. I refuse to allow the Other to ruin this, as it has ruined so many things before.

As I draw closer, the campfire's flame rises like a cobra poised to strike. Although my approach has been as silent as a shadow, and the seraph's back had been towards me, it stands up and turns to look right at me, its eyes glowing like bronze mirrors. Outlined by the flickering light, it appears twisted yet awesome, like a once-mighty tree withered by blight.

"I mean you no harm," I say, holding my hands up, palms turned outward.

There is no sign of fear in its posture. After all, how could I pose a threat to one such as it?

"I have come to ask a favor..."

The golden glow in the back of the derelict's eyes flickers then goes out. It has lost interest in me. Seraphim are notoriously hard to engage in one-on-one encounters. Their agenda is unknowable, even to those such as myself, who have been permitted brief glimpses into their mysteries.

"I need your help..."

The seraph returns its gaze to the fire, turning its back to me. Panic rises like blood in my throat. If I can't get this seraph to pay attention to me, then I'm screwed, Estes' screwed, Judd's screwed—in short, we're *all* screwed.

I move closer to the seraph, but it doesn't turn to look at me or show any other sign of acknowledging my presence. It merely sits before its trash-fed fire, eyes turned inward, as silent as a dead man's heart. Talking to it is about as much use as cutting water with a sword.

I place my hand on the seraph's shoulder. Heat jumps up my fingers and through my arm, as if an invisible flame is raging under its skin. Although it feels like I'm pressing my palm against a hot stove, I don't loosen my grip. I pull on the seraph's shoulder, turning it back around to face me. My arm feels like I've plunged it into a vat of boiling water up to the shoulder. The seraph stays mute as a turtle, staring off into space with unfocused eyes.

"*Look at me, damn you!*" I grit between clenched teeth. I give the seraph a shake, hoping to elicit some kind of response, but it remains as impassive as a glass of milk.

The heat radiating from the creature is so intense I feel like a piece of candy melting on a summer sidewalk. My pain is quickly giving way to anger. I can feel rage bubbling in my head, like crude oil working its way to the surface. A demon-born fury spreads through me like a virus, bringing with it a wrath as naked as bone. I feel as if I'm standing on a crumbling ledge, suspended high above a windswept precipice. Any second now I'll lose control, and the Other will emerge. But I know that, once in command, the Other will flee as fast and as far away from here as it can go, like a monkey desperate to escape the coils of a python.

I'm playing with dynamite, but I need the temporary insanity born of intense, dark passion to do what comes next, because I would never dare it in my right mind. I shove the seraph backward, sending it into the campfire. Sparks fly up from like a cloud of burning bees. The seraph's hair and coat catch fire with a dry, puffing cough, but still it doesn't open its mouth or cry out. It slowly regains its footing as its skin burns and blisters, chunks of melting flesh dripping from its body like tallow from a candle. As it turns to face me, its head splits open like a cicada's husk, unleashing a brilliant, cold light that burns like a fire in a blizzard. Something tells me I've gotten its attention.

The seraph stands revealed, its pretense of humanity destroyed. Although I am so frightened my stomach is full of static electricity, I can't keep from staring. It's slightly taller than a man and humanoid in appearance, but with transparent skin, like that of a medical teaching model. But instead of bones, blood and other viscera on display, there are arteries of lights, veins of brilliance, and organs that glow like radiant jewels.

It hurts to look upon its fearsome beauty, even with my shades on. Tears of blood well at the corners of my eyes, but I can't turn my gaze away, despite the Other's screams of horror. The desire to flee from the thing standing before me is no simple fear, but some deep, primordial instinct, the kind hardwired into all animals, whether natural or unnatural. Although it has not lifted a hand against me, a part of me recognizes the seraph as being as dangerous to my wellbeing as a cougar is to an antelope's. Mercifully, the seraph reforms its mortal guise, dousing the agony of its beauty as easily as pulling a window shade against the glare of the sun. It looks at me through its outward countenance of an unkempt street person, its eyes shining like opals held before a fire.

"Will you help me?" I whisper, my voice dry as a paper flower.

As if in response, the seraph looks up at underbelly of the bridge works hanging over our heads. I follow its gaze and feel my breath freeze within my chest.

Above us are dozens of seraphim squatting along the I-beams and concrete supports of the twin bridges like so many shabby gargoyles, their lambent eyes glowing in the darkness.

I should have known better. Where there's one, there are often others nearby. Or did they simply pop into existence upon receiving a summons from their fellow seraph that he was under attack? To tell the truth, I don't know if they are actually capable of individual existence. Maybe they're like bees and wasps, and share some sort of hive consciousness. I clear my throat and open wide my arms, to show I harbor no weapons. The seraphim peer down at me with unblinking eyes, like a parliament of owls come to judge a barn mouse.

"I stand before you unarmed. I have come to ask a favor of you, not to do harm. I only ask that you hear me out."

The seraphim grouped overhead wink out, only to reappear before me, gathered in a rough semicircle, with me at its center. It's almost enough to make me turn tail and run for all I'm worth, save that I now recognize one of their number. It is Fido. Or what I have come to know as Fido. The seraph tilts its head and touches a filthy finger to its mouth, then points at me.

I frown and shake my head. "I will speak to you with words, not my mind, for I fear to let you in my head, old friend. I do not pretend to understand what you have become, but I do know that you were once like myself—perhaps even worse. At one time you were all murderers, killers, monsters… *enkidu.* You fed on the blood of innocents and feasted on the darkness at the heart of humankind. I don't know why you are here on earth, or what plans you have for mankind. But I do know you can drive forth demons, because the one inside me is terrified of being in your very presence.. This is why I have sought you out. There is a man named Jack Estes… he was killed by a vampire, and within a few hours he'll be resurrected as one of the undead. I promised I would never let that happen to him."

I receive a mental impression, brief but vivid, of an axe cutting through Estes' neck, sending his head flying. I close my eyes and grimace, trying to rid myself of the sight.

"No! I *don't* want to damage his body! I have a means of returning him to life—but I have to first rid the body of the vampire's seed."

Another image flickers through my mind, this one of Estes squatting naked and empty-eyed, his body smeared with feces and blood, chewing hungrily on a severed arm. The vision is so sharp and detailed, I smell the reek of human waste mixed with spilled viscera. It is as if I am looking directly into the future, instead of being shown something that might occur. The ghoulish apparition shakes me, but I do not allow it to shift my resolve.

"I know what reanimating a human corpse can lead to. But that is *not* what I propose to do. I have a soul waiting to enter the body. You yourself know which one I'm speaking of. You helped me harvest it."

The assembled seraphim turn their heads as one towards Fido, who nods slowly, and then they all return their unblinking gaze to me. They simply stare at me, as impassive as stones. Their expressionless faces trigger my frustration.

"You think you're so high and mighty? So much more evolved beyond me? You're no different now than when you were *enkidu*!" I snarl, spitting on the ground in frustration. As if in answer to my plea, the assembled seraphim waver like images on a dying television set and wink out, one by one, returning to wherever it is they go.

Defeat, as bitter as bile and thick as blood, crowds the back of my throat.

"Damn it—you fuckers *owe* me!" I shriek, snatching up chunks of broken concrete scattered at my feet and hurling them at the disappearing seraphim. "That's right! Run away! That's all you sons of bitches are good for anyway, being enigmatic and disappearing when you're really needed!" A fist-sized chunk of pavement passes through Fido's chest and lands with a splash in the river.

This is what I get for depending on others to do the right thing. You would think I would know better than to rely on anyone beside myself by now. Whenever I've counted on someone to help out whenever I've really needed it, I always ended up disappointed. Monster or human, it's always the same—you can't trust others worth shit.

I snatch up a chuck of breakwater the size of an engine block and lift it over my head, only to find myself alone under the bridge, with nothing but the Father of All Waters for company. With a cry born of grief as much as rage, I shotput my final missile into the river, sending up a spout as large as the spume from a whale.

I stagger drunkenly and slide to my knees on the filthy river's edge. I can't bring myself to look heavenward, but instead stare at the reflection of the moon floating on the surface of the dark water of the Mississippi, as blind and cold as the eye of a drowned sailor.

17

VéVé looked up from the pot of gumbo simmering on the kitchen stove as the headlights cut across the kitchen window. Sighing, she turned off the gas ring and dried her hands on the apron cinched about her waist. She could tell by the slam of the car door that whatever happened in New Orleans had not been good.

"They would not help," VéVé said simply, as Sonja entered the room. Sonja nodded sharply but said nothing. VéVé moved forward and took her friend's hands in her own "Honey, you got to recognize that there are times when things are beyond your ability to set right. This is one of 'em. You have to let go, otherwise you're just tormenting yourself for no earthly use."

Sonja took a deep breath, steadying herself as best she could, then blew it back out. "You're right. I can't put it off any more. Where is he?"

"Still in the basement. I got Levon keepin' flies off him."

"Let's get it over with, then."

As VéVé opened the cellar door, a damp, earthy smell, like that of a cave, rose to greet them. She turned an old-fashioned twist-switch just inside the door and a solitary light bulb flared into life at the foot of the stairs, illuminating the dirt floor and brick walls pock-marked by lichen and mold.

"Hope you don't mind me turnin' on the light," VéVé said as they descended the steep wooden stairs. "I realize you can see perfectly well in the dark, and Levon…well, it's been a long time since day or night mattered to him at all. But I'm afraid my eyesight's nowhere near as sharp."

Estes' body, still wrapped in the velvet stage curtain from the strip club, lay atop an old picnic table in the coolest part of the cellar. Levon stood over the corpse like a bizarre scarecrow, staring into nowhere, a flyswatter clutched in one hand.

"That's enough for now, Levon," VéVé said, waving the zombie aside. The flyswatter dropped from Levon's dead fingers as he stepped back to await his next command.

Sonja gazed down at Estes' face for a long moment before peeling back the makeshift shroud. Once the body was completely exposed, she glanced at VéVé and nodded. The voodoo priestess took a white kerchief from her apron pocket and tied it about her head, chanting a prayer for the dead under her breath.

Sonja reached inside her jacket and withdrew Estes' silver Bowie knife. Normally it would take a hacksaw to sever a human head, but given her preternatural strength and the sharpness of the blade, it would only take two, maybe three cuts to do the job.

Jack Estes was gone. All he was and ever could be fled with his final breath. The thing stretched out on the table before her was a husk; nothing more than dead, senseless meat defiled by the taint of the *enkidu*. By destroying this corrupted vessel, she would prevent yet another member of the undead from walking the earth and save the lives of countless others. So why were her hands trembling? Why did her heart ache as if it was being squeezed in a tourniquet? She closed her eyes and bit her lower lip until something like blood came to her mouth.

She placed the Bowie knife against Estes' exposed throat. She had performed this act a thousand times before, without hesitation. Estes would feel nothing; indeed, he was already far removed from any pain and sorrow. She leaned forward and pressed her lips against Estes' pallid brow in a final kiss farewell. His flesh was as cold as something dredged from a pond.

As she pressed the blade against the bloodless skin, the back of her scalp began to rise, as if a frigid wind had blown across her spine. The light bulb hanging overhead brightened from sixty to one hundred watts before bursting with a sudden pop, plunging the cellar into darkness deeper than a bad dream. VéVé gasped in alarm, her prayer forgotten.

There was a crystalline chiming sound, as if all the bottles on the mojo tree were being rattled in unison, and a pale, coruscating light, like that reflected off a pool of water, crawled its way across the cellar walls, stopping at the foot of Estes' makeshift bier.

"Sonja, what's goin' on?" VéVé whispered fearfully.

"I'm not sure… but maybe my trip to the city wasn't a waste of time, after all."

A man with long tangles of greasy hair and sunken cheeks, dressed in a baggy gray raincoat and mismatched high-top tennis shoes, a filthy wool watch cap pulled down about his ears, materialized before them. He shuffled nervously, moving from one foot to the other, and swung his head from side to side with the rhythmic constancy of the autistic. Although the features were radically altered, there was something about how the seraph held himself that reminded Sonja of someone she used to know.

Levon lurched forward, placing himself between his mistress and the mysterious intruder, causing lights to fly from the seraph's eyes like sparks from a blacksmith's forge.

"It's okay, VéVé," Sonja said, holding up a hand to stay the zombie's attack. "This creature is known to me."

VéVé took in the seraph's unkempt appearance, wrinkling her nose in disgust. "Is this the one you told me about? The one y'all called 'Fido'?"

Sonja shook her head. "No. It is another. Once, not so long ago, this was the Noble who sired the vampire who created me."

VéVé frowned. "What exactly does that mean?"

Sonja turned and favored her friend with a twisted smile. "This is my grandfather."

The seraph's rocking to-and-fro became more pronounced, his head turned so that it looked at Sonja from the corners of its eyes, as if frightened of making full contact.

"*Pangloss*." Sonja whispered the name, but the seraph flinched as if she had shouted it at the top of her lungs.

She received a mental image of herself, a blazing halo the color of blood crowning her head, carrying a frail old man through dark and winding catacombs deep below the streets of New York City.

"Yes," she replied gently "I remember. I helped you reach the necropolis. I was with you when you died."

The seraph shook his head so violently it looked like it was in danger of flying off his shoulders. Sonja's mind filled with a jumble of images, most of them too painful to recall.

"You're right," she replied quickly. "You did not die. You transmuted."

Sonja saw a vast sea of faces, some human, some not. Some of the faces shone like lanterns, while others were cast in shadows as black as oil. The majority of the faces were neither alight nor in eclipse, but somewhere in between. One of these faces, she realized with a start, was her own.

"I'm sorry," she said, shaking her head. "I don't understand what you're trying to show me. Did you come here to help me?"

Pangloss's head halted its extreme side-to-side movement. The seraph stepped forward, peering intently at Estes' body, his nostrils flaring like those of a hound as he sniffed the moldy air. The seraph's eyes shone like jars of honey held before a fire. A pale and diffuse light surrounded Pangloss's right hand like a halo around the moon. Sonja stepped back, motioning for VéVé to do the same.

The seraph's fingers pushed against Estes' brow, passing through skin, muscle and bone without the aid of a scalpel or the shedding of a single drop of blood. As she watched his hand disappear into the dead man's cranium, Sonja was reminded of an old shaman she once knew who would stand motionless in a mountain creek, patiently waiting for a fish to swim by so he could snatch it from the water.

The thing Pangloss pulled from Estes' skull, however, looked like no fish spawned of any ocean known to man. Its skin was black and shiny as wet latex, and it had a large, wedge-shaped head, like that of a pit viper. It opened a sucker-like mouth, exposing concentric rings of sharp fangs, and gave voice to an ultrasonic shriek, like that of a bat. Its tiny red eyes gleamed with malevolent intelligence as it lashed its long, whip-like body in a desperate attempt to escape. It lacked legs and arms, but possessed what looked like vestigial wings jutting from what might have been stunted shoulder blades. The seraph held the thing at arm's length, gripping it tightly behind the hinge of its jaws, as it hissed like an angry bushmaster.

Sonja stared in sick fascination at the thing. So this was what vampires really looked like, once stripped of their human hosts. No wonder they were obsessed with personal appearance and worked so hard to surround themselves with beautiful people and nice things. The realization that such a creature was burrowed deep inside her own psyche made her stomach tighten.

Pangloss studied the *enkidu* for a long moment, a look of visible disgust on his face. Then the seraph opened his mouth, displaying teeth as strong and white as a tiger's, and without a moment's hesitation, bit the struggling vampire's head off and spat it onto the floor. Its body jerked in his hand like a garden hose, squirting foul-smelling black goo like rancid jism.

Sonja grimaced like an African mask and looked away, disgusted by the display. Although she had no idea how seraphim disposed of *enkidu* and other possessing demons, she certainly hadn't expected a geek act. But now it was very clear to her why the Other was always nervous in the presence of seraphim.

Pangloss tossed aside the rapidly decomposing carcass of the *enkidu* and turned to face Sonja. The Other was scrambling around inside her skull, frantic as a trapped mouse, but she was helpless to flee, even if she had wanted to. The seraph's golden gaze nailed her to the spot as surely as a fakir's flute holds a cobra in its sway.

Pangloss lifted his crooked, befouled fingers and tapped his chest, then pointed to her own heart, a quizzical look on his seamed face. Sonja received a vision of herself glowing like a Japanese lantern.

"No, grandfather," she said, shaking her head. "I've existed this way far too long to go back now. Chances are I could not *stay* human, no matter how hard I tried. I know too much about the Real World. While I cannot return to what I once was, neither am I ready to go forward. Not yet, anyway. I thank you for the offer, though."

Pangloss regarded her for a long moment, as if deciding whether to accept her words, then nodded his shaggy head. The glow behind his smoked-honey eyes grew as strong as headlights, becoming brilliant enough that Sonja had to avert her gaze. Then the light was gone, and with it Pangloss, plunging the cellar back into crypt-like darkness.

VéVé reached into her apron pocket and produced a book of paper matches and a small white votive candle. The light from the candle cast distorted shadows that flickered across the faces of the vampire standing to the left of her, the zombie standing to her right, and the corpse on the table before her.

"That's some family you got there, girl," the voodoo priestess said, shaking her head.

Sonja stared down at the tiny blue bottle glowing in her fist. "Yeah," she said, her voice tight with unshed tears. "I know."

"Excuse me, ma'am?"

The nurse manning the visitor's reception desk looked up from her charts at the a slightly built man, dressed in an Armani suit and sporting elaborately braided gray hair. She had seen many strange things working at the Wexler Memorial Institute, so the visitor's choice in coiffure didn't rate so much as a raised eyebrow.

"Yes, sir?" she replied, without missing a beat. "May I help you?"

"I have an appointment with Mrs. Hawley."

When the visitor spoke, the nurse detected a distinct British accent. She checked the appointment book that lay open before her. "You must be Mr. Jennet. Mrs. Hawley will be with you directly."

Jennet nodded solemnly and stepped aside to study a sofa-sized batik painting of seagulls in flight that hung on a nearby wall. A couple of minutes passed before he was joined by a middle-aged woman dressed in a sensible pantsuit and a waist-length white coat with the Wexler Memorial Institute emblem stitched on the right breast. She held a clipboard and a manila file under one arm.

"Mr. Jennet?" She extended a hand in greeting, flashing the high-wattage smile of a professional administrator. "I'm Joanna Hawley. I spoke with you over the phone."

Jennet bowed slightly at the waist as he took her hand. "Thank you for taking time out of your busy schedule, Mrs. Hawley."

"Nonsense! I always have time for the family and friends of our residents. Would you like to see the ward for yourself?" She did not wait for his answer, but began walking down the hall with a brisk, measured stride.

"Of course," Jennet said, falling in beside her.

"As you can see," Mrs. Hawley said, motioning to the well-lit corridors and pastel-colored walls, "we here at the Wexler Memorial Institute believe in maintaining a pleasant atmosphere; one conducive to the comfort, and eventual recovery of our residents."

An elderly man, seated in a wheelchair parked outside the door of his room, flashed a toothless smile and nodded a greeting as they passed.

"That's Mr. Doherty," Mrs. Hawley explained, without breaking stride. "He's here to recover from a stroke. The majority of our residents are seniors, but we have more than adequate facilities for younger residents, such as Mr. Lazarus. Ah, here we are: MIW. That stands for Memory Impairment Ward."

They paused before a large metal security gate that separated the ward from the rest of the building. Mrs. Hawley produced a specially coded plastic card and swiped it through the computerized locking mechanism on the door.

"Please don't mind the security, Mr. Jennet," she said as she pushed open the heavy metal door. "None of the residents in MIW are violent. This is done simply as a precaution against any of them becoming lost. Most of the residents suffer from Alzheimer's, and they have a tendency to wander off if you're not looking."

"Of course. I understand perfectly," Jennet said, smiling politely.

"Mr. Lazarus should be in here with the others," Mrs. Hawley said, pushing open the swinging double doors that lead to the communal day room.

A dozen or more "residents" were seated in a large room with narrow gunslit windows that allowed slices of sunlight to travel across its brightly painted walls. While most looked to be in their seventies, there were a handful of younger men and women scattered about, watching television, reading magazines, playing Ping-Pong, and assembling jigsaw puzzles.

"Ah, there's Mr. Lazarus," Mrs. Hawley pointed to a man with shoulder-length white hair seated alone at a table nearest the windows. Lazarus was dressed in peppermint-striped flannel pajamas, with matching terrycloth robe, and diligently making his way through *Mike Mulligan and His Steam Shovel*, brow furrowed in concentration.

"He's been making remarkable progress," she stage-whispered. "As you well know, when he first came here, he was incapable of walking or talking, much less feeding or cleaning himself. Now, less than six months later, he's doing so well we're giving serious consideration to graduating him from the Memory Impairment Ward into the Assisted Living Wing. Yes, we're quite proud of Laz."

"Beg pardon?" Jennet said, raising an eyebrow. "What did you call him?"

"That's the staff's pet name for Mr. Lazarus. It's just that, well, we've never been informed as to his Christian name..."

"That is the only name he needs," Jennet replied. "I'm sorry, my good woman, I did not mean to sound so... harsh. It's just that, well, Mr. Lazarus's parents are no longer living and his only remaining relative—the one who sees that his bills here are paid—is his grandmother. The sad condition your staff originally found him in was the result of illicit drug use, and she is desperate to keep the family name out of the papers. That's why he was sent here. The family knew of your facility, back when it was called Elysian Fields, and is keenly aware of its reputation for discreteness."

"Who, exactly, *is* Mr. Lazarus' grandmother?"

"I'm not at liberty to tell you that right now. I'm sure you appreciate the situation," Jennet replied curtly, the temperature of his voice dropping noticeably.

"Oh. I, um, see..." Mrs. Hawley nervously glanced down at her clipboard, aware that she had crossed into hazardous territory with her visitor.

Jennet's calculated smile returned to his lips as he reached into the breast pocket of his jacket and withdrew a small black-and-white photograph. "However, perhaps this picture of Mr. Lazarus' beloved Nana will help jog his memory..."

"Thank you, Mr. Jennet," Mrs. Hawley said, carefully sliding the snapshot into the manila file folder. "Would you like to speak to Mr. Lazarus yourself? He has been tested recently and found to possess the verbal acuity of a five-year-old. He can answer most questions put to him now, provided they are about his life here at the Institute."

"No. That won't be necessary. It would just confuse him. Mr. Lazarus and I never had any dealings with one another. I merely represent his grandmother's business interests. Speaking of which," he smiled crookedly, handing her a stiff white business envelope, "is a cashier's check acceptable?"

Mrs. Hawley's smile regained its previous wattage. "It will do most nicely, Mr. Jennet."

***

Jen slid behind the wheel of the ebony Lexus, sighing with relief as the car door closed solidly behind him.

"How is he?"

. Sonja sat in the back of the car, the collar of her leather jacket turned up as far as it could go, her shoulders hunched against what sunlight made its way through the darkly tinted windows.

"He's no longer crawlin' and shittin' himself, it's that's what you're askin'," he replied, tossing a sheaf of photocopied medical charts and case notes over his shoulder and onto the seat beside her. "Read all about it."

Sonja thumbed through the Xeroxed pages, nodding occasionally. "He's maturing rapidly. Excellent. Did he see you?"

"I don't think so."

"Good. Did you give them the photograph?"

"I fed 'em the song and dance about our friend in there being the last black sheep of a thinning flock. They bought it, just as you said they would. Luckily our Mrs. Hawley didn't recognize Lazarus' beloved "Nana" as Dame Margaret

Rutherford. Then again, I get the distinct impression that as long as th' check doesn't bounce, I could say he was Prince Mongo of bloody Mars and they wouldn't have batted an eye."

Sonja glanced through the rear window at the entrance of the sanitarium, a sour look on her face. "They may have changed the name since I was locked up in there, but this place still makes its money seeing to it that the dirty little secrets of the rich and famous are swept under the rug. As long as Lazarus' bills are paid, they won't do anything to rock the boat. When the time comes, we'll present them with a suitable family history for him, along with a modest fortune. And, if he ever fully regains his senses, he'll be free to start clean, the way he should have the first time, without parents to avenge or monsters to slay."

Jen turned around in his seat and stared at his kinswoman, shaking his head in amazement. "I'll be damned if you don't still love him."

"Don't be redundant, Jen. Besides, the man in there is a complete stranger to me. How can I love someone I've never met? And I intend to keep it that way; I can't risk triggering a residual memory in Lazarus, whether it belongs to Judd or Estes. The last thing I want is for him to remember me."

"Fine, then, if that's how you want it," Jen shrugged. "But if you truly loved these men, and they loved you, why erase yourself from their lives?"

"Because it's not safe for humans to be around me, Jen. Every 'normal' man I've ever been with has come to an unpleasant end because of me. Even those who had the ability to see into the Real World, like Chaz and Palmer, ended up getting the worst of it. I'm like radioactive waste: I contaminate those around me, even without trying."

"Where does that leave me, eh?" he sniffed.

"You don't count. You're suspended somewhere between heaven and hell—just like me."

"So you're sayin' I'm so filthy the dirt won't show, is that it?"

"I mean no disrespect, cousin," Sonja replied, smiling crookedly. "In your own way, you're as incorruptible as a saint."

"Thanks for th' compliment. I guess. And speakin' of the divine—why didn't you allow Pangloss to remove the Other? Without it, you could have somethin' resemblin' a normal life with Lazarus, without fear of his being tainted."

"I still need the Other, at least for now. How else can I hope to track down and slay Lord Noir? I promised Estes I would avenge him, and I will, even if it takes a dozen decades."

"You do realize what you're getting yourself into, don't you? Noir wants you to give chase, and that's exactly what you're doin'."

Sonja scowled, shaking her head. "No. You're wrong. I'm doing this for Jack."

"If that's what you want to believe," he said, rolling his eyes. "But this is how it always begins, y'know."

"How what begins?"

"The Ennui. I've seen it plenty of times. You find yourself obsessin' over perceived injustices, holdin' grudges, takin' the slightest insult and blowin' it up to apocalyptic proportions. You'll eventually latch on to anything that'll justify a blood feud, so you can pass the time and keep yourself busy… anything to keep you from thinkin' about the futility of it all."

Sonja stared at Jen, her mouth compressed into a thin line. She wanted to tell him he was full of shit and didn't know what he was talking about. She wanted to tell him she was different from the others, that her anger was righteous, not a self-serving excuse for violence for violence's sake.

Instead, she said nothing, for fear he would hear doubt in her voice… and that she would hear it as well.

Afterword

Some people make their midlife career decisions after passing the Buddha on the road. In my case, it took my coming down to Georgia to understand what was necessary for me in order to continue to grow as a writer. I have taken this time in my life as a sign to move further into mainstream fiction, focusing in particular on stories set in the South of my birth. I have been intending to walk this path for some time now, but, whenever the time came, it had always been easier to write another Sonja Blue novel than to strike out on something new.

After ten years of chronicling the adventures of Sonja Blue, I have, to be frank, grown weary of the task. It is entirely feasible that I will one day, possibly sooner rather than later, find myself eating these words with a large side-order of crow. However, should I feel the need to pen another Sonja Blue adventure, it will probably be less than novel length. And, of course, there is the chance that a theatrical film or television series might inspire me all over again.

I appreciate the interest and enthusiasm shown my work by those of you who have followed my writing so faithfully over the last decade. I hope those of you who have enjoyed my writing will be willing to follow me from the shadowy haunts of horror into the uncharted territory I am heading into. I can't promise much, but I can guarantee that whatever I end up doing, it will no doubt be weird and more than a little twisted.

Nancy A. Collins
Atlanta, GA
June 10, 2002